more ...

"SHADES OF NICK AND NORA AND THE OTHER GREATS OF THE STYLISH '30s AND '40s."
—*Washington Times*

* * * *

CAROL HIGGINS CLARK, a writer and actress, is the daughter of author Mary Higgins Clark. She has starred in television, film, and theater productions, and for many years has worked as editorial assistant and researcher on her mother's bestselling novels. Carol's first novel, *Decked,* began the highly acclaimed Regan Reilly mystery series, became a *New York Times* bestseller, and was nominated for an Agatha Award for Best First Novel. Her second book, *Snagged,* was also a national bestseller. Carol Higgins Clark, a graduate of Mount Holyoke College, now divides her time between New York and Los Angeles.

ICED

Published by
WARNER BOOKS

BY CAROL HIGGINS CLARK

Decked

Snagged

Iced

Published by
WARNER BOOKS

ICED

CAROL HIGGINS CLARK

A DOVE BOOK

WARNER BOOKS

A Time Warner Company

WARNER BOOKS EDITION

Copyright © 1995 by Carol Higgins Clark
All rights reserved.

Cover design and illustration by Bill Sloan

Warner Books, Inc.
1271 Avenue of the Americas
New York, NY 10020

Visit our Web site at
http://warnerbooks.com

 A Time Warner Company

Printed in the United States of America

Originally published in hardcover by Warner Books.
First Printed in Paperback: June, 1996

10 9 8 7 6 5

For my nieces and nephews, in order of appearance
Elizabeth, Andrew, Courtney, David, Justin and Jerry
With love

I would like to thank Dr. Larry Ashkinazy, a good friend and fine dentist, who encouraged me to visit Aspen and who allowed me to have some fun with his character in this book.

"I am a man more sinn'd against than sinning."

William Shakespeare
(Also the sentiments of one Eben Bean)

PROLOGUE

Friday, December 23

W E'RE ALMOST THERE," Judd said quietly to Willeen, his partner in crime and in love, as he turned from
the main road onto the private lane that led to the Bonnell
home. It was five minutes before three in the afternoon,
and the clouds over the surrounding mountains promised
another snowfall for the holiday skiers at Vail. Judd's eyes
darted about. Just before the moment of breaking the law,
every nerve in him vibrated. But this job had been elabo-
rately planned and should be foolproof.

He had contacted Monsieur Bonnell using the name of
a reputable art dealer with impeccable connections. Monsieur Bonnell was only too happy to invite him to inspect
at close range the Beasley painting that was being offered
for two million dollars.

"Now remember," Judd said to Willeen as he drove up
to the sprawling two-story stucco house, "we know that

the housekeeper left at one o'clock, but in case there's anyone else there, you have your Mace ready."

"It's ready."

On the off chance Monsieur Bonnell was looking out the window, they were wearing salt-and-pepper wigs made out of the finest human hair and had taped on fake gray eyebrows. Willeen had on a pair of bottleneck glasses that disguised her considerable sex appeal and Judd was sporting tinted sunglasses.

They parked in the driveway, positioning the dark gray sedan for a quick getaway, walked briskly up the steps to the front porch and rang the bell.

There was no answer.

A biting wind made Willeen shift from one foot to the other. "Did Claude get things screwed up?" she asked impatiently.

"Claude never gets things screwed up," Judd growled, his tone low and annoyed. "You heard me talk to Bonnell an hour ago. He confirmed the appointment."

Judd studied the knob expectantly, then noticed that the door was not flush with the frame. Cautiously, he put his hand on the knob. It turned easily and he pushed open the door. Instantly he grabbed his own can of Mace from his pocket.

He nodded to Willeen. "Let's go," he whispered.

As they stepped over the threshold, Willeen touched his arm and pointed to the security panel by the front door. The green light was on, indicating it was not armed.

They started down the hall.

"Do you think you should call out to him?" Willeen asked. Then she gasped as a muffled groan came from the closet on the right wall. The muffled sound was followed

by loud thumping against the door in what could only be termed desperation.

A dreadful suspicion attacked every fiber of Judd's finely tuned criminal makeup. The map Claude had prepared for him showed that the painting was over the mantel in the living room to the right of the entrance hall.

"Ohhhh pleassssse, nooooo," he cried. With Willeen at his heels, he raced from the foyer, through the archway, circled around a couch, avoided a cocktail table and screeched to a halt in front of the raised hearth.

He looked up and stared. Big baby tears welled in his eyes, clouding the blue contact lenses he had affected as part of his now unnecessary disguise.

The ornate gold frame was still in place, hanging uselessly, deprived of its function to enhance an artistic masterpiece. Instead of surrounding the Beasley painting of the railroad station in nineteenth-century Vail, it now framed the rough gray stones of the massive chimney.

"It's happened again," Judd wailed. "That friggin' Coyote beat us to it!"

1

ASPEN

Saturday, December 24

Eben bean loved to ski. The magic, the joy, the excitement of it thrilled him. It made him feel free. And that was very important to someone who'd spent five years in the slammer. The ski slopes of Aspen Mountain, with their sweeping views of the surrounding Rocky Mountains, the very essence of nature in all its glory and splendor did his soul good. It was also a lot better for his nervous system than the claustrophobic view he had had from the bottom bunk in his tiny cell. He'd never gone to sleep without the nagging worry in the back of his mind that his hulk of a cellmate would strain the bed frame, which had supported the weight of scores of outlaws, to its breaking point.

"Now I lay me down to sleep,
I pray the Lord my soul to keep.
If I get squashed before I wake,
I pray the Lord my soul to take"

he had prayed nightly for those five of his fifty-six years.

Since his confinement, Eben had developed a total love for the outdoors in all seasons. Neither rain nor sleet nor dark of night wiped the smile off his face, just as long as he wasn't surrounded by a chain-link fence. Even taking out the garbage had become a treat.

Of course, just because Eben loved to ski didn't mean he was very good at it. As a matter of fact, he wasn't very good at all. Just last week he had lost control and careened into the path of a fellow skier. She had desperately tried to avoid him but ended up taking a nasty spill, resulting in a very painful broken leg. Broken in two places as a matter of fact. Eben had watched as the ski patrol carefully strapped her into a sled, trying to ignore the slurs that the victim was spewing about his character. Oh well, Eben thought to himself. Sometimes it's a healthy thing to let yourself vent your anger.

He tried to make it up to her. But he heard that the poinsettia he'd spent at least fifteen minutes picking out and delivered to the hospital himself was ordered out of her sight the minute she read the card. Not that he didn't understand. Being in traction for six weeks didn't sound like much fun.

And this was going to be a fun week, Eben decided, as he completed his first run of the afternoon at Aspen Mountain. It had taken a little longer than usual to get down. He'd stopped for a late bite at Bonnie's, the bustling cafeteria-like restaurant on the slopes, which was crowded with

skiers eager to refuel their bodies after a hard workout. It was one of a very few places on the planet where celebrities slogged through a lunch line carrying their own trays. Eben had hung around the picnic tables on the deck outside, where skiers clad in designer skisuits and sunglasses congregated to see or be seen as they nibbled their chosen edibles.

Sitting alone, Eben had felt a little unappreciated by mankind in general. But tonight, he thought, I'll be the center of attention. They'll all be looking at me at the big party. Okay, he thought, so I'll be in a Santa suit. In a way, it was very freeing. He could act like a dope and everyone would think it was cute. He liked to dance around swinging his sack, ho-ho-ho-ing his way through the crowd.

It was Christmas Eve, and almost everyone was in a good mood. People were actually nice to each other the world over. Christmas was a great time to call a truce, no matter what religion you were. Hmmm, he wondered. I wonder if the lady with the broken leg would accept a holly wreath from me. Probably not, he decided as he dug his ski poles into the ground and awkwardly propelled himself in the general direction of the gondola. "Mush," he mumbled. "Mush."

Eben popped his feet out of his skis and hoisted them over his shoulder as he took his place in line. It was more than a fifteen-minute ride up to the top. This was the only lift where you had to take your skis off. The gondola was enclosed and you sat with anywhere from one to five other people, sometimes conversing, sometimes eavesdropping, sometimes lost in your own thoughts as you took in the unbelievable beauty of the mountains.

As Eben waited for the next free gondola to swing around, he realized that he would have it all to himself.

There was no one behind him. It was getting late. People were heading back for their après-ski drinks, their Jacuzzis, and their preparations for the evening's activities. Many of them would be at the ritzy party tonight, just waiting for his big entrance.

Nervously, Eben dropped his skis in the side pocket of the gondola and awkwardly clumped into his seat. He was always afraid that he'd be half in when it surged forward, or he'd fall and they'd have to shut it off as he hoisted himself up from the ground. That had happened more times than he'd care to remember on the lifts where you have to push yourself hurriedly off the chair and down the hill when it was time to disembark. It was usually a steep incline and more than once Eben had taken a belly flop. One of the lift operators had suggested that Eben try skiing at Tiehack, the mountain for beginners, which was just down the road. "It's a lot easier, Eben," he had said. Yeah, well, it's a free country, Eben had thought as he skied off. Besides, he liked to have his lunch at Bonnie's.

Eben settled himself in and stretched out sideways in the gondola. This way he had a view of the skiers swishing down the steep slopes above and at the same time could admire the charm offered by the village of Aspen below, a landscape dotted with snow-covered brick and wood buildings, ensconced between the protective surrounding mountains. When you were packed in with a bunch of other people, you either had to sit facing front or back.

This isn't such a bad life, Eben thought as he listened to the creak of the lift and the gentle blowing of the wind. He never thought he'd enjoy life without crime, but after he was hatched from prison five years ago, he decided that that was it. A master of separating jewelry from the bejeweled, he had enjoyed considerable success until the

unfortunate evening when he unknowingly targeted the wife of the police commissioner of New York. The occasion had been a dinner at the Plaza Hotel. Employed by the waiters' union thanks to fake identification, Eben had gone around collecting dirty dishes while plying his true trade. Until that moment it had been a very successful night. A Rolex watch and a ruby pendant were concealed in the floating remains of a Banana Surprise.

As it turned out, the police commissioner's photographic memory had already identified Eben and he had been watching him. An on-the-spot arrest was made, much to the oohs and aahs of everyone at the surrounding tables and the disappointment of the dinner speaker, who had just reached page eight of his address. In the confusion that followed, many of the guests who'd fallen into an involuntary trance sensed the opportunity to put themselves out of their misery and seized on it immediately. Jolted awake, they jumped from their seats and scurried to the coatroom with a grateful nod to the handcuffed Eben.

In the five years he'd spent up the river, Eben had mused that he'd been stealing jewelry since he was sixteen. He comforted himself with the thought that thirty-odd harmonious and profitable years were enjoyed by almost no one else in his profession.

However, five years as a guest of New York State had permanently soured Eben on the prospect of a return visit to the penitentiary. When he was given a measly check, an ill-fitting suit and the address of his parole officer, he had one fleeting moment of regret for the friends he'd made behind bars. They'd even put together a party of sorts in the TV room the night before he was sprung. One friend's wife had baked a seven-layer cake and as a tribute to his particular skills had filled the layers with plastic toy

watches. Swallowing over a lump in his throat as the whole room burst into "Auld Lang Syne," followed by "For He's a Jolly Good Fellow," Eben had said to them, "You're the only family I've ever known. But I still don't want to come back."

In his days as a thief, Eben had come to enjoy a bit of gracious living. He was particularly fond of renting nice houses. Post-prison, he realized that he would never be able to afford such luxury from the fruits of honest labor. While flipping through a copy of *Architectural Digest*, he started to get depressed but then happened upon an ideal solution. It occurred to him that every one of the estates he was looking at probably had a caretaker. Kidney-shaped pools with their very own waterfalls needed to be maintained, velvety lawns needed to be raked, long winding driveways needed to be blown clear of snow to make way for luxury vehicles.

Many a time Eben had made his leisurely way through an estate house after disconnecting the alarm, while the caretaker sat in his apartment over the garage drinking beer and watching mud-wrestling on television. Eben had decided that the only way he was going to come even close to living the good life again was to be a caretaker. Of course the old-fashioned way was to marry into it, but so far Eben had found no prospects.

To be totally insignificant-looking had been a great advantage when he was pursuing his life outside the law. Medium height, mousy hair, brown eyes and average features constituted a nightmare for police sketch artists. Horn-rimmed or frameless glasses, colored contact lenses, various hues of hair rinse contributed to his makeovers, enabling him to elude police for so long. Now he had put

on a little extra weight that he wasn't proud of, but at least he didn't have to worry about disguising it.

He'd won the drama medal in the eighth grade after starting out playing the third wise man in the school Christmas pageant and then had gone on to star, ironically enough, as the Artful Dodger in *Oliver Twist*. The zealous director should never have called in the magician named Slippery Fingers to teach me all those tricks, he often thought. It became too easy to relieve people of their gems. After his arrest, the only chance Eben had to exercise his acting skills was when he played Santa Claus for the children of inmates at the annual family Christmas party.

Which leads me to where I am today, Eben thought as he looked down from his perch. The slopes that a short time ago had been dotted with skiers were now virtually empty. The clouds that had blown in only a few minutes ago opened up and it began to snow. The thick soft powder immediately began to obscure the mountain peaks on the horizon.

Eben began to hum "Frosty the Snowman." This was perfect. He'd have one more run down the mountain, then go home and get ready for his big night. He quickly switched his humming to "Santa Claus Is Coming to Town."

At the top of the mountain Eben disembarked, grabbed his skis and clumped over to the area where people threw their skis on the ground and got ready for their run. Eben pulled on his goggles to protect his eyes from the blowing snow. Someday I'll be a great skier, he thought. But right now I'm glad that there aren't many people around and I have more room to myself.

He started down the hill, ambling from side to side, practicing the snowplow, which so far was the safest way

for him to navigate the slopes, all the while repeating the commandments he'd learned on his *Even You Can Ski* video. He'd watched the tape over and over in the privacy of the guest suite of the Wood home, where he was the caretaker in residence. He'd been so lucky to get the job.

He liked working for important people like Sam and Kendra Wood. They owned a home in Aspen but weren't there very much. Eben was in charge of keeping the place in shape. The Wood family was flying in tomorrow for the Christmas vacation. Their houseguests, the mystery writer Nora Reilly and her husband Luke, would be arriving with them. Eben had been busy getting everything ready. He still had to clear his stuff out of the guest suite, which he secretly used when he was alone. No one was the wiser for it, and Eben enjoyed living like a king. His quarters were perfectly adequate, but the little garage apartment could get drafty at times and it didn't have a big screen TV or plush carpeting or a Jacuzzi in the bathroom. Eben was always careful about leaving everything spotless when it was time to clear out, a bittersweet task at best. He loved it when the Wood family came into town and he was always truly glad to see them but he also had a great love for the big comfy bed and heated towel racks that he wouldn't get to enjoy again until they packed their bags and winged their way back to New York. Give and take, that's what life is all about, Eben thought.

He was so proud of the place that he'd even gotten a little daring about showing it off after he'd had a few drinks. I probably shouldn't have brought them back last night, Eben thought as he slipped and fell. Who would have thought, when he went into town last night for a beer and a burger at the Red Onion, Eben's favorite, a famous old mining-day saloon where he felt comfortable relaxing

around the historic wooden bar and under the old historical photographs, that he would run into Judd Schnulte? What a surprise that had been. And it could have been a terrible problem. No one in Aspen except his friend Louis knew that Eben had been a jailbird, and he wanted to keep it that way.

He needn't have worried. When Judd saw Eben, it was hard to tell from both their horrified expressions who had more use for a panic button.

"My girlfriend's in the can," Judd had said nervously.

"How long will she be in?" Eben asked sympathetically.

"You never know with women. She's always complaining about the long lines in ladies' rooms."

"I thought you meant our kind of can," Eben responded with a laugh, and then lowered his voice. "You know, a house of correction." He patted Judd on the shoulder. "We always did call you Mr. Smoothie."

"Yeah, well, whatever you want to call it, she doesn't know about my life in the cage. And I'd really like to keep it that way," Judd said, with almost a warning tone that slightly annoyed Eben.

"It's our little secret," Eben assured him. "I'm trying to make an honest living too. I've got a dream job, but I wouldn't have it if they didn't think they could trust me." As he talked, Eben wondered if all the members of the five million support groups that had sprung up for every conceivable problem felt the same queasiness when they ran into each other in public. Life was so much simpler when the one club everyone had in common was the T.G.I.F. group. Thank God it's Friday. Of course, being inmates together wasn't quite the same as being in group therapy, but it was a secret that the rest of the world didn't need to know.

Eben could see that a new girlfriend might not look kindly on a previously unmentioned incarceration period. What was it that Judd had been locked up for anyway? Eben racked his brains. I've got it! he thought as Judd's girlfriend joined them. He was an art thief.

Judd put down his beer. "This is Willeen. Willeen, say hello to Eben here. We know each other from way back."

She's a cute-looking gal, Eben thought. He extended his hand. "How do you do."

"My pleasure." Willeen smiled as she squeezed Eben's hand and held it just a little bit too long. She had blond hair, freckles and a pouty mouth. Eben figured she was probably about forty. Judd still looked the same to him: a good-looking Mr. Smoothie with brown hair and brown eyes, about the same height as Eben, late forties. Eben remembered him as being sharp-tongued but funny. They make an attractive couple, Eben thought, even though Judd is not practicing the honesty-is-the-best-policy theory of relationships these days.

"So what's this job, Eben?" he asked.

Over a beer he explained. It was nice to chat and brag about the fancy home he was in charge of. They sat down in one of the booths by the bar and ordered dinner. Feeling good, Eben boasted a little about his upcoming gig playing Santa at the famous Christmas Eve party at Yvonne and Lester Grants' house. Willeen obviously read the gossip columns.

"The Grants' house?" she repeated, impressed.

"Yes," Eben said proudly. "Yvonne Grant has a big party every year and really likes to do it up. Everyone brings their kids, so naturally they want Santa there too. It's so much fun. You should see me all dressed up!"

"We'd love to." Judd had laughed.

"But how, honey?" Willeen asked. She turned to Eben and put her hand on his arm. "We're not invited to the party," she said with a flirtatious pout.

Eben was pretty relaxed at this point. He usually didn't like to bring anybody back to Kendra's house. But his Santa suit was in the bedroom there and it was Christmas. . . .

"Come back to my place for a nightcap!" he'd blurted. "The Wood family is coming on Christmas Day. I'm sure they wouldn't mind."

Judd had insisted on paying the check and the three of them headed out into the night together.

Now in the light of day Eben felt a little guilty about it. Oh well, he thought as he snowplowed back and forth. No use worrying about it now.

The snow was really coming down and Eben's goggles were starting to fog up. It was perfect Christmas Eve weather, but Eben was glad when he made it to the bottom. He hurried to his car and secured his skis in the rack on top. I'll be home in a few minutes, he thought, and I'll heat up some cider, take a nice hot Jacuzzi, and get ready to ho-ho-ho.

"Eben."

Eben turned his head as he was opening the door to his car. Judd was running toward him.

"Hi, Judd. What's going on?"

Huffing and puffing, Judd told him. "Willeen was supposed to pick me up but she had some trouble with the car. Would you mind giving me a lift to the place where we're staying?"

Eben tried to sound cordial when he was really anxious to get home. "Well, sure, Judd. Where did you say it was?"

"It's just a few minutes outside of town. Not too far."

"Hop in."

They drove along chatting amiably, heading in the opposite direction of the Woods' home. Eben stole a peek at his watch, hoping that they'd get there soon. He didn't have much time now.

"Turn here," Judd finally said. He led Eben up a heavily wooded rural road to an old Victorian farmhouse.

"I see you decided not to go the condo route, huh?" Eben said.

"We like an old-fashioned kind of place with a little bit of privacy," Judd replied. "Why don't you come in for a drink?"

"Thanks, but I can't." Eben didn't know why all of a sudden he felt uncomfortable. "I told you I've got to go be Santa."

Judd pulled out a gun from under his jacket and pointed it at Eben's head. "Don't worry about Santa. Nobody believes in him anyway. Now get in the house."

As his life passed before his eyes, Eben desperately wished he'd obeyed his instinct that morning to remove his things from the guest suite and wipe out the tub.

2

SUMMIT, NEW JERSEY

Saturday, December 24

REGAN REILLY LEANED back on the big overstuffed couch in her parents' den and balanced a cup of hot tea in her hands; she was mesmerized by the twinkling lights of the sizable Christmas tree in the corner. Gaily wrapped packages were cozily arranged around its trunk. Tinsel glistened from its branches.

You'd never know it was a fake, Regan thought. She turned her gaze to the flames lapping evenly in the fireplace. You'd never know the fire was a fake either. Three red felt stockings hanging on the mantel, embroidered with the names Regan, Luke and Nora, completed the perfect Christmas-card scene.

The old grandfather clock in the hallway started to bong. Five o'clock and all is well, she thought.

So where are my mommy and daddy?

Her father, the owner of three funeral homes in the Summit, New Jersey, area, had gone out to take care of a few errands and her mother had gone into New York City to have her tooth repaired by their friend, Dr. Larry Ashkinazy, otherwise known as Mr. Drill, Fill and Bill.

Regan, a private investigator who lived in Los Angeles, was home with her parents for a few days before they all headed out to Aspen on Christmas Day. Regan was going to stay with a friend who was opening a restaurant and inn out there. She and Louis had met three years ago in traffic school in L.A., both having been nailed by the same cop in a speed trap on the Santa Monica Freeway. Rather than get points on their licenses, they had each opted for the choice of attending traffic school, which meant classes run by stand-up comedians. Louis, an occasionally successful dilettante, was a co-founder of the Silver Dollar Flapjack Chain, and he had confided to Regan his dream of someday opening up a restaurant of his own in Colorado.

Now, at age fifty, Louis had finally achieved his goal. He had sold his house in L.A., invested his last red cent, and had begged and borrowed the rest. His new restaurant was called the Silver Mine, and there would be a kickoff party there on December 29 to benefit the Rescue Aspen's Past Association.

While Regan stayed at the Silver Mine, her parents would be the houseguests of Kendra and Sam Wood. Sam was a prominent Broadway producer. Kendra, an actress who had starred in one of Nora's television movies, was about to make her Broadway debut in Sam's upcoming production.

Regan put down her teacup and pulled the requisite multi-colored afghan on the back of the couch around her. She snuggled into the arm of the couch, the only arm around, when the phone began to ring. She picked up the cordless phone next to her, willing her voice to sound bright and holidayish.

"Hello."

"Reilly!"

"Kit!" It was one of Regan's best friends. They had met ten years before, in college, when they'd both spent their junior year abroad, at Saint Polycarp's in Oxford, England. They'd become fast friends when at the first evening meal they'd deemed the cafeteria food unfit for human consumption. Dumping their trays, they headed downtown for spaghetti, which they ended up living on all year. Regan sat up on the couch. "How are things in the land of the insurance policy?"

"Hartford's all right. I'm trying to get into the spirit before I head to my parents' house for dinner."

"I don't suppose you're nibbling on any of that fruitcake your company sends out?" Regan asked. "Unless of course you keep a power saw in your apartment."

"No way. We had about a dozen left over from last year. We sent them out to people who canceled their policies."

"So how else are you getting into the spirit?" Regan asked.

"Well," Kit sighed. "I bought some mistletoe."

"I admire your optimism."

"Very funny. You know what we're heading into, don't you?"

"No. What?"

"The start of the Bermuda Triangle. And believe me, it's deadly."

Regan frowned. "What are you talking about?"

"Christmas, New Year's Eve, and Valentine's Day. The three worst holidays for single women. Will you get a present for Christmas, a date for New Year's, a lone flower on Valentine's Day?"

Regan laughed. "I have a feeling that on February fifteenth I'm going to be zero for three."

"Why?"

"Well, I'm sitting here staring at the presents under the tree. Every single one that's labeled 'Regan' has handwriting that looks suspiciously like my mother's. New Year's Eve in Aspen should be fun, but I'm sure it'll be a group affair. But that's okay. Ever since Guy Lombardo died, New Year's Eve just hasn't been the same. Valentine's Day I don't want to even think about. Now"—Regan paused slightly for emphasis—"you *are* coming to Aspen, aren't you?"

"I think so."

"I think so's not good enough. I know you're off next week."

"Well, I should go in and clear up some odds and ends before the end of the year."

"I thought you sent out all the fruitcake."

Kit laughed. "I've checked the flights. I'll probably be there by mid-week."

"What do you mean, probably? There isn't anything else stopping you, is there?"

Kit hesitated. "No."

"What is it? You bought mistletoe. Are you dating somebody?"

"Well, I've had a few dates with this guy in my health club. He seems really nice. I just thought that if he wanted to get together over the holidays, you know . . ."

"Yeah," Regan said, "but if he doesn't ask you out for New Year's Eve, you'll be sitting home alone banging pots and pans together at midnight."

"I've thought of that."

The phone clicked in Regan's ear. "Hold on a second, Kit."

"Hello."

"Doll! It's me."

"Louis!" Regan could picture him fluffing his hair, pushing it behind his ear and then patting his head. "I'm just on the phone with Kit."

"Is she coming?"

"I hope so. Hold on." Regan clicked back to Kit. "It's Louis. Let me call you back."

"I'll be here hanging the mistletoe."

As Regan got back on the line with Louis, she could hear him giving orders in the background. "Louis? Hellooooo. LOUIS!"

"Yes, darling. We're a little crazed."

"Isn't that good?" Regan asked. It was an important time for him. Reaction to his restaurant over the holidays, and the party on the twenty-ninth, would make or break him.

"Yes, I guess so, darling. Don't mind me, I'm just a wreck. I thought I'd try and reach you and make sure you'll be in tomorrow night. I can't believe it'll be Christmas!"

"I know," Regan said. "I'll be there. My parents and I are flying out tomorrow afternoon on the Woods' jet."

"Hold on, Regan. WHAT'S BURNING?" he yelled. "TAKE THE BREAD OUT OF THE BROILER, FOR GOD'S SAKE!"

Regan chuckled. "You do sound busy. I'd better let you go. I'll see you after dinner at Kendra's."

"Anything special you'll want to eat while you're here, darling?"

"Whatever you're serving. Oh, but one thing."

"What?" he asked quickly.

"I love it when the bread is served nice and hot."

Louis mumbled what Regan was sure was an obscenity and hung up on her.

3

NEW YORK CITY

Saturday, December 24

LARRY WILL THIS HURT?" Nora Regan Reilly garbled from underneath the mask that covered her nostrils, sending nitrous oxide swirling through her brain.

"Just a few more minutes, Nor," Dr. Larry Ashkinazy replied amiably, holding an instrument that looked suspiciously like a cuticle cutter in his hands. "That's some nasty tooth. I'll turn up the gas a little more."

"I have to walk out of here on two feet," Nora croaked as she felt herself flying out of the dentist chair.

"No problem, Nor. I'll get you fixed up in no time and then I'm on vacation." He leaned into her mouth and squirted the offensive tooth with a spray of water as a sputtering suction device hung from Nora's lip.

Nora stared straight ahead at the rows of holiday cards hanging on the venetian blinds. Outside the window, on Central Park South, snow was beginning to fall. It was Christmas Eve, and last-minute shoppers were scurrying by. Feeling woozy, Nora found herself wondering but somehow not worrying about what the drive back to New Jersey would be like.

This nitrous oxide does make you relax, she thought dreamily, but I'd rather be home with an eggnog. She closed her eyes as Larry picked up the drill. The sight of it was bad enough, but the sound was much worse. The whirring would make anyone's legs turn to jelly, not to mention the fact that it completely drowned out the relaxing light music Larry piped into his office.

As Nora breathed in and out, she had the crazy thought that the radio station had been playing the same song the whole time she was in the chair. Come to think of it, it sounded like the same song every time she was in the chair. But then she couldn't remember what it was. Everything was blending together.

A few minutes later, Larry proudly stepped back. "All done!" He turned to his assistant. "Give her straight oxygen."

Nora wiped the accumulated grit from around her mouth and leaned over to the gurgling metal bowl that was just within spitting distance of the chair. Larry's assistant, Flossie, handed her a Dixie cup that held barely enough water to drown a single ant. Nora swished it around in her mouth and aimed for the bowl. The water, flecked with traces of silver filling, was sucked down the pipes faster than you could say "Roto-Rooter."

"Thanks for coming in today, Larry. I couldn't have gone on vacation with that tooth bothering me."

"For you, anything," Larry said as he stood nearby, writing on her chart. "I'm glad Flossie was free to come in and help me out for a few minutes."

Nora watched him as, deep in thought, he made his notations. Larry was a boyishly handsome guy of forty-two with jet-black hair and eyes. His skin was tanned ninety-nine percent of the year, thanks to his frequent trips to places like South Beach in Miami. He was an eligible bachelor and loved every minute of it.

"I'm so glad Regan's going to Aspen," he said as he folded the chart. "She'll have the greatest time. There are so many guys out there that a girl could look like Lassie and she'd still have a good time."

"My daughter doesn't look like Lassie," Nora mumbled as she ran her tongue across her teeth.

"I know, so she'll have an even better time," Larry said earnestly. "I'll tell her where all the parties are." He wrote the name of his hotel on a business card that identified him as "Dentist to the Stars" and handed the card to Nora. "Merry Christmas," he said and gave her a quick kiss on the cheek.

As he hurried out of the room, Nora's head started to clear. She heard him in the hallway talking into his ever-present pocket recorder, which he called the friend that never talks back.

I've got to get going, Nora thought, as she started to get out of the chair.

"Flossie," Larry called as he came back in to assist Nora. "Let's make an appointment for Mrs. Reilly for mid-January and then I'm headed out west!"

"I'm going as far as New Jersey if you need a ride," Nora found herself saying.

"I think," Larry said, laughing, "that we better put that

oxygen mask back on for a few more minutes. We want you to get wherever you're going in one piece."

Nora leaned back in the chair and closed her eyes. So much rushing around at this time of year, she thought. Getting everything ready for Christmas. It would be good to get to Aspen, where she and Luke could unwind at Kendra's home. Regan would be staying nearby. They could all just be lazy and enjoy the rest of the holiday season.

So why did Nora have the feeling in the back of her not-yet-clear mind that it wasn't going to work out like that? She always cheered herself with the thought that if something bad happened, she could always turn it around and use it in one of her murder mysteries.

"Nor," she heard Larry saying. "I bet you get a lot of good material in Aspen."

"That's what I'm afraid of," she said as she took an extra-deep breath of oxygen.

dangling over nothing from a bulletin board, a locket and a dewy little reminder to a couple wishing hands in hand along the street came rushing down at her. Cheying them advice on everything from friendship and love to not keeping out of harm. "What a mess," Regan told aloud. "Things are never that simple."

Regan wasn't entirely sure why neither she nor mother had ever gotten around to tearing them down. Her mother had recently removed the forms at work over her own desk. Regan had had on her desk since the Year One. But she was probably hoping that some of the smarmy goodness urged by these oversized greeting cards would rub off on somebody. Regan smiled to herself. Meanwhile, the posters chirped cheerfully, proclaiming their dear sentiments of love, and friendship. Of them she'd turn out to be an accurate authority.

"Oh, well," Regan said as she pulled the suitcase off the bed and slung the strap over her shoulder.

4

SUMMIT, NEW JERSEY

Sunday, December 25

Hurry up, regan," Nora called up the stairs. "The car is here."

"I'm trying to fit everything that Santa brought me into the suitcase," Regan yelled back down. "He was very good to me this year."

Regan lay down on top of her suitcase, stuffing the protruding sleeves and hems inside as she tugged at the zipper. "This zipper's teeth are more deadly than a shark's," Regan muttered as a silk dress narrowly escaped being chewed up. She finally stood up. "Done."

Regan looked around her room for anything she might have missed. Testaments to her adolescent years still adorned the walls and bookshelves. Scripted posters

depicting everything from a bumblebee atop a flower and a dewy field at sunrise to a couple walking hand-in-hand along the Jersey shore stared down at her, offering their advice on everything from friendship and love to the meaning of life. "What a crock," Regan said aloud. "Things are never that simple."

Regan wasn't really sure why neither she nor her mother had ever gotten around to tearing them down. Her mother had recently removed the ENTER AT YOUR OWN RISK sign Regan had had on her door since the Year One, but she was probably hoping that some of the syrupy goodness urged by those oversized greeting cards would rub off on her daughter. Regan smiled to herself. Nowadays, the poster of that couple proclaiming their deepening love and commitment would probably be used in an ad for multicolor condoms.

"Oh, well," Regan said as she pulled the suitcase off the bed. "This room brings back the optimism of my youth, the feeling of being sixteen . . ."

"Regan!" Nora called again, pulling her back into the present, her thirty-first year of life.

"I'm coming. Ma, how come you never taught me how to pack a suitcase properly?" she asked as she rolled her valise down the hall and clunked it down the steps.

"It's always my fault," Nora said with mock indignation.

"No, it's not," Regan said as she observed all her mother's baggage. "No one ever taught you."

Nora laughed. "Nanny always schlepped out on the bus with everything she needed in two shopping bags."

Luke came out of the bedroom. "I hope the plane will be able to get off the ground with all that dead weight."

"Dad, speaking of dead weight, isn't there something depressing about us riding in a hearse on Christmas Day?

Everyone stares into the windows with such sad expressions."

"It's the only car that would fit all our bags," Luke said dryly. At six feet five, he towered over the two women. He had silver hair and what Nora liked to call Jimmy Stewart good looks. Nora was five feet three inches short, she always said, with blond hair and a patrician face. I fall somewhere in between, Regan thought. She was five feet six inches tall with coloring known as black Irish: dark hair, blue eyes, and skin so white she could get a sunburn at 6 A.M.

"One thing we'll never have to worry about is having anyone accuse us of being normal," Regan observed.

"Normal is a little dull, don't you think, dear?" Nora asked. "Besides, nobody is normal. Just scratch the surface."

"The problem with us is you only have to sniff, not scratch. We're going to pull up to a private plane in an extra-long vehicle with curtains on the windows."

"Kendra won't mind. She'll think it's fun," Nora commented as she locked the front door behind them. "Doesn't that Christmas wreath look pretty?"

Luke and Nora got in front with the driver. Regan squeezed in the back, pondering the day when she'd be riding in this same space in a horizontal position, her eyes shut for good.

Forty-five minutes later, after listening to the special "Imus in the Morning" pretaped Christmas show, they pulled up to Kendra and Sam's private plane. People along the highway had stared into the windows of the hearse and had been taken aback to see the passengers laughing and the driver pounding his fist on the steering wheel as he guffawed.

Thank you, Imus, Regan thought as she chuckled at the nationally popular DJ's imitation of a deranged Santa, for making us seem even weirder than usual.

"Merry Christmas!" Kendra greeted them. Her flaming-red hair and sea-green eyes were vibrant. Sam stood beside her, white-haired with crisp blue eyes and a dazzling smile. They looked like an ad for the good life.

"Welcome!" Sam boomed. "Regan, it's good to have you."

"Thanks for letting me hitch a ride." Regan smiled. "This is the only way to fly, huh?"

"Where's your boarding pass?" Sam asked her.

"What?" Regan said with a puzzled expression.

Sam slapped her on the back. "Just kidding. But you don't get any frequent-flier miles for this trip."

Regan laughed. "I'll make the sacrifice."

Onboard, the Woods' sons, fourteen-year-old Greg and fifteen-year-old Patrick, were playing video games. They look so young, Regan thought. They were both good-looking kids. She wondered how many girls their age were staring at their bedroom walls at that very moment, nursing broken hearts over these two, deriving whatever comfort they could from their favorite passages about romantic misery.

The boys smiled up at her, their slightly self-conscious expressions a contradiction to the rows of earrings they were sporting. God, I feel old, Regan thought.

Kendra was passing out champagne. "Regan?"

"Thanks, Kendra." Regan took a sip, feeling the bubbles tickle her nose. "Louis wants you to be sure and be at his party. He's really excited about it."

"We have our tickets," Sam said. "Just what Aspen

needs, another nightspot. I hope he doesn't fall on his face."

"If he does, they'll have to cart him off to the funny farm," Regan commented. "He'll never recover."

"Opening a restaurant is a high-risk venture," Sam said.

"Yeah, like producing a Broadway play." Kendra laughed.

"My business might not be the most exciting," Luke said, "but I'm happy to say it has the lowest failure rate of any business in this great land of ours."

"We're all happy for you, dear," Nora told him.

"Seriously, Louis is lucky he landed the benefit party for the Rescue Aspen's Past Association," Kendra said. "I hear the competition for it was fierce. He managed to butter up the committee."

"He told me he really wants to make his place a part of the Aspen ideal," Regan said.

"What's that?" Luke asked. "Sounds like New Age mumbo-jumbo."

"Dad." Regan rolled her eyes. "It's serious. Aspen doesn't want to get overdeveloped. Because it's become so popular, they're having a real struggle to keep a small-town flavor. Louis is going to be displaying the works of local artists in his restaurant, and he's also promised to sponsor weekly literary gatherings in the back room."

Greg looked at Regan and yawned.

The old generation gap rears its ugly head, Regan thought.

"What do they do at those gatherings?" Sam asked.

"Everyone gets up and reads what they've prepared. It could be a short story, it could be a poem. Some people might bring a guitar and sing a song."

"I'll stay home and watch my toenails grow that night," Luke drawled.

"Dad, you're impossible!" Regan reached out for a champagne refill.

"It's a throwback to the old coffeehouses," Kendra said enthusiastically. "Nora, you'll have to go and read them one of your stories. You'll scare the pants off them."

Nora put down her glass and dramatically cleared her throat. "It was a dark and stormy night . . ."

Sam laughed. "The wind was blowing hard against the windowpanes . . ."

"A shot rang out . . ." Nora continued.

"And I got called into work," Luke muttered.

Kendra's laugh was a deep, hearty, pleasing sound. Regan looked at her and smiled, glad to see that she seemed totally relaxed. In her mid-forties, Kendra was a fine actress whose entire career up until now had been in television. Regan knew that Kendra had confided to Nora that she was nervous about her Broadway debut.

"Okay, folks," the pilot said. "We've been cleared for takeoff. Be sure your seat belts are fastened."

As Kendra buckled herself in, she said, "Next stop Aspen and the smiling face of our caretaker, Eben . . ."

5

ASPEN

Sunday, December 25

Louis was filled with a sense of nervous well-being. Things were going well. There wasn't a single empty table for the Christmas brunch.

The place was bustling as waiters took orders and refilled coffee cups and champagne glasses, diners greeted each other with air kisses, and children clutched their favorite toys, which had been opened just hours before. Christmas music played softly in the background, and outside, a light snow was falling.

Everything is perfect, Louis thought as he smoothed down the lapels of his red velvet smoking jacket. If only I can keep this up and pull off the big party Thursday night, then I might be able to get some rest.

For months now, as the cost had mounted to put the restaurant together, he'd felt like the Cowardly Lion in *The Wizard of Oz* : too scared to sleep and afraid of witches flying overhead on a broom. For Louis they all had the faces of his investors.

The Grant family was seated at one of the central tables. They had had the big party last night and were part of Aspen's high society. Yvonne and Lester had two young children. For the last few years they had thrown Christmas Eve parties where the children of all their friends got to enjoy a visit with Santa Claus. Yvonne was gesturing to Louis.

He hurried over. Yvonne was a beautiful woman, with none of the signs of fatigue that most young mothers exhibited, especially during the holidays. She looked refreshed and rested. Well, why not? Louis thought. She probably hasn't washed a dish in ten years.

"Louis, dear," she said as she rested a well-manicured bejeweled hand on his arm, "I really must call my housekeeper and ask her to make extra apple pies for tonight. I forgot to tell her we invited some people to stop back again."

Without another word, Louis reached into his pocket and pulled out his cellular phone, a must in finer eating establishments. He flipped it open and ceremoniously handed it to her. "Madame . . ."

"Thank you." Yvonne started to press the numbers, then frowned. She turned to her husband. "Sweetie, what is our number again? I always get it mixed up with the house in Hawaii."

Lester took out his black book and checked. "Allow me," he said lovingly as he took the phone from her and then handed it back.

Yvonne smiled at her children and picked a piece of imaginary lint off her designer sleeve as she waited for Bessie to pick up the phone. "Josh, honey," she said to her son, "why don't you have a few more bites?"

"I don't want to," the four-year-old replied.

"Just a few itty bitty bites for Mommy?"

"No."

"Okay." Finally she spoke into the phone. "Bessie, what took you so long to answer?" Her smile quickly faded. "What are you talking about? Hold on. Lester, the Guglione painting in the library ... did you move it?"

"Of course not!"

Yvonne started to hyperventilate. "Bessie went in to vacuum a few minutes ago and noticed it was gone. Nobody should have been in there last night. The children and nannies were in the family room and the rest of us were in the living-room area. Who could have taken it?" She turned to her children. "Did you see anybody go in the library?"

Josh spoke up. "No one except Santa. He asked me and I told him there was a little bathroom in there but he might be too fat to use it."

"Santa!" Yvonne screeched. "He took that priceless painting! Where could he have gone with it?"

"He said he was headed back to the North Pole," her five-year-old daughter Julie replied practically. "It's a long way and he had to go tinky before he left."

Louis felt a flash of fear sweep through his body as the other diners began to stare. What have I done? he thought.

As they approached Sardy Field, the airport at Aspen, Regan looked out the window. What a sight to behold, she thought. The snow-blanketed Rocky Mountains surrounded

them. Bold and powerful with their rugged terrain yet quietly beautiful, they seemed to welcome the plane as it began its descent.

"Look at those evergreens," Nora said, gesturing to the rows and rows of stately trees sweeping up the mountain-sides.

"Awesome," Greg muttered as he peered out the window.

"Radical," Patrick agreed.

"Kind of reminds me of our Christmas tree at home, huh, Mom?" Regan asked.

"I dragged that tree over my shoulder all the way up the basement steps," Luke protested.

"In three pieces in a cardboard box," Regan said. "With the screws rattling around at the bottom. Dad, you're a regular Paul Bunyon."

"It's the thought that counts," Nora said.

"I love the view, but I can't wait till we're on the ground," Kendra remarked. "The approach here always makes me nervous."

"We are way, way, way above sea level, yes, sir," Sam said. He turned to Luke and Nora. "You've got to take it easy on your first day here. No matter what kind of shape you're in, the lack of oxygen at this high altitude can cause problems. Light-headedness. Fainting. An occasional heart attack. And that's before you hit the slopes."

"Sam, please." Kendra winced.

"Sorry, honey. Besides, I don't need to tell these folks. They've been skiing before."

"Maybe so, but I hope there's a bunny hill," Nora commented.

"It doesn't look like it from here," Regan said. "But you'll do fine."

"Ever since she dislocated her shoulder on an icy slope in New Jersey, Nora's been a little nervous in the wintertime," Luke explained to the Wood family.

"That's a shame," Kendra said sympathetically. "Which ski area was that?"

"Reilly's Lodge." Regan chuckled. "That icy slope was our driveway."

A few minutes later they landed amid a sea of private planes. There was no sign of Eben, so their luggage was brought inside the tiny airport.

Kendra looked around expectantly. "He's always so prompt," she murmured.

Sam shook his head. "A real Johnny-on-the-spot."

Kendra hurried over to one of the pay phones and dialed the house. She stood tapping her foot as the connection went through, glancing at her watch. "It's four-fifteen. I can't believe he's not here. It's the machine . . . Eben, it's Kendra. We're here at the airport, and I was wondering where you were. We'll be waiting out front."

"Eben's bound to be along any second," Sam assured Kendra. He turned to the Reillys. "This guy is really good. You couldn't find a caretaker like him in a million years. Treats the place like it was his own. Always a smile. He's a pretty good cook and even knows how to serve a dinner party. He used to be a waiter."

Regan had heard the story from Louis about the night Eben the waiter tried to separate the police commissioner's wife from her necklace.

Fifteen minutes later, Sam pronounced, "It's time to make an executive decision here. Let's all pile into a couple of taxis."

After negotiating the baggage into two vehicles, Kendra

got into the first cab with Regan, Nora, and Luke. Sam and the boys followed.

"What a glorious place this is," Nora said as they drove along, admiring the views of the mountains from both sides of the cab. The sky was darkening and they headed up into the hills, passing stately homes along the way.

"I always have so much energy when I'm here," Kendra said. "There's something in the air." She leaned forward and instructed the driver to make a right at the private bridge.

After the turn, the narrow gravel road they traveled was surrounded by snow-covered spruce and pines. "It feels like the forest primeval," Nora breathed. "It's wonderful."

But when they approached the sprawling log house nestled against the mountainside, Kendra was shocked to see that it was completely dark. No welcoming lights. No signs of life. "I don't understand it," she murmured. "I hope nothing happened to him." She dashed out of the cab, keys in hand.

Nora, Luke, and Regan scrambled to follow her.

Kendra quickly unlocked the door and pushed it open. "The alarm isn't on."

Not a good sign, Regan thought.

The side door led into the open area that encompassed both kitchen and family room. Kendra flipped on the light. The kitchen was in perfect order except for a few dishes in the sink, a personalized cereal bowl that said EBEN in big orange letters and a matching EBEN mug.

"Where did he ever manage to find dishes with such an unusual name?" Nora wondered aloud. "Regan, remember when you were little and used to cry because we could never find anything with your name on it? Not a license plate for your bicycle, not a key ring, not a—"

"Mom, please," Regan said as a sense of impending doom drew closer.

Kendra opened the dishwasher. "It's full," she said flatly. "The caretaker cottage has its own dishwasher." She hurried to the breakfast bar and flipped on the lights that illuminated the sitting area of the room and gasped, "Oh my God."

"What?" Regan croaked.

"There, and there, and there, and there." Kendra was pointing at blank spots on the walls. "My paintings," she wailed. "My beautiful paintings."

Please don't let it be Eben, Regan prayed, trying to remember the name of the saint in charge of hopeless causes.

6

IDA BOYLE OPENED the door of her daughter Daisy's oven to take a peek at the turkey that was roasting inside. "Umm-hmmm," she murmured to herself. She poked a fork at the bird's opening in an attempt to retrieve some of the stuffing that looked so golden and crunchy.

"Mom!" Daisy said from behind her. "What are you doing? You're not supposed to open the oven while it's cooking."

"Just testing, my dear, just testing. I'm not ruining anything. I cooked a lot of turkeys before you were even born and your father always thought they were delicious." Ida turned to her as she blew on her fork. "I hope we didn't add too many onions."

Daisy pulled out a chair for her mother at the kitchen table. "This group will eat anything. Now sit down, Mom, please. You're on your feet too much."

"If I sit down too long, I'll never get up," Ida said as she eased herself into a seat. "Maybe you could rub my back a little."

Daisy, a trained masseuse who serviced the tired and aching muscles of skiers in the Aspen area, complied. She put her hands on her mother's shoulders and started to massage.

"How's that?"

"You're the best, Daisy. That's why you're always so busy."

Daisy was forty-six years old. She'd come to Aspen from Ohio in 1967, when she was eighteen. Word of Aspen's free spirit and "anything goes" attitude had reached the growing number of hippies all over the country. Fresh out of high school, Daisy had jumped into her red Volkswagen bug and driven cross-country with a couple of her girlfriends. They hadn't planned to settle in Aspen, just maybe spend the summer there and then move on to California, where flower power was really going strong.

For Daisy, it was not meant to be. At a sit-in in Aspen, she met Buck Frasher. She noticed him across the crowded green, wearing love beads that matched hers. Cupid struck. Buck came over to her and never left. How square, Daisy sometimes thought. I of all people never thought I would get married so young. She and Buck had settled happily into life in Aspen together and never looked back.

Buck got a job giving snowmobile tours during the winter. During the summer he worked in construction. Daisy became a traveling masseuse, visiting hotels and private homes, her clients ranging from Hollywood stars to regular folks with aching backs.

"Feel better now?" Daisy asked as she released her hands and headed for the sink.

"A little," Ida said as she reached back and caressed her shoulder under her brown polyester jacket. It was her favorite outfit, the jacket with the matching skirt and pale

yellow blouse with the ruffle around the collar. Even though Ida worked at the dry cleaner's, the best part of it was that it was wash-and-wear.

Ida was in her mid-seventies. She had a pleasant face framed with salt-and-pepper hair, large glasses, and an understanding smile that greeted customers who brought in their stained clothes and were upset that they might never be able to wear them again. She always promised that they would try their best and if that wasn't good enough to remove those pesky stains, then darn it, they'd run those dirty clothes through the machine again. If all their efforts failed, Ida had the sad task of putting a bright orange sticker with a frowning face on the ticket. She hated that.

Ida still lived in Ohio but came out to spend a couple of months every year with Daisy and her family. A local dry cleaner always needed extra help, and Ida's experience at the One-Hour Cleaners back in Columbus had gotten her hired for some part-time work when she was in town. She kept an autograph book behind the counter, and when the stars came in, she always got them to sign it for her.

She also took a secret delight in going through their pockets, hoping that they left something interesting that she could tell the girls about when she went back to Ohio in the spring. But of course, she always returned everything.

"You're the eyes and the ears of the world," her boss always said, but she never did anything to threaten his business. She didn't even put up that much of a stink when he told her to leave her camera home. The stars in Aspen don't like having their pictures taken when they're running around town doing their errands like everyone else.

"Honey, what time are we going to eat?" Buck asked from the family room, which was an extension of the kitchen. He was a hearty, bearded man who was at the

moment sitting on the floor playing with six-year-old Zenith and seven-year-old Serenity, the children who arrived one after the other after years of unexplained infertility.

"It just goes to show what can happen when you forget about trying so hard," Daisy always preached to anxious would-be mothers among her clients.

Daisy and Buck gave their children the names they had picked out so long ago when they decided it was time to go forth and multiply.

Buck got up, walked over, and helped himself to a stalk of celery that was lying on the counter.

Daisy pushed back her long brown hair. "About six," she said. She hadn't changed much at all from her hippie days. She always said she wouldn't know what to do with all that mousse and spray and gel some women put into their hair. Not to mention the fact that the aerosol cans wreck the ozone layer.

The phone on the counter began to ring. Buck picked it up. "Merry Christmas."

Ida turned to Daisy. "He shouldn't say that. What if they're Jewish?"

"Don't worry about it."

" 'Happy Holidays' would be more appropriate . . ."

Daisy motioned for her mother to be quiet as she saw the concerned expression on Buck's face.

"Kendra, I haven't talked to Eben in a few days." Buck leaned on the counter. "When I saw him on Friday he said he was heading out of town to do some shopping."

"Who's Eben?" Ida asked.

"A caretaker we know," Daisy whispered. Finally she couldn't stand it anymore. "Buck, what happened?"

Buck covered the phone with his hand. "Kendra and

Sam Wood just got into town with their kids and some guests. Their artwork is missing, Eben is gone, and there's no sign of forced entry."

"Oh wow!" Daisy exclaimed.

"Kendra Wood is a lovely actress," Ida observed. "Who are her guests this weekend? Anybody famous? If so, I'd like to get their autographs."

7

EBEN HAD HAD a terrible night. And to think it had been Christmas Eve. It just wasn't fair. He knew he should never have trusted old Mr. Smoothie. Hell, Judd had never been very nice to him back in their days of confinement. Why the change of tune now? *If I'd had my thinking cap on, I would have been suspicious. How often does a leopard change his spots anyway?*

And sweet little Willeen. *Give me a break.* She had a pretty tight grip when she yanked his arms behind him and helped Judd snap on the handcuffs. Judd knew that Eben's fingers worked like magic at removing jewelry, so he also tied a rope around his wrists with double knots that would have made Houdini pause.

Eben was not only scared but was also homesick for Kendra's house. Tears welled in his eyes as he once again thought that even if he did get out of this alive, he'd probably never get his job back. Not after Kendra realized

he'd been taking advantage of all the little luxuries the house had to offer. Like sleeping in the guest suite.

If only, he thought. Eben knew that one of the most painful things a person can do is mull over all the "if onlys" in his life. Like the endless hours in prison, this newfound free time was getting him started again. If only the police commissioner hadn't been watching him. If only he'd wiped out the tub. If only he'd been born with the innate ability to make tons of money. If only he'd been born into a family that wanted him. Oh forget it, he decided. No use torturing myself. I've got Judd and Willeen for that.

Eben rolled a little bit sideways on the bed. This blanket smells as if some drooling dog spent a lot of time snoozing here, he thought. No one is ever going to find me. This place is remote.

The door to the bedroom opened. Willeen was standing there in her black stretch pants and cheerful holiday sweater. "Are you having a nice Christmas?" she asked sarcastically.

"Never been merrier," Eben answered.

"Well, you sure helped to make ours a better one," Willeen said. "We got lots of nice presents, thanks to you."

Last night they had gone out after securing him to the bedpost. Hours later they returned, flush with victory. Judd was decked out in the Santa suit, the cap and fake beard in his hand.

"Willeen makes a good Rudolph," he'd told Eben. "She was waiting in the car for her secret Santa, protecting the pretty pictures we took off Kendra Wood's walls. When I got out of the party I jumped in and we dashed out of town."

How galling, Eben had thought. Judd and Willeen had

cleaned out Kendra's house of all her art and then had gone on to the Grants' party, where they'd pulled off another heist. So much for the Christmas moratorium of peace on earth and good will toward men.

And to make it even worse, they had grabbed most of Eben's clothes from his room at Kendra's. Now everyone would think he was the thief and had run out of town. No one would be thinking kindly of him!

"Would you like a little snack?" Willeen asked now. "A little Christmas porridge?"

"You're not going to poison me, are you?" Eben retorted, only half kidding. He had no idea what they were planning for him, but he was worried. How could they ever let him out of there alive when he knew what they had done?

"Eben, you're our Christmas blessing," Willeen said.

"I'm sure not one of the three wise men," Eben muttered.

As Willeen walked out of the room, Eben could hear Judd's voice in the living room. "Willeen, this stash should save our butts with Claude. He'll blame us for not beating the Coyote to that painting that was stolen in Vail. But the party on Thursday will put us over our quota in the group's sales club."

"Yup, the Beasley will save our butts," she agreed.

Oh my God, Eben thought. Does that mean that Judd and Willeen are planning to steal old Geraldine Spoonfellow's Beasley painting from Louis's party? Spoonfellow is famous for making a stink about law and order. If anything happens to her property in Louis's place, she'll have it closed down. Louis will be ruined. He's probably halfway there already if everyone in town found out that he's the

one who recommended a jailbird to Kendra Wood. Tongues must be wagging all over the Roaring Fork Valley.

Eben tried to breathe steadily. He felt himself getting light-headed, as if becoming detached from reality, floating above his handcuffed, shackled self. This can't be happening, he thought. They will probably kill me. Why didn't they kill me right away? Maybe because they'd be stuck with my remains. After they steal Geraldine's painting, they'll be hotfooting it out of town. I don't think they'll want me along. They won't leave me here to talk about them. So . . .

Eben forced himself to cease and desist the dreary path on which his thoughts were leading him.

Trying to be an optimist, he whispered to himself, "If I do have until Thursday, maybe I can figure out a way to bust out of here."

What a way to spend the holidays.

8

NOT EXACTLY WHAT I expected to find at Kendra's house on Christmas afternoon in Aspen, Regan thought. It reminded her of the story of the three bears. Eben was missing, but his presence was everywhere. After Kendra phoned Eben's acquaintances Buck and Daisy, and while they awaited the arrival of the police, they'd begun to walk through the house.

"Somebody's been sleeping in the guest bed," Kendra said, her voice and finger shaking in unison as she pointed out that not only had her house been robbed and her art was missing, but her caretaker had enjoyed the pleasures of the guest suite as well.

They were all standing around the spacious room. Obviously Eben had made himself very comfortable. Several books on how to ski were scattered on the king-size bed. The television was pulled out from the armoire and tilted for better viewing. The pillows were propped up just so and a bottle of Vicks and a box of tissues were placed

within handy reach of the bed on the handcrafted night table.

"Eben loved the smell of Vicks," Kendra said flatly. "He told me one of his few good memories of the orphanage was standing in his crib when he was sick and inhaling the steam from the vaporizer. It made him feel loved."

"I would have bought him a vaporizer for his own room," Sam grunted. He picked up and leafed through a stack of adventure and mystery magazines that were piled on the chaise longue. With a disgusted look he remarked, "I should have known about that guy."

"He seemed so trustworthy," Kendra protested. "He said that he wanted to take care of a nice house because he'd never gotten the chance to live in one while he was growing up. It's just so hard to believe he would do something like this."

I'm going to have to tell them, Regan thought miserably. She had met and liked Eben when he worked for Louis in Los Angeles a couple of years ago. That was when Louis had had a small catering business. But she had also known that Eben had spent five years in the clink for jewel theft. When Louis told Regan that he had recommended Eben for a job with Kendra Wood, Regan had ignored the warning voice in her head that told her Kendra should be made aware of Eben's background. Now, as one after another of the paintings Kendra had loved were noted as missing from the walls, Regan's guilt deepened. She felt a tug at her arm.

"Regan, what's up?" Nora whispered. "You look as if you've seen a ghost."

Regan shook her head as the front doorbell rang.

"That will be the cops," Kendra said. She darted for the door, returning with two police officers. "This used to

be known as the guest suite," she explained. "But it's obviously where my caretaker took up residence."

"He has very good taste," the cop, who introduced himself as Officer Dennis Madden, observed dryly.

"I'm on the next shift in this room," Luke remarked. "The last guy checked out in a hurry."

The other officer, a slender young woman who looked to be in her late twenties, raised her eyebrows. "Did you have any knowledge of him playing Santa Claus for the Grants last night?" she asked Kendra and Sam.

"Last year at their party he stepped in for someone who got sick at the last minute," Kendra said. "Eben said he had been a department-store Santa years ago and loved it. They asked him back this year. Why? Didn't he show up?"

"Unfortunately, yes. Today they discovered a blank spot on the wall in their library. A Guglione painting is missing." She glanced down at her notes. "We talked to the Grant children and they said that Santa 'had to go tinky' before he left for the North Pole. He asked to use the bathroom off the library. Nobody else from the party went in there. The kids said that his bag looked full when he left."

"Oh my God!" Kendra cried. "Yvonne is a friend of mine. Sam, that painting is worth a fortune. I can't believe that Eben could have done this!"

"How much did you know about him when you hired him?" Officer Madden asked.

Kendra looked at Sam. "We had placed an ad but hadn't found anyone we felt comfortable with. Then an acquaintance we'd met in Los Angeles through Regan, Louis Altide, recommended Eben. Said he'd known him for years. Louis lives in Aspen now. He just opened the Silver Mine Inn."

Regan inhaled sharply. I've got to tell them now, she

thought. Here goes nothing. Or everything. "Kendra," she began.

Kendra looked up at her. "Yes, Regan."

"There's something you should know about Eben. Something I should probably have told you before . . ."

The whole group waited.

Regan found herself cringing as she mouthed the words, "Eben spent a few years in prison."

"For what?" Kendra's voice rose.

"Jewelry theft."

Kendra and Nora both unconsciously grabbed at their necklaces.

"Why didn't you say anything before this, Regan?" Nora asked.

"I didn't find out until after Kendra and Sam hired him and he was already working here. I didn't think it was my place to interfere."

Kendra hesitated, then said, "If you knew before I hired him, it might have made a difference. But he did do a good job and I wouldn't have fired him if I had found out." She paused. "So he's an ex-con?"

"No wonder he never wore stripes," Sam said.

"Did Louis know when he recommended him?" Kendra asked.

Regan gritted her teeth. "Wel-l-l, I guess so. But he seemed to be such a nice guy and so accommodating. There was nothing Louis asked him to do that he wasn't perfectly happy to do."

"That much is true," Sam grunted. He waved his hand around the room. "We just didn't know how much in perks he was taking on his own. And how much he was planning to take."

"I was thinking of giving him a raise." Kendra sighed.

"He was so agreeable. You know, I looked in the refrigerator and he'd done some of the food shopping." Then she looked at Regan and shook her head. "Regan, I'd have given him a break if I were in your shoes. Louis is a different story. The way he praised Eben I thought he was his long-lost brother."

Officer Madden had his notebook out and began firing questions at Regan. "What name did this guy go under? Was that his real name? Where was he in prison?"

"He was in prison in New York State. I think it's his real name but I don't really know."

"I'll talk to this Louis guy. Some friend," the cop muttered. "Pass off a jailbird on you."

Deep in thought, Regan wandered over to the bathroom and glanced inside. This place is bigger than my living room, she thought. All done in tones of apricot, there was a large Jacuzzi, a separate shower with a gleaming glass door, a toilet set off on its own with a view of the snowy mountains right in the backyard, and a long countered area with two sinks and a mirror covering the whole wall. You could have an aerobics class in here, she mused. A pair of big black boots with jingle bells attached sat under the counter on a green towel.

"Look at these," she called as she picked them up and carried them into the bedroom. "Wouldn't these be the type of boots you would wear if you were going to play Santa? They look as if they are all shined and ready to go. Even the bells are attached. But there's no sign of the rest of his outfit."

"We can check his apartment," Sam said.

The policewoman, Officer Webb, opened the closet door. A man's terry-cloth bathrobe was hanging by itself. A few brightly colored polyester shirts were on the floor. Several

hangers were askew. "It looks like someone might have left here in a hurry."

You would think that anyone who loves his Vicks would have brought along his terry-cloth bathrobe, Regan mused. People get attached to their bathrobes like children to their security blankets, wearing them to tatters, often throwing them away only after a long-suffering family member buys them a new one.

Nora had her arms folded and a thoughtful look was on her face. "Maybe he came back here after he was at the Grants' and then took off."

"That would be taking a big risk," Regan said. "If they discovered right away that the painting was gone and they knew who Santa was, this is the first place they'd have looked for him."

Officer Madden nodded in agreement. "That's right, ma'am."

I hate being called ma'am, Regan thought.

Regan was still holding Eben's clunky boots. "Well, since it looks as if he left here of his own volition, I say there's something strange about him not taking these with him."

"Very often when criminals are in a hurry, they make stupid mistakes," Officer Madden said flatly. "But I wouldn't wear boots with bells if I wanted to make a quick exit and disappear."

Regan was agitated. The whole thing didn't sit right with her, and she was determined to find out what the hell had happened. When she'd met Eben at Louis's place in California he'd told her how much he enjoyed being a caretaker. "I get to live in the place while the owners are away making money to support it." When Louis admitted

Eben's past, she had questioned him on the recommendation to Kendra.

Louis had said, "Regan, I believe Eben when he said that he wouldn't even steal a salt shaker from a restaurant. He hated prison."

What had changed his mind?

Luke was talking. "As I was saying, why don't we check Eben's apartment and see what else he might have left behind?"

Not bothering to put on their coats, they exited the side door and headed back to the garage apartment. The door was unlocked and they hurried up the steps.

This place isn't so bad, Regan thought. The living room was small but cozy, with a little kitchenette at the end.

Sam pushed open the door to the bedroom. "The bed is neatly made," he pronounced. "Why wouldn't it be? He probably hasn't slept in it for months."

Well, Regan thought, I can see why he preferred the main house. The room was small. A portable television was resting on a folding chair near the bed. But the quilt is cheery enough, and you can't knock the view of the Rockies. And it's certainly peaceful.

In Los Angeles, Regan regularly had to scare off a group of early-morning walkers who often paused outside her first-floor bedroom window for a loud chat before they went on their separate ways. It always called for an indignant "DO YOU MIND?" Eben didn't have to worry about that here. It was a perfect place to find solitude. Or a perfect place to be secluded if that's what you wanted, she thought.

Ceremoniously, Sam opened the closet. A couple of sweaters were folded on the shelf. A handful of work shirts, jeans, and corduroys were hanging on old wire hangers. Scuffed-up shoes were thrown around the closet floor.

"Not many clothes here, Luke," Sam said. "No Santa suit, either."

"Come to think of it, I don't think he owned a suit," Kendra said. "As I recall, he had a blue blazer that he sometimes wore." She turned to Luke. "He wasn't the type to get too dressed up."

"No sign of a blue blazer, no, sir," Sam said.

The top drawer of the dresser was not closed properly. It looked as if it had gotten stuck on the tracks when someone tried to shove it shut. It squeaked as Sam pulled it open. "It looks to me as if he didn't want to leave without his socks and underwear. A man can't do without those, now can he?" He held up a raggy pair of B.V.D.s and two mismatched socks. "I can't say that I'm surprised he left these behind."

"Sam!" Kendra shook her head.

"Yes, sir, here's a man who knows that you should never wear underwear with holes in it. What will the emergency-room personnel think if you get hit by a truck?"

Regan always thought that the doctors and nurses in emergency rooms probably had better things to do than discuss the state of their patients' underwear.

"Well, he obviously didn't care about what we thought when we found it," Kendra observed.

"Need any more rags for the maid?" Sam asked before he dropped Eben's personal effects back into the drawer.

"Eben was the maid!" Kendra moaned. "You're just trying to make me feel better."

"Let's check the bathroom," Nora suggested.

They all shuffled over to the doorway. The bathroom could best be described as functional. White tiles, white toilet and small sink, white bathtub with a green vinyl shower curtain. Regan doubted that the towel racks were

heated. In a way Regan couldn't blame Eben for being tempted by the amenities in the guest-suite luxury bathroom, like the Olympic-size Jacuzzi. *But that didn't make him an art thief.*

The police officer opened the medicine cabinet. Another source of potential embarrassment, Regan thought. She had a friend who at parties would always make sure to use the bathroom before leaving in order to peek in people's medicine chests and behind their shower curtains.

But Eben's medicine cabinet was empty except for a bottle of Tums on the top shelf. Stress, Regan thought. There was no sign of a toothbrush. There hadn't been any toilet articles in the bathroom of the house, either. Another sign that he had planned his departure.

"You say you met Eben Bean through Altide?" Officer Webb asked. "Did he have other references?"

"No. Louis was so enthusiastic and Eben was currently working for him, so we just accepted his word." The betrayal was starting to get to Kendra. Her face turned scarlet. "I can't believe Louis did this to us. I could throttle him."

There was a phone in the caretaker apartment. She went over to it, dialed information and got the number of the Silver Mine. When she was put through to Louis, she did not mince words. "I just want you to know that your highly recommended caretaker friend has ripped us off. You may already know about the Grants' painting. Ours weren't nearly so valuable but they were expensive, and they were selected for very personal reasons over the past twenty years."

Sputtering could be heard from the other end of the phone.

He'll be a basket case by the time I get there, Regan thought.

Kendra cut through the tearful apologies. "Oh, shut up,"

she said as she slammed down the phone and marched out of the apartment.

Over dinner, Sam and Luke made a determined effort to cheer up Kendra. "We've got each other and our children," Sam said, "although they seem to avoid us in favor of the VCR. Come to think of it, I'm surprised Eben didn't put that in his sack too. And we have our good friends."

"Don't forget your health," Luke added. "Your most valuable possession." He paused. "Of course if it went on for everyone indefinitely, I'd be out of business."

"One time years ago, the police came to our home when we weren't there because the alarm had gone off," Nora contributed, as she ground pepper over her salad. "When they saw the mess in Regan's room they were sure someone had broken in."

"Mom!" Regan protested.

Nora shrugged. "Oh, honey, it's a good story. Well, thank God, we got home before they started dusting for fingerprints. We had to inform them that that was the natural state of affairs in Regan's room. The wind had tripped the alarm," she explained.

"Thank you for sharing," Regan said as she helped herself to a piece of bread. She tried to sound light-hearted, but inwardly she was troubled. I'm a trained investigator, she thought. I knew Eben was a thief. Not the kind of thief who had one brush with the law but one who'd been a career criminal until he picked on the police commissioner's wife. I'm going to find out what happened to him.

Then she laid down the bread. *Not, what happened to the art and where Eben had taken it, but what happened to Eben?* Why did some instinct warn her that this was not a cut-and-dried case of a recidivist felon?

9

REGAN, THANK GOD, you're here!" Louis screamed as the cabdriver helped her into the lobby with her bags.

From the expression on his face, Regan could see that Louis was in his frantic mode. "It's going to be all right," she assured him. "Say, you've got a classy joint here."

For a brief, shining moment, the terror evaporated from his countenance. "I know," he acknowledged.

The lobby had a clubby atmosphere, with oriental rugs covering the old oak floor, high-back chairs, a grand fireplace big enough for a weenie roast, glass-topped tables supported by antlers. Antlers, Regan realized, seemed to be a big theme in Louis's decorating. They were also sprouting from the chandelier and peeking under lamp shades.

Red wallpaper was the background for numerous paintings and portraits. Beyond the reception desk, a grand staircase led to the second floor.

"The restaurant's in the back," Louis explained as he

picked up her suitcase and headed for the stairs. "Let's drop your bag in your room first."

Regan followed him across the lobby. As they passed the reception desk, the clerk, who had the tanned look of a perennial skier, called, "Louis, do you want me to get someone for the bags?"

"Too late now, Tripp," Louis shot back as he trudged up the steps.

He's tense, Regan decided. Louis's receding brown hair was pulled back into a little ponytail. Flecks of gray were evident, probably multiplying by the minute, she thought. Despite the fact that he was a nervous wreck, in his splendid red dinner jacket and gray slacks Louis still looked the part of lord of the manor.

"Where did you get all these great portraits?" Regan asked, pausing to examine them briefly as she ascended to the second floor.

"They just look expensive," Louis said defensively. "I started collecting them when I bought this place. You'd be amazed how many people dump their ancestors' portraits into garage sales. They give an old place like this atmosphere."

"How old is it?" Regan asked, as they reached the second floor.

"Exactly one hundred years old. That's one of the reasons I got the big benefit. This place was originally the Silver Mine Tavern, built by Geraldine Spoonfellow's grandfather. She's the moving spirit behind the Rescue Aspen's Past Association. She's donating a painting to the association and it will be on view here at the party . . . if the party stays here."

Regan's room was near the staircase. Louis led her into

it. "It's my best," he said, waving his hand. "Hope you like it."

"I love it," Regan said as she took in the old-fashioned wallpaper, fluffy quilt and sleigh bed. "It makes me feel like Emily Dickinson. Maybe I'll write a poem."

As the words rolled off her tongue, she knew they weren't falling on appreciative ears. She waited.

Louis sank into the green velvet rocker by the window. "Regan," he moaned, "I'm in big trouble." Nervously he smoothed the hair on the sides of his head and pulled at his ponytail. "There's a lot of money invested in this place."

"It looks it," Regan agreed and then wished she hadn't said that.

"I have all my own money in it and investors' money and it's very important that this place starts to make some of that money back."

"Running a restaurant is tough," Regan said and realized she should maybe go for a Dale Carnegie course. Think positively. Make the other fellow feel better. "You'll make it back," she added lamely as she thought about Sam's comments on the plane.

"Regan, the dinner-dance is the key," Louis said, his voice cracking with strain.

"I know it's an important night for you."

"It's more than that. I didn't go into it all over the phone, but that Geraldine Spoonfellow, a grande dame of Aspen if there ever was one, discovered a painting of her Pop-Pop in her barn. It's over one hundred years old."

Regan squinted. "Her what?"

"Her grandfather. That's what she calls him. It's a Beasley and it's been appraised at three million dollars. That's the painting she's donating to the association. In the new

museum they'll have a special room for it. It features Pop-Pop and some other miner trudging down the mountain from their silver claim. On Thursday night, they're going to give the painting its first public exhibition and they're also going to sell silver nameplates and use them to decorate that room."

Louis took a deep breath. "Beasley's done for Colorado what Remington did for the West and O'Keeffe did for the desert," he explained nervously.

"And Monet did for outdoor picnics," Regan added.

"Oh, Regan." Louis laughed in spite of himself. "Anyway, that's why we're getting so much media coverage and interest from every social climber in Aspen. We're fully booked. I've paid a publicist. *People* magazine is coming. I've pulled out all the stops." Louis paused to catch his breath. "Now because of Eben everybody is mad at me. They're talking about moving the affair to one of the other restaurants. If they do, I'll start the New Year by filing for Chapter Eleven."

"Who's talking about moving the party?" Regan asked.

"Well, isn't Kendra mad at me?"

"Yes."

"I know her friends the Grants are mad at me."

"Bingo," Regan said.

"You're a big help. Yvonne Grant called to scream at me after Kendra let her know about Eben. What do you think the Rescue Aspen's Past Association—isn't that a dumb name?—is going to think? I'm tied to the felon who just ripped off two prominent Aspen citizens."

"I don't think they'll be very happy," Regan agreed. "But, Louis, we can't be sure that Eben is guilty."

He looked up at her, astonished. "Why not? The trouble with me and you is that we're nice, kindhearted optimists.

In other words, we're big dopes. I should have laid it out for Kendra, and then, when I blabbed about him to you, you should have decided to warn her."

"Thanks for including me," Regan said sardonically. "Share the guilt. Why did you have to tell me about his record in the first place?"

"I'm sorry," Louis apologized. "Regan, the cops are coming to talk to me in the morning, after they get a full report on him. Will you sit in with me?"

"I wouldn't miss it for the world."

10

The man known to the art world as the Sleuth had spent a highly entertaining Christmas Eve. He had thoroughly enjoyed the remote cottage where Willem, Aned and their daughter Lana Elion were staying. He was able to hook up a cable through the phone line there, connecting his equipment to the hidden cameras. An electronic whiz, he could not only hear but actually see their every activity on the sophisticated portable televisions that were one of the tools of his trade.

At first, when he'd heard Willem and Aned making their vacation plans to kidnap Lana and sneak the art from the Grimes and the Woods, he had toyed with the idea of once again beating them to it.

Then he'd decided that would be a serious mistake. The art in the Woods' home was a little common to the taste of the wealthy patrons, even the cosmic sculpture which was a genuine prize, even worth the risk of stealing.

There was no need to hurry himself for Thanksgiving,

10

THE MAN KNOWN to the art world as the Coyote had spent a highly entertaining Christmas. He had thoroughly bugged the remote cottage where Willeen, Judd and their unwilling guest Eben were staying. He was able to hook up a cable through the phone line there, connecting his equipment to the hidden cameras. An electronics whiz, he could not only hear but actually see their every activity on the sophisticated portable televisions that were one of the tools of his trade.

At first, when he'd heard Willeen and Judd making their pathetic plans to kidnap Eben and steal the art from the Grants and the Woods, he had toyed with the idea of once again beating them to it.

Then he'd decided that would be a serious mistake. The art in the Woods' home was a trifle compared to the value of the Beasley paintings. Even the Grants' million-dollar Guglione painting was not worth the risk.

The Coyote was saving himself for Thursday night.

That the whole Aspen community would be in an uproar over the supposed guilt of that poor slob, Eben Bean, was nothing short of a gift to him. No one would even consider the possibility that Eben would return to attempt to remove the Beasley painting in front of six hundred spectators.

The Coyote leaned forward. There wasn't much to watch now. Willeen and Judd were on their way into town to hobnob in the Timberline with the people out for a belt on Christmas night. Eben Bean was staring at the ceiling. His arms were moving, so he was probably trying to undo the knots Judd had tied so carefully.

"Go for it," the Coyote said aloud. "I wish I could help you, pal. You've been a big help to me."

After he turned off the set, he felt restless. Maybe he'd go out for a glass of cheer. He deserved it. In the morning, when he was rested and fresh, he'd mull over the plan Judd and Willeen had concocted to steal the about-to-be-donated Beasley on Thursday the twenty-ninth.

And he'd work out all the details of his scheme to add another Beasley to his collection.

11

Eben slept fitfully. Being tied up didn't help. He had dreams of a line of Santas marching toward him, ringing their bells and yelling, "Merry merry merry Eben." *I wish this were a dream,* he kept thinking. When he finally came out of it and awoke, he was flooded with relief, until he realized again where he was. *From bad to worse and back again,* he thought.

Gray winter light was beginning to filter through the ratty shade. *I feel as stark and hollow as this room,* he thought. *Normally I'd be getting up soon and fixing a pot of Kendra's fresh-ground gourmet coffee. Then I'd sit at the big butcher-block table, read the local papers and get ready to take on the day. But this dawn felt incredibly lonely, as dawns can when you're alone and have got no plans, nothing in particular that needs to be done. Like the*

days back in prison. He shook his feet, which were chained to the foot of the bed. "I don't think I'll be going anywhere soon," he mumbled softly.

Eben's body ached. His muscles were cramping up but good. Normally he liked to sprawl out in his sleep, planting himself in the middle of the king-size bed at Kendra's house and getting her money's worth out of every inch of the mattress. With his hands tied behind him, there weren't too many positions to get comfortable in. When he tried to rest on his back, the only parts of his body that got any sleep were his hands. He'd spent several cheerless minutes trying to shake out the pins and needles.

I could use Daisy to give me a good massage, he thought. He'd known Daisy and Buck ever since Buck had done some construction work on the house. A couple of times Eben had splurged and hired Daisy, and it had been well worth it. He always felt like a new man after the massage, and Daisy was good company too. So relaxed. "Not a hassle," was her favorite expression. He would have liked to have gotten to know them better, but he kept mostly to himself. Sometimes they had invited him to dinner, but he usually declined. He didn't want to get too close for fear they'd find out about his past. A deeper sense of gloom struck Eben's heart. I bet they know now, he thought.

Last year there'd been a nice little write-up in the local paper on the Grants' party. Eben had been a little disappointed that they hadn't used one of the pictures he was in, but he was happy they mentioned the "spirited" Santa who made the "children of all ages" smile and laugh. What did they have to say about Santa this year? he wondered. Santa the Swindler?

It wasn't until about eight o'clock that he heard voices in the living room. The walls were thin and the place was

small. On top of that, Eben had been blessed with excellent hearing. But as he listened, he was shocked to realize that it was not Willeen and Judd talking.

"I enjoyed meeting the Smiths from Arizona. It was their first time at the Timberline too," a cultured woman's voice was saying.

"He's in reinsurance, dear," a well-modulated man's voice answered back.

Who are they? Eben wondered. Should I try to attract their attention? Who could they be? Then, at the next words, he realized what was going on.

"Geez, Eben, it's a pain in the ass trying to talk nice," Willeen yelled. The door swung open and she walked over to the bed. "Did we fool ya?"

"You deserve an Academy Award," Eben said sourly. "But I'd keep your day job."

Judd joined Willeen. "We took elocution lessons. They were expensive."

"Demand a refund," Eben snapped.

Willeen laughed heartily. "You're a card, Eben. Hey, Judd, let's let Eben stretch his legs and use the can. Eben, you can even sit in the living room and have breakfast with us. But don't try anything."

"I won't," Eben replied as Judd freed him from the bed.

A few minutes later, Judd was pouring coffee into Eben's cup. A gun lay on the table next to Willeen.

Eben sipped the bitter black brew and almost choked. "Do you have any sugar?" he asked.

"Oh, yeah," Willeen said. She got up and flipped on the radio.

"You picked a fine time to leave me, Lucille," Kenny Rogers was singing mournfully.

Eben found himself tapping his foot.

When the song ended, Marty, the DJ, said, "Well, that's a song the Wood family could be singing this morning, referring, of course, to their caretaker, Eben Bean. Come on now, Eben, how could you do it? We at the station are hereby nominating you for America's Most Ungrateful Criminal."

Judd's laugh was a series of braying snorts punctuated by slaps on his thigh.

"But seriously, folks," Marty continued, "the police are putting up Eben's picture around town and want you to be on the lookout for him. Of course he's probably in Tahiti by now!"

Willeen widened her eyes and pointed at Eben. "There he is!"

"Shut up, Willeen," Judd ordered as he turned up the volume of the radio.

". . . possible link between Eben Bean and a Mace attack three days ago on an elderly dude in Vail in which a painting worth mucho bucks was stolen," the DJ concluded.

"Oh my God." Eben's tone was barely audible.

"Perfect," Willeen declared as Judd snapped off the radio. "Everything is working out just beautifully."

The clock on the nightstand that used to hold Eben's Vicks and tissues read eight-fifteen.

"Darling, I can see why that Eben fellow slept in this bed. It really is rather comfortable," Nora murmured as she rolled over and faced Luke.

Luke pulled her close. "Nothing like helping yourself to a few perks. Remember the guy I had at the first home who kept stealing the flowers?"

"Wasn't he dating a bunch of girls at the same time?" Nora asked drowsily.

"I'll say. I knew something was up when we got to the cemetery to bury a client and there weren't as many flowers in the hearse as there'd been at the home. That it was Valentine's Day made it even more suspicious. When we got back I pretended that I was thinking of buying a car like his and could I get a look at his trunk space." Luke chuckled at the memory.

"When I opened it, there were two big bouquets staring us in the face. One was from the Moose Lodge and the other was from the Shriners."

"That's terrible," Nora said as she rubbed her eyes. "Thank God he didn't have a bigger trunk. Or the only flowers around your client's grave would have been the daisies he eventually pushed up himself."

"You're sick," Luke declared.

"It runs in the family. Ohhh"—Nora stretched her arms—"I guess it's time to get up. It's so nice not to have to hurry."

Luke kissed her. "I'll jump in Eben's shower first. Sam said we should take a day to get used to the altitude before we ski, so why don't we take them out to lunch? It'll take their minds off all those blank spaces on the walls."

"Let's hope we don't pass too many art galleries," Nora said as she pulled the covers around her. "I'll just rest my eyes for a few minutes longer."

Fifteen minutes later Luke opened the bathroom door and stepped into the bedroom, drying his hair with a scraggly hunter-green towel.

As he had expected, Nora was fast asleep. He tiptoed over to the bed, leaned down, and was shocked when her arm reached up and grabbed the towel.

"I'm going to do this to you when I'm in one of your caskets," she threatened, then looked with distaste at the

towel she was holding. "Where did you get this rag? Surely Kendra's decorator didn't select it."

"A towel is a towel, my dear. It was in the linen closet in the bathroom. As far as I can tell, it was serving its purpose until you so rudely grabbed it."

Nora sat up and pushed back the apricot quilt. "Look at this. It's disintegrating." A shower of green nublets had settled on the bed, and some had drifted onto the beige carpet.

"Would you have minded if they matched?" Luke asked.

"Oh, be quiet," Nora chuckled as she swung her legs onto the floor, walked across the room, and shut the bathroom door behind her. She turned on the shower and glanced at the thick monogrammed towels on the racks. A suspicion formed in her mind. I'll bet anything Eben brought in his own towels when he stayed here, she thought.

Twenty minutes later she was convinced that her guess had been accurate. When Luke helped her make the king-size bed, she noticed a slip of paper between the nightstand and the dust ruffle. When she picked it up she realized it was a receipt from the Mishmash Bargain Store in Vail. The items purchased included a dozen bath towels at ninety-nine cents each. The date on the receipt was December 23.

"Luke, look at this," Nora said, showing him the receipt. "Your towel might be brand-new."

Luke studied his wife. He recognized the analytical frown of Nora the mystery writer's investigative mind. It always amused him that Regan had that same expression when she was puzzled.

"He just bought them a few days ago," Nora said. "Why wouldn't he take them with him?"

"He must have taken some of them," Luke said. "There aren't more than five or six in the closet."

"Then he might have forgotten them," Nora reflected, "but on the other hand, the fact that he was in Vail could be significant. Maybe he has a connection there. I'm going to call Regan and talk to her about it."

12

AT NINE O'CLOCK on Monday morning, Regan and Louis met with Detective Matt Sawyer, who had been assigned to investigate the Christmas-weekend thefts.

The information Sawyer gave them about Eben's background was not pretty. Regan had known that Eben had not been a first offender when he was sent off to prison but she had had no idea of the extent of his lawless past. With increasing anxiety she listened as the information on Eben's rap sheet was laid out for them.

When Detective Sawyer read that during his plea bargain Eben had confessed to thirty years of jewel thefts, even boasting that he could have lifted Queen Elizabeth's crown from her head during the coronation ceremony, Regan thought Louis was going to burst into tears.

Louis's feeble protest that he hadn't realized the scope of Eben's activities obviously did not impress Sawyer.

"Mr. Altide, you're new here," Sawyer snapped, scowling at him. "We take great pride in this community. Aspen

is a place where celebrities and wealthy people come to get away from big-city life, to feel free and safe. A lot of the local people wish they would stay home, but that's the way it is. It is our job to protect them."

His voice rose a pitch. "We can't do our job if people like you recommend convicted felons who admit to a long history of grand larceny for positions that give them entry to these people's homes. Thanks to you, Mr. Bean was able to shop at leisure in the Wood home and walk out of the Grant house with a masterpiece in his sack."

Dismayed, Regan listened, knowing that this was exactly what everyone in town would be thinking. But the next words out of Sawyer's mouth chilled her. "On the other hand, the Woods and the Grants may have been lucky. Three days ago, on the twenty-third, an elderly man in Vail was Maced and tied up in a closet. A Beasley painting was taken from his home. Luckily he was wearing his medical-alert necklace and was able to summon help when he recovered consciousness."

There was a knock on the office door. Louis barked, "I said do not disturb! Damn it! Doesn't anybody ever listen to me?"

"Kendra Wood obviously did when you recommended Eben Bean to her," Sawyer said sarcastically as the door opened and one of Louis's young attractive waiter/clerk/receptionists looked in.

The staff here reminds me of the Up with People group, Regan thought.

"Brendan, what the hell is so important right now?" Louis demanded.

"I'm sorry, Louis," he said, "but Regan's mother is on the phone and she says it's important."

Louis grabbed the phone on his desk and handed it to Regan.

"Mom, what's wrong?" Regan asked quickly. Then, as she listened, she frowned. "Oh boy, that is important. Thanks. I'll fill you in later." She hung up the phone and looked directly at Sawyer. "My parents are staying in the suite Eben was using at the Woods' house. This morning my mother found a receipt from a store in Vail on the bedroom floor. It's dated December twenty-third."

Louis finally burst into tears and laid his head down on his desk. "I'm ruined," he wailed. "Completely ruined."

13

Wᴴɪʟᴇ ʜᴇ ᴡᴀꜱ eating breakfast, the Coyote observed the antics of Willeen and Judd practicing the King's English for Eben's benefit. He shared their delight that Eben was being linked to the crimes that he and they had committed independently. "Poor bastard," he muttered as he used his buttered toast to mop up the last of his sunny-side-up fried egg.

After Willeen and Judd had again secured Eben in his makeshift holding pen and gone back to the kitchen, the Coyote paid rapt attention as they once again went over their plans for the benefit.

So, when the time is right, Judd and Willeen will strike too, huh? They plan to ring in the New Year with something to hang on a client's wall. Well, we'll see about that.

14

REGAN HELD LOUIS'S hand as Detective Sawyer phoned his counterpart in the Vail Police Department and tersely informed him that Eben Bean might very well have been in Vail on Friday.

As Louis continued to sniffle and moan, Regan pulled out her handy pocket tissues.

The detective gave Louis a dirty look as he struggled to absorb the information he was receiving from Vail.

"Keep the rest," Regan said, handing Louis the dainty package of tear absorbers. "I'm afraid you're going to need them."

"You're a big help," Louis mumbled as he dabbed his eyes.

Regan watched as Detective Sawyer's round face creased into lines that straddled his forehead. He probably was only in his late forties, she guessed, but he didn't look as if he spent a lot of time on the ski slopes or his NordicTrack. His jacket bulged at the seams and he seemed to wear a

permanent disgruntled expression. But his eyes showed a keen intelligence and it was clear to her that he was listening to vital information.

A moment later, when Sawyer dropped the phone back on the hook, it became obvious that her guess had been right.

"If your friend Eben did pull the Vail robbery, he had a lady friend along with him to help him carry out the Beasley painting. Not that anyone had to eat that much spinach to have the strength to lift it—they cut it right out of the frame."

"A woman was with him?" Regan asked.

"Yeah. The poor old guy was dazed and confused. When he came to in the closet, he heard a man and a woman."

Regan turned to Louis. "Did Eben have a girlfriend?"

"How am I supposed to know?" Louis protested.

Regan was becoming exasperated. "Well, Louis, how much did you see him? . . . What are you doing, Louis?"

Louis took his hand off his wrist. "I was taking my pulse. I'm getting overexcited."

Regan didn't dare look at Sawyer. "Louis, come on. What do you know of Eben's social life around here?"

"He kept to himself. He didn't want anyone to know about his past. What a joke, huh? When I first got here, he stopped by when we were doing the renovations. After we opened last month he'd drop in for an occasional beer, always on a night he was going to the movie theater down the block. He loves the movies."

"He had plenty of time in prison to develop a fondness for them," Sawyer said wryly.

Regan ignored the remark. "So he liked going to the movies. What else?"

Louis looked up at the ceiling as if the next answer would materialize there. "He mentioned something about going to McDonald's after the show."

Sawyer's face took on that you've-got-to-be-kidding-me look. "If you were such good friends, why didn't he eat here?" he asked.

"He likes Big Macs," Louis said defensively.

Detective Sawyer stood up. "I don't think there's anything more we can do here," he said. "I assure you I'll keep in touch. I trust you'll be sticking around, Mr. Altide?"

"If I'm not run out of town," Louis sighed.

When the door closed behind Sawyer, Louis turned to Regan. "Regan, this is your vacation. You came here to ski. Forget about me."

Regan took in the pathetic demeanor of her friend. "A friend in need is a friend indeed," she assured him.

"How corny, Regan. I can't believe you said that." He gave one final blow on the last tissue.

"I can't believe you told me to forget what's going on. How can I forget it? Thanks to you I'm an accessory after the fact." She paused. "Besides, you know me. I like to ski, but it wouldn't compare with the satisfaction of tracking down Eben-eezer."

In Los Angeles, Regan had just finished a case where she had traced a guy using stolen credit-card numbers. He ordered merchandise to be delivered to an address that was temporary, to say the least. Regan had been only too happy to deliver the purchases to him in person, ending his shopping spree for good. And, as always when a case like that wrapped up, she felt anxious to take on another challenge.

She just never guessed it would come so fast and hit so close to home.

Standing up, she said, "And I'm going to start by getting Kendra to arrange a meeting for me with the Grants. I want to hear firsthand the whole family's version of old Saint Nick's performance the other night."

15

IDA COULDN'T GET her mind off all the excitement
going on in Aspen as she spooned out the pancake batter
into perfect circles in the frying pan. She couldn't get over
the shivery delight of being close to celebrities who had
just been robbed. To think that a star like Kendra Wood
and her husband Sam the producer had called her daughter
Daisy practically the minute they knew. She couldn't wait
to hear the reaction from her bridge club when she got
back to Ohio. This morning she'd talk about it with the
customers who came into the store with their dirty holiday
clothes.

As she stood there watching the batter bubble, she
counted the blueberries in each pancake. Fair is fair, she
thought, and the kids would notice any difference in the
blueberry count.

"Zenith! Serenity!" she called. "Grandma Ida's pancakes are almost ready!"

Daisy appeared in the kitchen in her flannel bathrobe. Stretching her arms, she yawned and said, "Thanks, Mom. You didn't have to do that."

"My grandchildren mean the world to me. When I'm here I like to spoil them. Besides, that whole-grain cereal starts to taste like cardboard after a while, don't you think?"

"It's healthy for them," Daisy protested. She grabbed some oranges from the refrigerator and started cutting them up to make fresh-squeezed juice. "You're going down to work this morning?"

"God willing." Ida was concentrating hard. It was a delicate art, deciding when the right moment was to flap the jacks.

"Are you on the schedule?"

"Yes, dear."

"The kids and I are going to take an environmental-awareness walk this morning."

Her back to Daisy, Ida rolled her eyes.

". . . and then this afternoon they're going to a play group while I go over to Kendra Wood's to do a few massages."

"The crime victims," Ida observed. "They could probably use massages to ease the tension."

"Let's hope nothing else happens in this town. At least no one was hurt. I thought I knew Eben better than that. He just didn't seem like the type to do it."

"COME AND GET IT!" Ida bellowed. "Whoever did it, I hope they catch him and string him up," she said as she carefully arranged the steaming-hot pancakes on her grandchildren's plates. "In the meantime, we all better be on the lookout for strange happenings. I know I'll keep my eyes peeled." She turned to Daisy. "Maybe I should drive

you over to Kendra's this afternoon and wait while you work. It might not be safe to drive alone after dark."

"Mom, I'll be fine."

Darn it, Ida thought. I'd just love to meet Kendra Wood.

16

I THOUGHT YOU were going skiing early today," Bessie Armbuckle barked at her employers, Yvonne and Lester Grant. "Does this mean you're going to hang around for lunch?"

She's been a wreck since the robbery, Yvonne Grant reminded herself. She shot a warning look at her husband, who was never known to take guff from his employees: Be patient.

"We'll have lunch on the slopes, Bessie," she said patiently. "Right now we're waiting for Regan Reilly, a private investigator who is a friend of the Woods. She wants to talk to us about the other night."

"A private investigator?" Bessie exploded. "Haven't we had enough people around here asking questions?"

Yesterday afternoon, after they'd learned about the missing painting, there'd been an onslaught of police and media types. Aspen was teeming with photographers and reporters covering the activities of celebrities during the holiday

week. They'd gotten wind of the robbery not long after Bessie discovered it; the phone and the doorbell never stopped all day Sunday. In desperation, the Grants had escaped to a friend's house for Christmas dinner, leaving Bessie to hold down the fort. By now, Monday morning, her nerve endings were jangling.

"She wants to help us," Yvonne said patiently. "What time is your bus to Vail?"

"Not soon enough," Bessie replied.

After breakfast Lester had informed Yvonne that either she had to fire Bessie, give her a couple of days off, or spend the rest of the vacation without him. Bessie had jumped at the chance to go visit her cousin in Vail and get off her sore feet for a couple of days. "It's about time I had a day off," she added. "You people have run me ragged with your parties in New York, the party here, and the fancy caterers with their sloppy help who I had to clean up after. This is getting to be too much for me."

Yvonne's lips tightened. She was about to say, "Maybe it is," but when she looked at Bessie's weary and stress-filled fifty-something face, she knew that this was unusual behavior for her. She'd been with them for seven years now, traveling with them among their various homes; her dependability and efficiency made her aggressiveness bearable. Bessie's elbow grease had made every nook and cranny of their three homes sparkle. Yvonne knew that anytime anything went wrong in the Grant household, Bessie felt responsible. The theft of the painting was the biggest thing that had gone wrong since she'd been in their employ. She just needs to get away for a few days, Yvonne told herself.

The doorbell rang. Please let that be Regan Reilly, so we can talk to her and then get out of here. To have to

escape your own home, Yvonne thought wryly. How do these things happen?

Outside, Regan stood waiting, glancing around at the sloping street lined with condos. The house backed right into the mountain, which of course meant easy ski-in, ski-out access. Because the Grants lived in town, they didn't have as much property as Kendra, but Regan supposed that having the ski lift practically in your own backyard more than made up for it.

The stone exterior of the house was most impressive. A massive carved oak door was adorned with antique hardware. It looked as if it could have been ripped off from Saint Patrick's Cathedral. But it was no kindly cleric who answered the door asking, "What can I do for you, my child?"

Instead, a stern, hefty woman wearing remarkably unflattering steel-gray glasses and a gray uniform stood before her. Looking at the hairdo gave Regan a headache. The woman's locks were tightly braided, yanked back and plastered to her skull with hairpins that looked as if they had removed at least her first couple layers of scalp.

"Who are you?" she demanded.

"Regan Reilly," Regan answered in an equally brusque tone. Over the years, Regan had found that it was the only way to deal with the rude people of the world.

"Oh." Broom Hilda waved Regan in.

Regan stepped into the enormous entryway. A second-floor balcony framing the foyer on three sides and numerous doors leading God knows where made Regan wonder just how big the house was. To the right was an elevator. A must, Regan thought, after a hard day of skiing.

"Mrs. Grant," the woman bellowed as she led Regan across the marble foyer toward the back of the house,

through a family room with a movie-screen-size television, finally reaching a magnificent library with Chinese red leather couches and chairs. "She's here."

The terse announcement made Regan wonder what they'd been saying about her.

Yvonne and Lester Grant were sitting side by side having coffee. They both got up and shook Regan's hand. Yvonne was wearing a sleek black ski outfit and looked as if she were ready to do a photo shoot for *Vogue*. Lester was also decked out in the finest skiwear money could buy. Yvonne looked about forty. Her husband was probably ten years older.

"Kendra told me you were about to go skiing and I'm very grateful that you waited for me. I know you've talked to enough people about this already."

"That's for sure," the housekeeper mumbled as she started to leave the room.

"Wait, Bessie," Yvonne said. "Regan, would you like some coffee?"

From the look on Bessie's face Regan decided it was probably best to feign caffeine overload and declined the offer.

"What time did you say her bus was leaving?" Lester asked his wife after Bessie disappeared around the corner.

Yvonne laughed and turned to Regan. "That's Bessie, our housekeeper. She'll be taking the next few days off."

"Sounds like a good idea," Regan said wryly as she sat down.

Regan explained to them her involvement with Louis and her knowledge of Eben's background. "So you can understand why I really want to find out what happened."

"That makes three of us," Lester said.

"Five of us," Yvonne corrected him. "Kendra and Sam

would like their stuff back too. I only wish I had paid more attention when he was here the other night. But I was playing host to all my friends in the living room and the children were in the family room with that big red thief . . ."

"I was helping too," Lester said in mock protest.

Yvonne squeezed his hand. "Of course you were, darling. You're the perfect host." She leaned over and gave him a little kiss.

I may throw up, Regan thought. Instead she waited for them to denuzzle before steering the conversation back to the crime.

"So you both were in the living room," she said.

"It really was a great party." Yvonne smiled. "I wish Kendra and Sam and your parents and even you had been here for it."

Even me. "Why, thank you," Regan managed to say. "I'm sure it would have been a delight."

"Really," Lester said. "When you think that at the party itself everyone had a wonderful time."

"Especially Santa," Yvonne said and burst into gales of laughter, soon joined by her husband.

"Cookie, you're so funny," Lester choked.

Am I missing something? Regan wondered. I thought these two were upset about the theft.

"We're sorry, Megan," Lester offered as he struggled to regain his composure.

"It's Regan, honey," Yvonne said and the two of them started laughing again. When the hearty sounds of her mirth subsided, Yvonne said, "Regan, we're reading a book on stress management. It says that if you laugh at your troubles, they won't get the best of you."

"When did you start reading it?" Regan asked.

"This morning," Lester sputtered.

My timing is impeccable, Regan thought. It must be great to be so rich that you can laugh at the loss of a million-dollar painting. Maybe she ought to get a copy of the book for Louis. It would be a lot more helpful than tissues. "Was the painting insured?" she asked.

Lester's laughter stopped on a dime. "Of course!"

Bingo, Regan thought. It's a lot easier to yuk it up when you know there'll be an insurance check winging its way to you.

"All of our friends love our Christmas Eve party," Yvonne said. "A bunch of them have been calling asking if they're in any of the pictures of the party we handed over to the newspaper. I understand they're going to do a big spread on it." Yvonne's eyes widened. "It's amazing how much publicity we've gotten."

"Do you have any pictures with Santa?" Regan asked.

"Not a one. He was in and out of here so fast. . . ." Yvonne answered.

"Which was a relief," Lester said. "Last year he hammed it up so much, stopping to pose for pictures with every last guest. We had to practically use physical force to get rid of him. This year we left instructions with Bessie to let him do his thing with the kids and then get the hell out."

"Darling." Yvonne looked at him.

"Sorry."

"Bessie was in charge of everything."

"As usual," Lester added.

Yvonne ignored him. "She's sick of talking to people, but let me get her in here. BESSIE!" She paused. "BESSIE!"

"WHAT?" Bessie shouted back from down the hall.

She must be very good at cleaning, Regan mused. She's

certainly not here to give the children French lessons or offer tips on gracious living.

"Please come here," Yvonne called.

Bessie reappeared with an annoyed expression. "I was just getting out the vacuum. If I'm going to be gone for a few days—"

"Could you please get the children and bring them in here? I think we should all talk to Regan at once."

"Oh, all right," Bessie said begrudgingly and started down the hallway. "JOSH! JULIE! Your mother wants you!"

"Regan," Yvonne warned. "The children still believe in Santa Claus. Please be careful of what you ask them."

"We're trying to keep up the myth that Santa is alive and well and not a slimy . . ."

"Darling."

Lester closed his mouth and turned to Regan with a big smile. "Do you know how Santa spells his last name?"

"I think I do," Regan said.

"C-L-A-W-S," Lester said and started to chuckle. "I just made that up. Santa Claws."

Regan laughed. "Not bad."

"Not bad? I think it was pretty good, myself."

I have to get a copy of that book, Regan thought.

One of the many doors in the house slammed and two lively brown-haired, brown-eyed children ran into the room. Their skiwear obviously hadn't been bought at the local Ski Shack either. They jumped up and joined their parents on the endless couch, cuddling up and getting a few tickles from Lester before things calmed down. Your perfect nuclear richer-than-God family, thought Regan.

Bessie unloaded her body into a chair next to Regan. She sighed, folded her hands, and started twirling her thumbs. Regan got the impression that she was not the type who

could sit still for very long without getting mad at some-body. And she seemed nervous.

Yvonne stroked her daughter's hair. "Kids, this nice lady wants to talk to us about Santa."

"But Christmas is over," Julie said practically.

"I know," Yvonne said, "but she wants you to tell her about the Santa who came by here the other night."

"The one who stole the picture?" Josh inquired.

Yvonne glanced quickly at Lester. "We didn't say that, honey."

"But you were mad in the restaurant yesterday and said that—"

"Mommy was just reacting too quickly. We don't know who took the painting."

Julie looked thoughtful. "Do you think one of your friends took it?"

Regan tried not to smile.

"No, dear," Yvonne replied with a patience that did not seem heartfelt. "Now let's answer some important questions."

The two children turned their gazes to Regan. Their stares were the stares of little children who expected to be entertained, or at the very least not bored to death.

I'd better make this quick, Regan thought. She had the feeling that their undivided attention was a commodity that could disappear faster than the painting. She barely had time to form a question when Julie opened her mouth to speak.

"Last year Santa was nicer," she blurted.

"What do you mean?" Regan asked in that gentle voice she thought you were supposed to use with young children.

"Well," the little girl said and cocked her head, "he

was funnier and played with us more. This year he just gave us our presents in a hurry."

Josh extracted his thumb from his mouth. "The presents weren't too good either. Santa was cheap this year."

Julie started giggling. "Santa was cheap," she almost chanted. "Cheap, cheap, cheap." Within seconds Josh and Julie looked like miniature versions of their parents, laughing hysterically at the thought of Santa's stinginess. Had they read the stress-management book too? Regan wondered.

"Who wanted another stupid dump truck?" Josh asked.

"And who wanted another stupid doll that burps?" Julie added.

It was clear that Big Daddy Lester took that as a personal insult; he started to interject, but Yvonne stopped him. "Maybe next year Santa will have something you like better."

"Hope so," Josh said and resumed sucking his thumb. He leaned up against Lester's chest and crossed his legs.

"He's back in the North Pole now," Julie informed Regan.

"Yes, I know," Regan said. She knew she couldn't talk about Eben playing Santa in front of the kids. After all, she thought, you have to preserve their innocence. Better to have them think that Santa's cheap, not a thief. "So he just gave you your presents and left?"

"Uh-huh," Julie said. "We had lots of kids to play with, so we didn't care."

"But last year Santa spent more time with you?" Regan asked. "Was that fun?"

"He sang some songs with us. It was all right," Julie replied.

Josh looked up at his father. "Next year, can we have Barney instead?"

Poor Santa. He's going to be wiped out by a purple dinosaur, Regan thought.

"We'll see," Lester said.

Yvonne looked at Regan and shrugged. It was clear that Regan wasn't going to get too much more out of the kids. "We'd better get going, Regan. Why don't you talk to Bessie for a few minutes? She's the one who made the arrangements with Santa Claus."

Throw me to the lions, why don't you? Regan thought. "That would be great, if Bessie doesn't mind . . ." She didn't have to look at Bessie; she could feel her reaction.

"I've got a lot to do before I leave for Vail."

Yvonne gave her a look and Bessie knew that she was pushing her employer's envelope. "I suppose I could talk to you for a few minutes."

After the Grant family left for the slopes, Regan sat back down. The room took on a quiet, empty air. Alone with Bessie, Regan felt as abandoned as the room. She cleared her throat and figured it was best just to forge on. This was business.

"Did you know Eben Bean?" Regan asked.

"Just a little," Bessie said quickly. "Last year when he was Santa he made a mess of this place."

"What do you mean?" Regan asked.

"His boots were all muddy when he came in here. We'd had a little spell of warm weather and he went around the back of the house knocking on the windows, shouting, 'Merry Christmas.'" Bessie leaned forward in her chair. "'Merrrrrry Christmas. Merrrrrry Christmas.' I said, 'All right already. Enough's enough.' Then he tracked the mud into the house and I was following him around trying to

clean up after him. It made me look like the Grinch who stole Christmas, but I told him before he left to make sure his boots are good and clean next year or he's not setting foot in the door or down the chimney or however else Santa's supposed to let himself in.''

Regan's pulse quickened. ''What were his boots like the other night?''

''I checked them when he came in the door and I thought there was a wad of gum stuck underneath. I could have killed him. But he'd stepped on some kind of orange sticker you'd have to blast off. So I let him go. This place was such chaos.''

''Did you see him again?''

''No. He was in the family room with the kids and then went out through the library.''

''When was the last time you saw Eben before that?''

''He came to pick up the toys for his sack last Tuesday.'' She managed a slight smile. ''When you hire Santa, he needs to be supplied with the gifts.''

Regan, deep in thought, frowned. ''The boots are what bother me. At Kendra Wood's house my parents are staying in the room that Eben was using. There was a pair of boots in the bathroom that looked like the kind you would wear if you were dressing up as Santa. They even had jingle bells attached.''

''That sounds like Eben,'' Bessie said.

''But the boots Santa was wearing the other night didn't have bells on them?''

Bessie looked at Regan as though she were nuts. ''No. These were black cowboy boots. Like they all wear around here. You'd think you were in the Texas Panhandle.''

''I just don't know why Eben wouldn't have worn those

boots," Regan said. "As far as you could tell, you had no reason to suspect that it wasn't Eben in the Santa suit."

Bessie shook her head. "I barely looked at his face. I was more concerned about his feet and then I had to run into the kitchen to check on those caterers."

Regan stood up. "Thanks, Bessie. I understand you're going away today. But if you think of anything that might help in this investigation, no matter how trivial it seems, please don't hesitate to call me." Regan handed Bessie her number. Bessie's hands were shaking when she took it. Why does she seem so nervous? Regan wondered.

GERALDINE SPOONFELLOW SAT in her creaky old rocker, lacing up her well-worn high-top boots. She loved to get up early in the morning and breathe in the crisp mountain air. A lifelong resident of the Roaring Fork Valley, she felt a part of the land, of Aspen, of everything that went on in town. She personified the Aspen ideal of self-expression, which usually meant letting everyone know your opinion whether they wanted to hear it or not.

Geraldine's grandfather, Burton P. Spoonfellow, had been one of the early prospectors who struggled across the Continental Divide in the early 1880s and settled in Aspen, which was known as Ute City at the time. He staked his claim on a section of land and made a fortune in the silver that lay below. It was an exciting era until the year 1893, when the U.S. Government changed the currency standard from silver to gold.

"It blew my mind, Geraldine," he used to tell her as she snuggled in his lap and heard all the old stories of the

early pioneers. "I wanted to go to Washington to kick their fannies, but I stayed here and toughed it out. That's what you've got to do in life during the hard times, and you can be sure they'll be many. Keep your chin up and tough it out."

Geraldine would take her thumb out of her mouth long enough to say, "Yes, Pop-Pop," find a new section of her security blanket to whiff, then lay her cheek back against the scratchy comfort of Pop-Pop's turkey neck.

For Pop-Pop toughing it out meant living off the fortune he had already made. He took some of those funds and opened up a saloon in town, which only made more money for him. He married and had a son, Geraldine's father. When his wife, the blessed and saintly Winifred, died from dropsy, Pop-Pop and their son, Felix, lived alone together until Felix took his own wife, Imogene. She moved in with them, bringing back into the house the feminine touch that had been so sorely missed.

In that old Victorian house built in the shade of Aspen Mountain, Geraldine and her brother, Charles, had grown up basking in the attention of two caring parents and their beloved Pop-Pop. The great outdoors was at their fingertips, and they were taught to take advantage of the lakes and mountains and rivers long before anyone dreamed up *Field & Stream* magazine. They picked raspberries, fed the pigs, chickens, and rabbits, milked the cows and were pulled around in donkey and dog carts. Geraldine became a veritable tomboy, learning to keep up when Charles would run ahead of her up the mountain, her pace only slowed by the sight of an irresistible rock that just had to be picked up and fired at a nearby evergreen.

Aspen was a tight-knit community when Geraldine was a child. The population had dropped dramatically after the

silver crash in 1893, and the townspeople who remained stuck together during the quiet years that lasted until the 1940s.

Waffle suppers, hog roasts, church socials, canasta games played around the radio, while the children played run-sheep-run and kick-the-can, were all part of the life. The Volunteer Fire Department sponsored picnics, and occasionally a theater troupe would come through to provide a little entertainment.

Today Geraldine still lived in that same house, the only surviving member of the Spoonfellow family. Never having married meant Geraldine never moved out. "No decent girl leaves her home before she's a bride," her mother used to say. When she was fifty-seven, Geraldine broached the subject of getting an apartment in town, but her parents just gave her that look. The subject was dropped and never came up again because they both died a few years later. At age sixty, Geraldine finally had her bachelorette pad.

It was lonely sometimes, but, following Pop-Pop's advice, Geraldine toughed it out and made the best of it. With no family of her own, Geraldine became even more involved in the town's activities, arguments and political unrest. She had made friends and enemies of all ages and was a regular at every town meeting, always anxious to put in her two cents about the fight of the minute.

Outspokenness and assertiveness were valued Spoonfellow traits. "Make a difference in life," Pop-Pop had always preached. Geraldine had heeded his advice. Back in 1956, she had led the brigade that under cover of darkness had cut down all the billboards on Highway 82 because they were ruining the beauty of the Aspen area. There hadn't been a billboard in the area since. Geraldine's group made sure they were banned. Recently she'd joined the group

who drove their cars around city hall honking their horns in protest of the plan to establish paid parking in Aspen. The noise, Geraldine bragged, reached 114 decibels.

In July the *Aspen Globe* had started a series of stories focusing on the descendants of the original settlers of Aspen. Geraldine was among the first, interviewed and photographed in her home, posing proudly under the 8-by-10-foot portrait of Pop-Pop that hung on the dining-room wall. He had commissioned it when he opened the saloon. Wearing his Sunday best, he stood in front of the saloon with his walking stick, looking as proud as a peacock.

When the reporter asked to be shown around and was brought back to the barn, another painting caught his eye. Ever since the Spoonfellows gave up their animals, the big old barn had become the dumping ground for all their paraphernalia. "You'll never know when you'll find a use for it" was yet another family motto, and everything from Pop-Pop's wedding bed to turn-of-the-century kitchen utensils was scattered about.

Ted Weems, the reporter, an intense young man who fancied himself a history buff, started poking around. "Fascinating," he said, "just fascinating." When he pulled a large drop cloth off a painting, he nearly fainted. Staring him in the face was a picture of Pop-Pop in his mining days, coming down the mountain with a fellow miner. Lanterns in hand, they were followed by a line of workers slogging along, all with their own twinkling lanterns.

"Do you know what this is?" he asked Geraldine, trembling.

"A picture of my Pop-Pop. But I like the one inside the house better. In this one his face is dirty."

"Ms. Spoonfellow, it looks to me as if this is a Beasley painting!"

"Who's Beasley?" Geraldine had answered.

When the article was written up, a great deal of attention was paid to the fact that Geraldine did not even know she had an invaluable painting on her hands. One of the missing Beasleys, it had been called *The Homecoming*. Beasley was an artist who had traveled from mining town to mining town in the 1880s and 1890s, capturing on canvas the spirit of the times. The painting was authenticated and its value estimated to be at least three million dollars.

Licking their chops, the Rescue Aspen's Past Association got together and hatched a plan. A whole entourage, led by Ted Weems, who was very active in the association, drove up the mountain to Geraldine's homestead to pay a little visit. The motivation, of course, was to attempt to pry the painting out of her clutches for their new museum, which would be opening on the first of the year. But first they had to pay homage to Pop-Pop.

"*The Homecoming* captures the spirit of the early years, which of course were so important to your grandfather," one of them said to Geraldine in a hushed, reverential tone. "To have it hanging in our museum would be a tribute to him."

"What about his portrait?" Gerladine had asked practically. "Why don't you want that one?"

"Well-l-l-l," one of the committee members said, "we didn't want to be selfish. We thought you would want to keep it."

"If I give you *The Homecoming*, then I want a special room in the museum dedicated to Pop-Pop. Where both his paintings will hang."

It took about a nanosecond for the committee members

to nod their heads in unison, gushing about what a wonderful idea that was. They told Geraldine about the Christmastime benefit they were planning and how it would be the biggest event of the season in Aspen. She would have to come and be guest of honor. Geraldine, her civic-mindedness getting the best of her, offered to underwrite the benefit and let the ticket money go to the museum. "I have no one to leave my money to anyway, and as long as Pop-Pop's memory lives on . . ."

The committee members almost fell off their chairs.

A few weeks ago they had paid another call on Geraldine to bring her up-to-date on their plans for the party and the museum. They'd now decided to re-create entire rooms as they might have looked at the turn of the century and to give the museum-goers the feel of the old mining village. Maybe Geraldine had a few items in her barn that she'd wish to donate.

"That barn hasn't been cleaned out in decades," Geraldine said. "This might give me a good excuse."

"Anything, anything that might be of historical significance. I can help you if you'd like," Ted Weems had said.

Geraldine had declined the offer. "At first I'd like to be left alone with the memories," she'd said. "If I get good and depressed, I'll call you in for help."

Now, as Geraldine pushed herself out of her rocker, the stiffness in her bones made her feel every day of her seventy-five years. "Let's get going, girly," she said to herself. "The day is a-wastin'. If I'm going to get anything done in that barn, I've got to move."

She had already made a few interesting discoveries, like old spittoons that had been put to use in Pop-Pop's saloon and a pair of Pop-Pop's faded overalls that she thought they might hang on display to symbolize the work ethic.

Geraldine ambled past the painting of Pop-Pop in front of the saloon and saluted as she did every morning. She wanted to keep him home until the night of the party.

"I'll come down and visit you all the time," she said aloud as she buttoned up her jacket.

Geraldine pulled open the front door, stepped down on the porch and bent over to pick up the paper. She was about to chuck it inside the living room when the headline caught her eye.

"Damn it to hell!" she growled and charged back into her house to make a phone call.

18

THAT'S IT! I'M ruined!" Louis howled when Regan appeared at his office door.

Tripp, the young tanned clerk who'd been at the desk when Regan arrived, was standing there with a dejected look on his face.

"What happened?" Regan asked quickly, unzipping her ski jacket.

Louis waved his hands at Tripp. "Tell, tell, tell!" Louis's eyes were watery and his face looked as if his blood pressure must be as high as the altitude. In the corner near his desk a little humidifier was humming away, gently blowing a fine mist of cool air into the tense environment.

Tripp ran his hand through his sun-streaked hair. Regan sat down on an upholstered chair opposite Louis's antique desk. Tripp sat down in its twin.

"What?" Regan asked again impatiently.

"My buddy Jake, who works at a restaurant across town . . . it's a pretty cool place . . ." Tripp began.

Louis moaned.

"Anyway, he called me up a few minutes ago. I guess that Geraldine Spoonfellow, the one who's sponsoring the party and donating the painting, is bent out of shape because Louis recommended an ex-con for a job in Aspen and didn't tell anybody . . ."

"So?" Regan asked.

"She called over to this other restaurant and asked about their availability. She wants the historical committee or whatever to switch the big party from here."

"You see, Regan?" Louis asked plaintively.

"Why is it so important to her?" Regan asked.

"Because she's been on a crusade to take a bite out of crime. She's taking it out on me because that no-good Eben went back to his old tricks." Louis pounded his desk. "I'm having an anxiety attack."

"Take it easy, Louis," Regan warned. "Can I get you anything?"

"A cup of coffee?"

"No coffee now. You need something a little soothing. How about some herbal tea?"

"Whatever. Tripp, you go get it," Louis growled.

Shoot the messenger, Regan thought.

"Sure, man," Tripp said, glad to get away.

"Herbal tea for two and a plate of cookies."

Tripp gave him the thumbs-up sign, which made Louis scream, "Hurry up!"

"Tell me more about this Geraldine," Regan said when the door had closed behind Tripp.

Louis threw a file across the desk at her. Regan opened it and skimmed the article from the *Aspen Globe*. She looked up at Louis. "Let's go visit her."

"I'm afraid," Louis whined.

"Stop it. What's the worst that can happen?"

"She'll tell us she's definitely moving the party."

"Right."

"Which means I'm ruined. All those wonderful publicity people I've lined up for Thursday night. Everyone would have seen me in *People* magazine!"

"Louis, going up to see Geraldine can't hurt, it can only help; and furthermore, it's our only hope."

"Maybe tomorrow."

"Today, Louis."

"This afternoon."

"Now."

"Let's call first."

"No. She might not agree to see us."

"That's not polite. Didn't your mother ever tell you you're not supposed to just drop in on people?"

"Louis," Regan said firmly. "Get your coat on."

"What about our tea?" Louis asked.

"Maybe we can have a tea party with Geraldine." Regan stood up. "We'll make this very civilized." She reached for his hand and pulled him out of his seat. "This Geraldine sounds like a character. Let's go give her hell."

"If you say so," Louis said in a little voice as he thought of the angry faces of all his investors. "I could just kill that Eben. Look at what he's done to me!"

19

GERALDINE WAS OUT in the barn muttering to herself when Regan, followed by Louis, tried to locate her.

Geraldine's house looked, Regan thought, probably the same as it did when it was first built. Painted white with green trim, it was old-fashioned and charming. A barn was out back.

"Ms. Spoonfellow?" Regan called. They had seen that the barn door was open; when no one had answered the doorbell at the house, they had gone around the side to check.

"Maybe we should leave," Louis suggested.

"Come on, Louis," Regan insisted.

They stepped into the barn, their eyes slowly adjusting to the change in light. The place was filled with junk; Regan wondered if any animal had ever laid down its weary head on the straw-covered floor.

"Who's there?" a voice called sharply.

"Ms. Spoonfellow?" Regan asked.

"That's me. Who are you?" Geraldine snarled as she came into view.

"My name is Regan Reilly, and this is my friend Louis."

"How nice for you. What do you want me to do about it?"

"We wanted to talk to you."

"About what? I'm pretty busy here. I have a lot of odds and ends to rummage through."

"It looks as though you have quite a few interesting artifacts here," Regan said, lying through her teeth. "You could have some garage sale."

"Yeah, well, I'm donating what's good to the new museum in town. Other things"—she pointed to a canvas lying on the ground—"I don't know what to do with."

"What is it?" Regan asked.

Geraldine waved her hand dismissively. "I bought it for the frame. It's just a beat-up portrait of some old geezer from France."

"Can I see?" Regan asked, bending over.

"I guess." Geraldine watched as Regan lifted the folded canvas. Staring from it, under layers of dirt and grime, was the corpulent figure of a white-haired aristocrat with a self-satisfied smile. He was wearing a velvet cape trimmed with ermine, silver slippers and hose. In one hand he held a plumed hat; in the other, a scepter. A throne could be seen behind him and a gold crown rested on the table next to him.

"I don't know what possessed those guys to dress like that and wear their hair long and curly," Geraldine said. "Don't you think he looks awful?"

Regan laughed. "I think he was in the height of fashion for his day. It must have taken him a long time to get dressed. Will you be giving this to the museum as well?"

Geraldine shrugged. "As I said, I only bought it because the frame is really nice and I wanted it for the portrait of my Pop-Pop."

"Your what?"

"My grandfather."

"Oh. Do you know who this is?"

"He's supposed to be Louis the Eighteenth of France," Geraldine said. "At least that's what the woman who sold it to me said. I didn't care who it was. The museum certainly won't want it. That guy never marched around Aspen. I'll get rid of it somewhere."

Louis had been hovering in the doorway. Regan's mind raced. This might be a good time to break the news of who he was to Geraldine. "Louis, did you hear that?" Regan asked him. "This is a portrait of King Louis! Don't you think this would look great hanging in your restaurant?"

"Wait a minute!" Geraldine snapped. "What restaurant?"

"I'm the one you're mad at," Louis said quickly. "Please listen to us!"

"YOU!!! You brought that lawbreaker into the bosom of this town and let him run wild among our youngsters?" Geraldine shook her head and stalked out of the barn. "You don't deserve to have the big benefit." She turned and pointed her finger at Louis. "The police force in this town has a wonderful motto." She straightened her back. " 'To share with all a safe and peaceful environment by encouraging mutual responsibility and respect.' You, sonny, showed no respect for Kendra and Sam Wood or for the Grants or for anyone in this paradise in the wilderness."

Louis's lip quivered. "I'm sorry." He turned to Regan.

"Let's get going. It's no use." He started down the driveway, his feet crunching in the snow.

"Louis, wait," Regan called. She turned to Geraldine, who was wrapped in a red-and-black jacket. "Ms. Spoonfellow, from what Louis tells me, and from what I've read about you, your grandfather was a silver miner who lost the potential to make a lot more money when silver was demonetized."

"Don't mention that snake President Grover Cleveland's name in my presence," Geraldine warned. "That was his big idea."

"Didn't eighty percent of Aspen go bankrupt?"

"Eighteen ninety-three was a terrible year, um-hmmm."

"But your grandfather, unlike a lot of other people, chose to stay here . . ."

"And tough it out."

"He didn't abandon ship, shall we say."

"That's right. He used his resources to open a saloon. He figured that people needed a place to go and forget their troubles. Have a few shots of whiskey, tell jokes, get drunk. Pop-Pop liked to bring people together."

"So why don't you give Louis that chance?"

"What's that guy got to do with my Pop-Pop? Don't mention them in the same breath, missy."

Regan paused and inhaled deeply. If she failed now, it was all over for Louis. "Ms. Spoonfellow," she said earnestly, "Louis is trying to open more than a restaurant. It'll be a place where he'll have poetry readings and society meetings and whatever else people want to gather for. The paintings of local artists will be on display all the time. If anyone is trying to promote the Aspen idea of keeping culture in this town, it's Louis. Like your Pop-Pop with his saloon, he just wants to bring people together. If you

have the party moved to that other restaurant, which is just another commercial joint, he'll be finished.''

Geraldine kicked a mound of snow with the tip of her boot. Her white hair seemed to blend into the snowy mountains in the distance behind her. The creases in her forehead deepened. ''What about that Eben fellow? He's a no-good varmint.''

''Louis was trying to give someone a fresh start. He thought that Eben wanted to pull himself up by the bootstraps and begin his life again. Like the old silver miners who came to Aspen looking for a new life. No one would have hired Eben if they knew he had a criminal record. The only thing Louis is guilty of is sticking out his neck for somebody.'' Regan paused. ''It didn't work out so well, but I don't think he should have to pay so heavily for it. If this town is anything, I thought it was open-minded. I thought it was a place where all different kinds of people can hang out together . . .''

''People who can afford it,'' Geraldine snapped.

''Still. People come here to ski and socialize and have some grog . . .''

''Peppermint schnapps is a local favorite,'' Geraldine observed.

''Peppermint schnapps, whatever,'' Regan said. ''This town was built by people taking chances, not by people who played it safe. Your grandfather was one of the first. I think he'd probably hate to see someone lose his chance before he even got started.''

Geraldine stared out at the mountains. Who knows what memories of Pop-Pop are flashing through her mind, Regan thought.

Finally, Geraldine said, ''I guess nobody's perfect. It's

getting nippy." She pulled the jacket closer around her. "Why don't you two come in for some coffee?"

Louis, who'd been quiet up until now, with one foot in front of him as though ready to flee if Geraldine attacked him, now looked as though he could have jumped three feet in the air. He clapped his hands together. "Do you by any chance have herbal tea?" he asked as they followed her into the house.

"Herbal tea is for wimps," their hostess said emphatically.

For the next forty-five minutes they sat and talked with Geraldine.

"Call me Geraldine," she demanded. "You find as you get older, fewer and fewer people call you by your first name. And the ones who do right away are just plain rude. If there's anything that bugs me it's these people who call on the phone and try to sell you something you don't need. They always start off with 'Hello, Geraldine, are you having a good day today?' Give me a break. The ones that really tick me off say, 'Hi, Gerry.' I just hang up on them. Anyway, with my family and most of my friends gone, I get to miss the sound of my own name."

Regan found the house to be cozy. A Christmas tree decorated with old family ornaments, framed pictures and holly adorning the mantel of the fireplace, the painting of Pop-Pop, floral curtains and an oriental rug—all gave the feeling that the house shared a history with its owner. The very essence of Geraldine oozed from every nook and cranny. Obviously all the junk had been relegated to the barn.

A bouquet of flowers was centered on the dining-room table, where they sat drinking their coffee.

"They're beautiful," Louis said, leaning over to inhale the pungent scent.

A faint smile appeared on Geraldine's lips. "I had a beau who used to go out and pick me a whole big bunch of forget-me-nots. That's why I like to keep fresh flowers around, to remind me of him. We used to go out to the Maroon Bells-Snowmass Wilderness and ponder our existence. We had great discussions out there about the meaning of life. Or we'd grab our fishing poles and go down to the Roaring Fork or Frying Pan rivers and try our luck at those flying fish. . . ." Her eyes glistened at the memory.

"When was this?" Regan asked.

"Last year. Besides Pop-Pop, Purvis was the smartest man I'd ever met. Then one day he woke up dead."

"That's too bad," Louis said sincerely, silently wondering just how you wake up dead.

"A bummer," Geraldine agreed.

Regan smiled to herself. She doubted that in all the years her father had run the Reilly funeral homes there had ever been anyone who came to pay their respects to the deceased and greeted the family with "What a bummer."

"We had fun together," Geraldine continued. "He was always interested in learning about everything. He hadn't lived here long and he wanted to hear all about the history of the town. Like I bet you didn't know that Ute City the mining town changed its name to Aspen in homage to the aspen tree that you find all around here?"

How have I survived so long without knowing this tidbit, Regan wondered, but dutifully shook her head no. Louis was paying attention with the fervor of a reformed student in danger of flunking out of school.

"The aspen is a member of the poplar family. They're so beautiful. Nothing gets my goat more than when those

hikers scratch out their initials in the bark. It lets the insects in and the trees start to rot. The only time I ever got mad at Purvis was when he started carving our initials in one of those trees. Of course he didn't realize until I explained it to him. Anyway, enough of that."

It seemed to Regan that Geraldine definitely liked to have an audience. With Purvis gone to the great beyond, Geraldine was obviously alone a lot and now seemed to enjoy their company. I'd have loved to see the way she interacted with Purvis, Regan thought. It was hard to imagine Geraldine with a man, especially since the spirit of Pop-Pop never seemed to leave the room. "I bet you had a lot of stories about your Pop-Pop you shared with Purvis."

"Pop-Pop was a character," Geraldine said. "He had so many adventures, you'd never get bored listening to him. I've tried to remember them all, keep them alive." She sipped her specially brewed coffee and picked at one of the blueberry muffins she had magnanimously placed on an old-fashioned plate that reminded Regan of the kind her grandmother had had. The grandfather clock ticked away in the living room. Or should I call it the Pop-Pop clock, Regan wondered.

"This coffee is delicious," Louis said as he drained his cup.

Geraldine almost pounded the table. "It gets you going in the morning. If I hear about one more person who needs to relax with their soothing herbs, I'm going to get sick." She licked her lips and set her mug on the old oak table. "Okay, Louis," she said with deliberation, "I'll skip making a fuss about having the party at your restaurant. God knows it would send that ass-kissing committee into a tizzy

if I made them change things now. I tell you, my hind quarters never felt so loved. Those people are really getting on my nerves. They think I can't see through their fawning. But . . ."

Regan and Louis waited for whatever the "but" was. There's always a but, Regan thought.

"I hope we don't have any more problems with that son of a gun, Eben. Aspen is a place we want to be proud of."

"For all we know he's hundreds of miles away from here by now," Louis said, anxious to get out of there before he did anything else wrong.

"Geraldine," Regan said, "I am a private investigator. I really want to find out what happened. You're the one who knows this town inside out. May I call you if I have any questions or need to talk to you?"

"Dial away. If there's any gossip going on, I usually hear it somehow or other." Geraldine looked across the table at Regan appraisingly. "You look like a smart young woman. I've been involved with a couple of private investigators lately and they haven't been worth beans. If the one on my feedbag now doesn't work out, I may talk to you."

"I'd be very glad to help," Regan said sincerely.

Geraldine turned to Louis and frowned. "Now listen. At the party, Pop-Pop's portrait better have a place of honor. The committee swore up and down that it would, but I'm holding you personally responsible."

Louis had been pressing his napkin up to his mouth, almost as a shield from anything Geraldine might hurl at him. "The best," he sputtered. "The best."

"Oh, I know that Beasley painting I donated that they say is so valuable will get top billing. I'd forgotten all

about it. I remember seeing it when I was a little kid, but Pop-Pop never liked it. The fellow in it with him was a friend who tried to double-cross him." Her face darkened. "A lot of bad blood between the two families. I guess that's why Pop-Pop shoved it in the barn. I certainly forgot all about it until that young reporter started poking around."

When they got up to leave, Louis slipped into the bathroom. Regan tried to make arrangements with Geraldine to buy the Louis painting.

"Take it," Geraldine insisted. "Make a donation to the museum in Pop-Pop's name."

A few minutes later Regan and Louis were tying Louis XVIII to the ski rack of Louis's car.

The weight of almost certain doom lifted from his shoulders, Louis was practically doing a jig. He looked as if he would break into song. Regan felt as if they should be in a grade-B musical.

"You didn't have to do this, Regan," Louis chirped.

"It was free, Louie baby," Regan said, "but I'll spring for the frame. Then we'll find a good spot to hang him."

"I feel as if I was almost hanged."

"You were, Louis. But we'll hang this Louis where everyone can see him when they walk in and pay their proper respects."

"Like it was his wake. You sound like the daughter of a funeral director."

"Gee, thanks. But the most important corpse at the party better be Pop-Pop's. The Beasley with Pop-Pop won't be unveiled until later that evening. Up till then it will be the portraits of Pop-Pop and Louis. What a pair."

"Legends in their own mind." Louis started to hum. "When this party is over, I'm going to be one happy man."

Regan didn't know why she had the nagging feeling that

it just wasn't going to work out that way. She realized she also had a burning curiosity as to why seventy-five-year-old Geraldine Spoonfellow was involved with private investigators.

20

Benbrooke was in the bathroom. It was very quiet for Elson. Very wrong, indeed. Willey and Judd had left a little while ago after dumping him, breakfast and shedding him back in the bed. He was still a little glad that he had to putall their pathetic dissents. They should pull off their boots under cover of darkness and for a few months that while they'd let be thought to himself. Even though he had the difficulty...

...

it just wasn't going to work out that way. She realized she also had a ticking difficulty as in very, seventy-five very not Deadline. Somehow was involved, with private indications.

20

B Y THREE O'CLOCK, the call of nature was very strong
for Eben. Very strong indeed. Willeen and Judd had left at
nine o'clock after feeding him breakfast and shackling him
back to the bed. He was still a little glad that he had insulted
their pathetic accents. They should pull off their heists under
cover of darkness and keep their mouths shut while they're
at it, he thought to himself. Even though he had that little
morsel to cheer him, he was still very depressed.

It's amazing, he thought as he watched the television
they had set up in the bedroom for him. It's downright
amazing how the urge to relieve yourself can wipe out
almost all thoughts of the rest of the universe.

As he watched the television, Eben couldn't believe that
Judd and Willeen had left it on for him today.

"Maybe you'll hear about sightings from people who
claim they've seen you," Willeen had said as she bent over
to find an outlet. "I can't promise you'll get great reception,
but beggars can't be choosers."

"I wasn't begging," Eben said wryly.

Willeen ignored him. "This TV is a piece of garbage. There's no remote control. So you'll be watching one station all day."

"Don't you hate when that happens?" Eben said to her.

Willeen chuckled. "Me and Judd always end up fighting over the remote control. You being all by yourself wouldn't have that problem now, would you?"

"It's one of the great pleasures of being alone," Eben said. "Judd was always picking fights in the TV room in prison. He never wanted to watch what everyone else did."

"He was probably doing it out of spite," Willeen said casually as she straightened up, Eben's remark just rolling off her well-toned back.

Now as Eben watched the small black-and-white set perched on the dresser, he was treated to another news brief that warned everyone to be on the lookout for him. The frizzy-haired newscaster looked both perplexed and alarmed.

"Eben Bean may be armed and dangerous. Be careful out there," he urged his viewers. "If you have any information, please call . . ."

"I never hurt a fly," Eben whispered as his eyes grew misty. I can't start crying, he thought, because I'll have to bury my face in this smelly pillow to wipe away my tears.

It was galling to hear that the state police had an all-points bulletin out for him when he was only a couple of miles away. So close and yet so far. Like so many things in his life.

Eben didn't doubt that Willeen and Judd would succeed in stealing the painting at Louis's party. That obviously had been well planned, and from the little conversation

he'd been able to pick up, he was sure they were part of a larger ring.

Had they pulled off that job in Vail? Eben didn't think so, based on their conversation he overheard yesterday. But it sounded right up their alley, and the newscaster, shaking his head in disgust, said that a man and a woman seemed to be involved. So they're probably trying to figure out who I've hooked up with. Ha, he thought. I haven't had a date since I moved to Aspen. And so much of my life before that, if you don't count the time spent in prison, was spent on the run.

The newscasts during the day had given examples of Eben's past crimes. Like the time he stole the Wellington family jewels. One of the necklaces, a string of flawless diamonds, had actually been replaced, probably by an unhappy relative, with pitted, poor-quality rocks one-tenth the value. It certainly hadn't been worth Eben's trouble shinnying down the drainpipe from the roof to the master bedroom. And of course no one would have believed that the good diamonds had already been stolen before he got his hands on the necklace.

When the news report went off, Eben rolled on his side and crunched up in the fetal position, a position he usually liked to sleep in. Maybe because he had been in the fetal position inside the womb the last time he had any contact with his mother.

Eben took a deep breath. Why are they keeping me alive? he thought. What do they have planned? When they were in prison together there'd been a rumor that Judd had killed a couple of people but it had never been proved. What's stopping him from killing me? Of course, right now they're both thrilled that I'm being blamed for their derring-do.

Suddenly Eben's blood froze. Are they going to try and make it seem that I'm responsible for the art theft at the benefit and then get rid of me? That must be the reason they're keeping me alive! How will they do it? Burn this house down with me and some of the cheaper art in it?

Eben heard a car pull up in the driveway. No such luck that it would be a wayward traveler asking for directions, a person he could scream to for help. Instead he heard the door open and Willeen's usual nasal voice. "We're here to walk you, Eben," she called.

She and Judd appeared in the doorway.

"We made a lot of nice friends today," Judd said. "You'd be jealous, Eben. We got the addresses of a whole bunch of rich people who told us to give a call if we come to their town."

Willeen giggled. "We figure we'll just drop in unexpectedly. Like when they're not home."

"Yeah," Judd said, "we're going back to do the whole après-ski number and make some more friends, but we figured we better give you some relief in case we don't come home before dinner."

"This is worse than having a dog," Willeen pronounced.

"Shut up," Judd said.

They both stared down at Eben as though he were the prize exhibit.

I feel like the lamb about to be slaughtered, Eben thought. I've got to find a way out of here.

BESSIE WAS GLAD to be getting out of town for a few days. Enough is enough, she thought. I've worked hard the past few days, between the party and getting ready for Christmas and the fiasco of the stolen painting. I'm not a robot and my nerves are frazzled.

Damn, she thought. That joker masquerading as the very essence of trust and goodwill, Santa Claus himself, really got her goat. If only I'd paid closer attention to him, but once I saw his boots were clean, that was enough for me. I had other things to worry about, like making sure those slowpoke waiters kept making the rounds with the hot hors d'oeuvres.

It was mid-afternoon and she was relaxing in her room, waiting until it was time to go down and catch the bus to Vail. One of the daytime soaps was on. "I don't know why I love these," she said to herself, "working for this family, I live through this crap."

Bessie had worked for the Grants for seven years, ever

since Lester and Yvonne had taken their vows to love, honor and cherish each other for as long as they both shall live. Bessie had given it a year, two at the outside, and was surprised and pleased that the Grants had lasted and she was able to build up her pension plan. Aside from Yvonne being a little snooty at times, they weren't so tough to work for. Hawaii, Aspen and New York weren't such bad places to hop among, even though it slightly annoyed Bessie that the Grants never bought her a first-class ticket. I'm the one who needs it most, she always thought.

As the woeful strains of the theme music of *To Love or Not to Love* played, the credits rolled over a couple who had just been reunited after he had been lost in the rain forest for seven years. "I wouldn't want to get back together with anyone that dumb," Bessie mumbled even as she brushed back a tear. When the embracing couple faded to black, a picture of Eben Bean was flashed on the screen.

Bessie stood up and ran to the TV as if it would make a difference, as if Eben would be able to hear her cursing at him. The fervent newscaster again recounted the story that Eben Bean had been in Vail the day of the other major art theft, and it was now believed he might be working with a female partner.

Bessie's heart started palpitating. Oh my God, oh my God, she thought. I can't believe it's happening to me again. I've got to get out of here. I'll go get a drink at the bar before I catch my bus.

As she scrambled around the room, gathering her belongings, she caught her reflection in the mirror. A sturdy woman with brown hair and eyes, it was hard to tell if she was in her late forties or north of sixty. She was fifty-six. She'd never married but had found satisfaction working

for four different families in the past thirty-five years. Having her own home was almost unfathomable, an alien concept, something that other people thought about but not Bessie.

She yanked the zipper of her tubular all-purpose paisley travel bag and quickly looked around the room for anything she might have missed. Whatever I forgot, Carmel can lend me, she thought. She'd left a message on her cousin's answering machine saying she was coming down for a few days. Carmel had always urged her to take some time off. And she would be good to talk things out with. Bessie couldn't believe that there had been a second theft.

She picked up her bag off the bed. "Let's go, Mary Poppins," she said to herself.

Fifteen minutes later Bessie was seated on one of the comfortable lounge chairs in a bar near the bus stop. Her chair was farther away from the fireplace than she preferred, but you had to get there pretty early to get one of those choice seats. Today she didn't really care. Usually she enjoyed watching everyone parade around like peacocks in their fashionable skiwear, but today she quickly ordered a gin martini and barely noticed her surroundings. A piano player was tinkling his heart out in the corner, but Bessie's jiggling leg was moving at three times the beat.

A couple came through the front door and walked over to the love seat right near Bessie.

"Judd, how about here?" the woman asked.

They sat down and the man crossed his legs in that macho position, with one foot resting on his knee, the sole of his black cowboy boot facing Bessie. It took a moment for her to notice, but when she did she froze. A raggedy orange sticker was stuck to the bottom of the shoe. She glanced at the rest of the boot and recognized the silver

scroll on the side. That was Santa's boot! She was absolutely positive it was the one she'd examined. But this guy wasn't Eben. I've got to call Regan Reilly, she thought.

She jumped up quickly, too quickly, just as the waitress came over with her drink.

"I've changed my mind," she said.

"But the drink is already made . . ."

"I'll pay for it," Bessie said and pulled out several bills from her wallet. With trembling fingers she laid them on the waitress's tray. She wanted to get to a phone as fast as possible.

As she turned to go, her purse slipped out of her hands. It landed at the feet of the man wearing the cowboy boots. When she bent over to pick it up, he leaned down to help. Her face was inches from the sole of his foot when their eyes met. His brown eyes darted between the sticker and Bessie. When a flicker of recognition passed over his face, her whole body shuddered.

"Thank you," she whispered and hurried down the long hall to the phone, her purse and travel bag flying behind her. She fished out Regan Reilly's number and dialed the phone.

A clerk answered and informed her that Regan was out. Could he take a message?

"This is Bessie Armbuckle. It's very important that I talk to her—"

A hand reached over and pushed down the receiver. Willeen and Judd were standing right behind her.

"Honey, we're going for a ride," he said. "Just act nice and nobody will get hurt. Make a fuss and there's no telling what will happen."

Bessie replaced the phone in its cradle and walked between them out the side door to the parking lot.

I CAN'T BELIEVE how late it's gotten," Regan said as she and Louis carefully guided Louis XVIII through the door of his restaurant. "It's four o'clock already."

"Time for a cocktail," Louis purred. "A drink to Geraldine. And to you for forcing me to face her."

"Sometimes you just have to face these things head-on," Regan said. "No matter what happens, you usually feel better for getting it over with."

"That might be true," Louis said. "But if Geraldine had refused to keep the party here, you'd be giving me smelling salts right now. Where do you want His Majesty to go?" he asked.

"Let's bring him up to my room. I'll keep him there until I drop him off to get cleaned and framed, which I'll have to do soon so he'll be ready for the party."

Tripp was just coming out of the office with message slips in his hands. "What a dude," he said appraisingly as he checked out Louis XVIII in all his regalia.

"He was the King of France," Regan said.

Tripp smiled at Regan. "I figured he wasn't an Olympic skier. I did take an art history course in college, you know."

Regan laughed. "Sometimes I like to state the obvious."

Tripp looked down at the messages in his hands. "Oh Regan, you just missed a phone call."

"Who was it from?"

"Some lady named Bessie Armbuckle."

Regan raised her eyebrows. "Oh really?" Tripp handed her the slip. "What did she say?"

"She sounded a little wired. She said she needed to talk to you but she hung up pretty fast. I was like 'whoa.'"

"I just met her today. She can be a little abrupt," Regan said. "She didn't leave a number?"

Tripp shook his head. "No. Also, some guy named Larry Ashkinazy called. He said to meet him at Little Nell. He'll be there between four and six. That place really hops at that time." He looked at his watch. "He must be there now."

Regan turned to Louis. "We were going to have a drink. . . ."

Louis waved his hand at her. "Don't worry, darling. Go have some fun. I've got to get ready for the dinner crowd anyway. We're pretty booked tonight. I'll have to go back to the kitchen and start bothering them. We'll get together later."

Regan smiled. It would be good to get out for a little while. She'd only been in Aspen for twenty-four hours and wouldn't mind seeing what the rest of the world was up to. "All right. But first I'm going to go upstairs and change. I'll give Bessie a call at the Grants' to see what's going on with her."

"Please, God, don't let it be anything that further incrim-

inates Eben," Louis said. "I'm going to be on an emotional roller coaster all week."

Don't I know it, Regan thought. Carrying the painting, Louis and Tripp followed her up the stairs. When she closed the door behind them, she immediately picked up the phone and dialed the Grants' number. Yvonne answered.

Regan introduced herself. ". . . so I was wondering if Bessie was there."

"No, Regan," Yvonne said. "We just came back from a wonderful afternoon of skiing. You should really get out there and try it."

"I know," Regan answered. "I intend to. So Bessie's not there?"

"She was taking the bus to Vail around this time. You saw her today. She's a little frazzled. We did have a lot of parties in New York and I think we wore her out. So we decided we should really give her a few days off to go down and see her cousin." Yvonne laughed. "For all our sakes."

Regan sat down on her bed. "She wanted to talk to me but didn't leave a number. Do you have her cousin's number?"

"It must be around here somewhere. I'll have to look. When I find it, I'll call you back."

"Thanks, Yvonne." Regan hung up the phone and sat there thinking. She couldn't get Eben off her mind. Where was he? Regan stood up. At least I've accomplished something today. For the time being, unless something else happens, Louis's party is still a go.

There was a knock at the door. Now what? she thought. She walked over and pulled it open. Standing in front of her was her good buddy from Connecticut. "Kit!" she exclaimed and gave her a quick hug. "You're here!"

"Am I ever!"

"Come on in!" Regan grabbed her suitcase. "I'm afraid to ask. What happened to the guy?"

Kit looked disgusted and fell back on the bed. "He told me his old girlfriend showed up with a Christmas present. A present she bought for him before they broke up."

"The oldest lie in the world."

"No kidding," Kit said. "Now they have to 'work some things through.' He said he'd call me 'when the dust settles.'"

"What did you say?" Regan asked eagerly.

"I told him to get a can of Pledge."

Regan laughed. "Good!"

"It's pathetic. I thought he was different. I thought this New Year's would be different. Like maybe I'd have a date."

"Well, I'm glad you're here. We'll have fun and I need you for moral support. You wouldn't believe what's been going on around here; I have to fill you in. But let's get ready. Mr. Drill, Fill and Bill is meeting us at Little Nell for drinks."

"Go, Larry," Kit said. "Nothing like jumping right back in the swim of socializing. I'll probably just meet a nerd and start to get all depressed again."

"No, you won't." Regan chuckled.

Kit rubbed her eyes and yawned. "By the way, Regan, I hope you don't mind sharing the room. Louis says they're all full but they can put a cot in here."

"That's fine," Regan said. "It'll be like our college days."

"Does that mean we're going to sleep till noon?"

"No. It means we can lie in bed and analyze everything

going on in this town. Maybe we'll catch a few criminals while we're at it."

"Criminals?" Kit sat up. "Reilly, I thought you were on vacation."

"I guess skiing isn't enough for me," Regan said. "Besides, we don't want things to get too dull, now do we?"

"Dull is all I know these days," Kit said wearily.

"Get ready," Regan said. "You never know who we'll meet."

23

Daisy DROVE TO the Woods' house, never tiring of the scenery of Aspen. The small Victorian picture-book houses, many of which were painted bright pink or lime green or turquoise, and trimmed in equally flamboyant colors, made her smile. Painted cows on mailboxes lent a certain whimsy. And, as always, the sight of the mountains in any season made her feel alive.

Everything in Daisy's life was going so well, even if her mother's three-month visits did get to be a little trying.

Christmas week was a busy time for her. With all the people in town to ski, massages were in great demand. Things stayed pretty busy through the winter months. Only in the spring did business quiet down a bit, but then the crowds came back in the summer for the music festivals and all the other outdoor activities.

As she pulled into the driveway, she found herself smiling. The Woods were nice people. She always enjoyed coming to their house. It's just so hard to believe about

Eben, Daisy thought, pulling her massage table from the car.

Kendra greeted her at the door. "Come on in, Daisy. We're drawing straws over who gets to go first. And none of us even skied today." She introduced Daisy to Luke and Nora.

"We had a tough day," Luke drawled. "It consisted of going out to lunch and coming back to read."

Daisy laughed. "That makes my job easier. You're already relaxed."

"I know what you mean," Luke said. "I work with bodies, and it's much easier when they've relaxed."

"Luke!" Nora squealed.

"What do you do?" Daisy asked innocently.

"I'm a funeral director," Luke said proudly. "Only after rigor mortis has passed can we prepare the body."

Daisy rolled her eyes. "I've worked on some bodies that were so stiff they felt like they were in the throes of rigor mortis. It's usually the first day of their vacation."

"Honestly, Luke," Nora said and turned to Kendra. "He never used to talk about his clients like that."

Sam, who had been stoking the fire, spoke up. "Well, why not? They can't talk back."

Kendra noticed Daisy looking around at the bare walls. "It's the minimalist look, Daisy."

"I just can't figure out what happened to Eben," Daisy said. "I didn't think he had it in him."

"The evidence is piling up," Kendra said matter-of-factly. "Nora found a receipt that shows Eben must have been in Vail the other day when there was a big art theft there."

"That reminds me," Nora said. "I want to talk to Regan about it. I wonder what happened with her today."

"Well, Nora, you get to go first. So why don't you call Regan when you're finished?"

"Sounds good."

"I'll sit here and figure out what we should do for dinner."

"Make reservations," Sam suggested.

Kendra turned to Daisy. "Now that my friend Eben is gone, we have no one to do the shopping and cooking."

"Except us," Sam said, sitting down and picking up the newspaper.

Kendra continued, "We'd planned to be lazy this week. Eben was good at taking care of everything when we were here. He left us some prepared food in there but not enough for the week."

"He got greedy," Luke mumbled.

"So now, disaster of disasters, we've got to figure out every meal for ourselves. And go out and do the shopping. What a pain."

Daisy hesitated. Her mother was a good cook, not gourmet, but she could make some decent dishes that would taste good, especially if you're starving after a day of skiing. And she could shop for them. Should she say something? She wouldn't recommend her for the White House, but Kendra and Sam were low-keying it this week and probably wouldn't expect seven-course meals. Why not?

"My mother," she began, "is in town visiting us from Ohio. She works part-time at the dry cleaner's but I'm sure she'd be happy to work for you a couple hours a day. She's a pretty good cook. Nothing too fancy . . ."

Sam put his paper down. "I knew I always liked you, Daisy. When can she start?"

24

WILLEEN SAT IN the back of the car with the gun they kept in the glove compartment pointed at Bessie's head. Bessie was resting uncomfortably on the floor.

"Hurry up, Judd," Willeen said. "Step on it."

"Willeen, the last thing I want to do is get stopped."

"It would serve you two right," Bessie shouted.

Willeen nudged her with the pistol.

"Shoot if you must this old gray head," Bessie said. "But you won't get away with it."

"Listen lady—" Judd started to say.

"Bessie's my name. Miss Armbuckle to you."

"Miss Armbuckle, we don't want any trouble—"

"That's why you dressed up as Santa and stole the painting. I should never have let you in the door." Bessie tried to get herself into a more comfortable position. At my age, I'm crumpled on the floor like a pile of laundry, she thought. She was so angry that her fear had subsided.

She was still in shock and, as usual, reacted by opening her mouth and letting it flap.

When the car finally stopped and Judd opened the door, Bessie started to feel a sense of dread. As long as the car was in motion, she didn't have to face what was really happening, like a baby who can ride in a car happily sleeping but the moment you stop to pay a toll starts to screech. Bessie's nerves reacted the same way.

"They're looking for you, you know," she said. "Regan Reilly is a young investigator staying in town and she's doing some first-class snooping."

Judd and Willeen exchanged a glance. They led her to the back door of the house, unlocked it, and turned on the kitchen light. Bessie's hands were tied with rope they kept with the gun in the glove compartment.

"Don't you two just think of everything?" Bessie had asked sarcastically.

Judd ordered her inside the house as Willeen went around turning on the lights.

Bessie wrinkled her nose when she got a good look at the place. "This joint could stand a cleaning."

"Maybe you're just the person to do it," Judd remarked.

"Fat chance," Bessie muttered under her breath.

"Say what?" Judd asked.

"Nothing," Bessie answered, wondering just what they were going to do with her. It didn't take long to find out.

Willeen opened a bedroom door off the living room. "Eben," she said. "We've got some company for you."

"Eben!" Bessie said. She couldn't believe her eyes. Sprawled on the double bed with his hands tied behind him was the man who was supposed to have played Santa, the man whose mug she'd just seen on television that afternoon.

"Will the real Santa Claus please stand up?" Judd joked.

Eben looked at Bessie. "Bessie! What are you doing here? Forgive me if I don't get up and shake your hand."

Willeen laughed. "I tell you, Eben, I love your sense of humor. Say hello to Eben, Bessie."

Bessie stared at him. "You're the slob who got mud all over my carpet last year. Which means you're the one who got me into this mess. If I hadn't been so worried about Santa's boots the other night, I wouldn't have been paying attention to this bird's shoes."

"A silly little thing called fate," Eben said tonelessly. To think I'd been longing for company, he mused. This is what I get. Mrs. Clean.

"Well, I got news," Judd said. "You two are going to have time to get to know each other because you're going to be sharing this bed."

"What?" they both protested in unison.

"What about the couch?" Eben asked. "I'll take the couch."

"It's not long enough and it doesn't pull out," Judd informed him.

Where's Bernadette Castro when you need her? Eben wondered. He'd give anything for one of those Castro Convertible couches that pull out so easily, even a child can do it. Like little Bernadette did in the commercials for her father's company all those years ago. If I get out of here alive, he thought, I'll have to write her a letter.

"Maybe you two will fall in love. You'll have lots of time to share your innermost thoughts and feelings. Just like me and Willeen. Right, honey?"

Willeen wrinkled her nose. "You don't share your inner-most—"

"Shut up." Judd turned to Bessie. "Now lay down. Eben gets a bathroom break and then he'll jump back in the sack with you."

"Another bathroom break so soon?" Eben said as Judd unshackled him. "I'm overwhelmed."

"No comments from the peanut gallery," Judd ordered.

"By the way," Willeen said to Bessie, "who is this Regan Reilly?"

Eben's ears perked up. Regan Reilly, he thought. Her parents were staying with Kendra and Sam. He'd met her through Louis, and knew that she was a private investigator.

Bessie realized that she shouldn't have blabbed about Regan Reilly. If Regan was going to be any help to her and Eben, she couldn't have these two losers after her. She'd have to keep it vague.

"Who is she?" Willeen demanded.

"A private investigator. She's here on vacation."

"Where is she staying?"

"I don't know." Bessie stared at them with a stone face.

"Fine," Judd said. "Just fine."

When he and Willeen climbed back in the car to head into town once again, Willeen looked worried.

"Who is this Regan Reilly, Judd? This is what I don't like about being here so long. We were supposed to spend the week skiing and meeting rich people and then get out of here after the party. Now we're baby-sitting and have the cops scratching their heads and sending out bulletins."

"Willeen, what do you want? After Eben saw me, we had no choice. We had to get him out of the way if we wanted to pull off the benefit job. It's all working out. Everybody thinks he pulled off the other jobs, so he's the one they're looking for."

"I hope that's the trail this private investigator Regan Reilly is on. I want to find out who she is."

"We'll find out, Willeen. Don't you worry. We'll find out."

T HE COYOTE WHISTLED as he showered and rushed to join the après-ski crowd. As he towel-dried he snapped on the television and stared in amazement.

"What the hell is going on now?" he said to himself.

As he dressed he hung on every word between Eben Bean and the broad being brought into his bedroom. "So, Eben, you got yourself a girl," the Coyote chuckled.

Several times he burst out laughing. He'd never been on a job that was this much fun. Willeen looked nervous. What were they saying? Regan Reilly is a private investigator? Let her investigate.

On the other hand, one of the cardinal rules in this business was not to underestimate anyone, whether it's the cops or your competitors. Judd and Willeen hadn't bungled the job in Vail. They had no way of knowing that he had a mole inside their ring. Theirs had actually been a well-planned heist. But as they'd learned, even the best-laid

plans can sometimes go awry. The Coyote laughed. His plan wouldn't fail.

He waited until Willeen and Judd, having secured Bessie and Eben, left to go back into town. As he turned off the TV, he waved good-bye to them. ''Maybe I'll run into you later, kids.''

26

AFTER HER UNEXPECTED guests left, Geraldine returned to the barn for another couple of hours. She hoped she hadn't made a mistake in being so generous to that Louis fellow, but she liked Regan Reilly. She seemed to be a square shooter and she was smart, not like some of those hippies who had invaded Aspen in the sixties and did nothing but pluck their guitars and sing about peace.

It was nearly five o'clock when Geraldine realized that she was stiff and cold. Except for a lunch pail that looked as though it must have been used in Pop-Pop's early mining days, the afternoon had been unrewarding. Everything she had looked through was junk. Pure and simple junk.

Geraldine was about to give up for the night when something made her stand on tippy-toes to make sure the shelf she'd been working on for the past hour had been completely cleared. Was there something still there? The overhead light dangling from a cord did not penetrate the dark corners where the shelf met the sloping roof.

She reached for the flashlight attached to her workbelt. She carried it to help ferret out possible hidden treasures that might be entombed under mounds of whatnots and useless debris. Pointed at the shelf, the beam spotlighted a thick book, like a bookkeeper's ledger or a photograph album.

Geraldine pulled over a chair, stood on it and stretched out her arm. The shelf was so deep that only the tips of her fingers could curl around a corner of the book cover. Tugging at it, she finally managed to yank it out. Quickly training the flashlight on the cover, she hoped against hope that it might contain early photographs of Pop-Pop and her family. She brushed the grit from the leather cover and gasped in joy as Pop-Pop's initials, in raised silver lettering, gleamed against the maroon leather. B.S.

Her eyes filled with tears as she opened the first page.

THE STORREY OF MY LIFE BY BURTON SPOONFELLOW

With both arms she hugged it to her. Barely remembering to turn out the light and lock the barn door, she rushed back to the house and poured herself some Wild Turkey. She lit the fire, positioned herself in the rocking chair that had been Pop-Pop's favorite perch, and glanced up at the portrait she so loved of him, standing in his Sunday best, stroking his goatee. She raised her glass to him and offered a toast.

"As you would say, honorable Grandfather, 'down the hatch.'" Geraldine swallowed the bourbon in one gulp and wiped her mouth. "Now I'm ready to find out your secrets." There was one she especially hoped he'd written about.

27

AS DAISY HEADED home in her Jeep, she hummed to herself. Everybody loves a massage, she thought. The Woods and Reillys had been appreciative of her hard work kneading their tensed-up muscles and relaxing their weary joints.

When she had worked on Kendra, Daisy had put on what she thought was her most soothing tape. Daisy liked it because it was the sounds of the ocean, waves lapping peacefully against the shore, with the cries of a few seagulls thrown in for atmosphere. Unfortunately it reminded Kendra of one of her favorite paintings, a seascape she had bought on Cape Cod, that was now among the missing.

"I think maybe you'd better change the tape," Kendra had said. "I'm getting aggravated."

"Not a hassle," had been Daisy's reply. "I thought you might like it because our bodies are made up of mostly water. And so is the whole planet. It's why we're drawn to the sea, ya know?"

"Just like Eben was drawn to my paintings," Kendra had said, shutting her eyes. Daisy knew they'd reached that moment where the client doesn't want to have to move another muscle, including her jaw. The massage would continue without another word exchanged. Daisy used this time to think about her TO DO list.

Now Daisy pulled into her driveway and smiled. It was good to get home.

Inside, Ida was standing in front of a bowl of ground meat, shaping patties with her hands. "Don't worry, dear, they're turkey burgers," she said as she pushed back her glasses with her knuckles.

Daisy laughed. "I didn't say anything." She hung her jacket on the wall rack by the back door where a jumble of coats and scarves was already hung and boots were resting on the floor in tiny puddles of melted snow.

Ida reached into the freezer, pulled out a box of frozen corn, and laid it on the counter. Picking up a hammer, she gave the box a good whack. "How was your day, honey?" she asked.

"Fine," Daisy said. "I've got some good news for you."

Ida looked up. "What?"

"I got you another job."

A pained, saddened expression came over Ida's face. "Another job? Do you think I'm around too much?"

"What? Of course not!" Daisy put her arm around her mother and thought, well, maybe a little. "I know you've been trying to earn some extra money and I thought that this particular job might be something you would like."

"I'm listening," Ida said, her face grim.

"Since Kendra Wood's caretaker disappeared, she doesn't have anyone to shop and cook and straighten up.

It would just take a few hours in the afternoon. I thought you might like to do it. It's just for this week."

"If she wants me all day, I'll dump the dry cleaner's," Ida sputtered.

Daisy laughed. "No, Ma. I don't want you to do that. It's a steady job and you like working there when you're out here."

"Not many celebrities have come in this year. It's been a little boring. But to work for Kendra Wood! And didn't you say Nora Regan Reilly was staying there too? She's my favorite author!"

"She's there with her husband," Daisy said.

"Didn't I read somewhere that he has some crazy job?" Ida asked.

"He's a funeral director." Daisy shrugged. "Somebody's got to do it. I'll call Kendra and tell her you'll be over there tomorrow afternoon." She walked over to the phone and began to dial.

Ida fluttered around the kitchen. "I've got to get some extra film for my camera."

Daisy put down the phone. "No camera, Mom."

Ida looked crestfallen. "But—"

"No camera," Daisy said firmly. "They're private people."

Ida waved her hand at her daughter. "Oh, okay."

As Daisy went back to dialing, Ida opened a jar of apple sauce with a strength she never knew she had. With gusto, she dumped the whole thing into a bowl. The mental Rolodex in her head was spinning off all the titles of the TV movies Kendra Wood had starred in. Ida couldn't wait to talk to her about every single one of them. Maybe then she'd pose for a few pictures.

28

KIT'S PRESENCE WAS like a shot in the arm for Regan. On the way over to Little Nell, Regan filled her in on the events of the last couple of days. "Do you remember Eben?" she asked. "He was at Louis's pool party in California a few years ago. He was helping to serve the hors d'oeuvres."

Kit stopped dead in her tracks. "I remember him! He was funny! As a matter of fact, he was serving me a drink when that producer was thrown in the pool. I said something to Eben about hoping she didn't lose all that jewelry she was wearing and he muttered that it was all fake anyway. Then he told me to be careful because the clasp on my bracelet looked bent."

"He said that?" Regan asked, incredulous.

"He said that," Kit confirmed.

"Oy. What else?"

"I asked him how he knew so much about jewelry."

"What did he say?"

"He got embarrassed and said he was just kidding. But he was right! The clasp on my bracelet was broken. Can you believe it?"

"Yes," Regan said as they resumed walking. "I'm afraid our friend Eben decided to broaden his horizons by expanding into the art world. And he knows his stuff there. The Grants' painting was very valuable. The painting from Vail was too. What I don't understand is why he went after Kendra's paintings after she'd been so good to him. As she said, they had more sentimental value than monetary worth. They weren't cheap but she liked them because they were bought on trips she and Sam had taken to Europe and Cape Cod."

"No thief like an old thief," Kit declared. "Once it gets in your blood . . . But I'm surprised too. It's like he was thumbing his nose at them. There was something about that guy that was endearing."

"I thought he'd turned over a new leaf," Regan said. "I swear, it just doesn't add up." She shrugged. "Well, it won't do any good to worry about it now. Isn't it a beautiful night?"

"Gawjiss," Kit said.

As they walked through town, they passed skiers heading home with their skis flung over their shoulders. All the watering holes along the way were crowded. The town felt alive. They looked in the glass front of Mezzaluna, which was packed with diners and barhoppers.

By the time they got to Little Nell the bar was filled to capacity. They had to wait in line behind a velvet rope until some of the après-skiers filtered out.

When the velvet rope finally parted and they were allowed to join the crowd, Regan turned to Kit. "Sound the trumpets." They squeezed their way through the well-

heeled revelers and headed for the bar, keeping their eyes open for the dentist to the stars.

"I see him," Regan said. "In the midst of the action."

Kit grinned. "Blinded by his dazzling smile, no doubt."

Larry was sitting at a corner table with two couples who were obviously just leaving. As they approached him, he jumped up.

"Regan! And Kit! I didn't know you were coming," he said, kissing them both.

"It was a surprise to me too," Kit said wryly. "But what do you know, I was freed up, so here I am."

"You two are going to have such a good time," Larry promised. "I already know of a couple of parties and I'll see if I can get you in."

"What do you have to do, promise them a free teeth cleaning for everyone you bring along?" Regan asked.

"You're mean to me, Regan." Larry laughed.

"No, I'm not. I'm the little sister you never had."

"There are lots of guys here. Do you want me to introduce you?"

Regan turned to Kit. "See, he's trying to get rid of us already."

Kit smiled. "Haven't we had enough small talk?"

Larry rolled his eyes. "You two. Let me get you something from the bar. It'll be faster. Here, sit down and hold the table."

He took their orders and slithered over to the bar, stopping to say hello to a few members of the female sex along the way.

"I think Moses crossed the desert in less time than it takes Larry to cross a barroom floor," Regan said as she looked around.

"I should have told him I have to be back in Connecticut

next week," Kit said, taking in the whole scene. "I'm so glad to be here."

"Me too," Regan said. "We'll have fun this week. Louis's party should be great." She rolled her eyes to the heavens. "Please, God, don't let anything get in the way of that party. Louis will freak."

"Here we go, ladies," Larry said, handing them their drinks as he took a seat.

"Thank you, Doctor," Regan said, holding up her glass.

"The good doctor comes through with the medicine," Kit said, taking a sip.

"Hi, Derwood," Larry said to a man who seemed to appear from nowhere.

"Hi, Lar. Okay if I join you?"

"Sure. Meet my friends Regan and Kit. Regan and Kit, this is my friend Derwood."

Derwood, a quiet, mild-mannered, mid-thirtyish guy who seemed attractive enough with his curly brown hair and hazel eyes, slipped into the chair next to Kit and sipped his beer. Within a few minutes it was determined that he was a computer specialist with his own business and hailed from Chicago. Unfortunately, Kit told him she was in the market for a new computer. For what seemed like an eternity he gave an earnest nonstop dissertation about hard drives, bytes, modems and printers. Even Larry couldn't get a word in edgewise. He rolled his eyes at Regan but then looked over her shoulder and gave a vigorous wave of his arm to a broad-shouldered, auburn-haired, athletic-looking man in his late thirties.

"Hi, Stewart," Larry called.

Regan turned to see who was the recipient of Larry's greeting. One glance was all it took. Hubba, hubba, she thought.

He was wearing a rust ski sweater that complemented his brown eyes and accentuated the reddish tones in his hair. His warm smile was attractive and seemed to be reflected in his eyes.

Kit noticed him too but was stuck hearing about the importance of keeping your computer disks from extreme temperatures.

"I wasn't planning on taking them skiing." Kit chuckled halfheartedly as Stewart the dreamboat sat down next to Regan.

Kit is ready to kill herself, Regan thought as they were introduced.

Stewart shook Regan's hand. "I guessed you were Regan Reilly. I met Larry last night when I was at a party and went into the bedroom to get my coat. He was in there talking into his pocket recorder." Stewart mimicked Larry holding the device up to his mouth. "Call Regan Reilly tomorrow."

They all laughed.

"Everybody's picking on me," Larry said.

"Would you have forgotten about me otherwise, Larry?" Regan asked.

"No. It shows I was thinking of you. I ended up telling Stewart all about you. He even read one of your mother's books."

"Several of your mother's books," Stewart corrected. "I seldom read fiction, but I really enjoyed them."

At least he didn't say he never bothers with fiction, Regan thought. She smiled. "I guess I should buy you a drink then."

"What? No way! I have a children's clothing business, you see. It's very lucrative . . ."

A woman with silky blond hair down to her waist tapped

Larry on the shoulder. He jumped up as though struck by lightning.

"Danielle," he crowed happily and yanked out the empty chair next to him. "Sit. Sit."

Larry on the stool next. He jumped up as though stung by lightning.

"Daniels," he curved sharply and yanked out the empty chair next to him. "Sit. Sit."

29

I DON'T BELIEVE this," Bessie said. "Our hands tied behind our backs, our legs shackled to the bedpost."

"And we're not even in love," Eben commented.

"Very funny."

"I hope you don't think this is my idea of a good time, Missy."

"My name is Bessie."

"Pleased to meet you."

Bessie harrumphed. "I believe we've met before. I wish we never had—then I wouldn't be in this mess."

"It was our destiny," Eben philosophized. "Are you so grouchy just because I had muddy boots last year? You should have had a welcome mat out for Santa to wipe his feet. Be a little considerate of my feelings. I'm getting the blame for everything."

Bessie grunted. "Chain of events. Our lives are subject to the stupidest little twists of fate. How was I supposed to know that doing my job, checking Santa's boots for

mud, would lead me to this?" After Judd and Willeen had gone back into town, Bessie had briefly explained to Eben, in caustic terms, her run-in with them in the bar. "We're in deep trouble."

The hours passed and they talked little. Judd and Willeen had turned off the television when they were getting Bessie tied to the bed and forgot to turn it back on before they left. No lights were left on in the whole house. The bedroom was pitch-dark.

"I don't know what we're going to do," Bessie said futilely. "I don't know what they're going to do with us."

"Why don't we get some rest?" Eben suggested. "There's an old saying that things always look better in the morning. Or something like that. Perhaps we'll be struck with inspiration and hatch an escape plan."

Bessie sighed and tried to get her head into a comfortable position. With her severe hairdo, it wasn't easy. The mounds of hair anchored to her scalp with numerous pins prevented her from sinking into the pillow. It reminded her of the days when women had to wear curlers to bed if they wanted to look half-decent. If she were home now, she would have removed every pin and brushed out her hair. At least one hundred strokes. The thought that she wasn't in her own comfortable bed with her few earthly possessions surrounding her made her miserable. "I hope you don't talk in your sleep," she said to the instigator of her misfortune.

"Sweet dreams," Eben replied and closed his eyes.

A half hour later they both snapped awake when they heard the back door open. A moment later Willeen opened the bedroom door and looked in on them. The bare lightbulb

in the hallway cast an annoying glare that shone right into their eyes.

"Hope we didn't wake you up," Willeen said.

She sounds a little tipsy, Bessie thought, blinking her eyes.

"You two must have to go to the potty, because I certainly do. Judd beat me to it, so I have to wait. We had the most wunnerful time . . ."

I wonder how many she belted down, Eben thought.

". . . and we had the most unbelievable stroke of luck. We got the business card of some guy who's the dentist to the stars." Willeen hiccuped. "Ah, excuse me. Anyway, I asked him what stars and he tells me Nora Regan Reilly. I say yeah, that name is so familiar. And he says she's a writer. I look at Judd and say out loud, 'Regan Reilly.' The dentist blurts out, 'She's here too! The daughter! Do you want to meet her?'" Willeen started laughing hysterically. "So we met Regan Reilly! Guess what, guys? She wasn't worrying about you. She was out partying. With some very handsome fellow at her side, I might add."

Judd joined Willeen in the doorway. She put her hand up to his face. "Not as handsome as you, of course, Juddie."

"Let's go to bed, Willeen. You've said enough."

"Sounds like an offer I can't refuse, baby," she giggled.

Oh my God, Eben thought. Was Regan Reilly in danger now? Bessie and her big mouth.

30

FOR HOURS GERALDINE had sat in the rocker, her shawl wrapped around her, engrossed in the attempt to decipher Pop-Pop's life story. She was having the worst time. Small writing, faded ink, terrible spelling, crossed-out words that nearly bore holes in the dried-up, brittle pages that felt like parchment—all made for slow going and called for frequent breaks to rest her eyes. The stream-of-consciousness writing—jumping from one subject to the next without any rhyme or reason—was really getting on her nerves.

"Who did he think he was?" she mumbled to herself as she delicately turned a page and positioned her magnifying glass. "James Joyce?"

Her momentary lapse into irritation was followed by a feeling of shame for herself and admiration for Pop-Pop as she read about him harvesting turnips on a farm in upstate New York when he was only twelve. Geraldine's lips moved as she mouthed what she was reading. "I was a skinny little thing in patched pants, trying to make a

living. Even after I'd had my saloon for many years, the sight of a turnip would still make me cry."

Geraldine looked up from the book, a little misty-eyed herself. He was so good to me, she thought. So understanding. Who but Pop-Pop would have had the talent to become one of the most successful men in Aspen? He'd really made the most out of his year and a half of grade school. And such a storyteller! Silver Tongue was his nickname when he was asked to speak at the annual Fourth-of-July picnic.

He had so much to tell, and so much to write down, his mind must have been a jumble. No wonder he skipped around so much. One minute the saloon, the next his trip out west at age fifteen, the next something happening at the mine. Did he write about *it* or not? Geraldine was dying to know.

She looked up at his portrait. "I didn't mean any disrespect. But it might take me days to find out if you wrote about that time or not. I've found someone who I think can help me, but she's only going to be here for the week. Otherwise, Pop-Pop, I could happily while away the hours drinking in every last detail of every day of your life that all seem to be included in this here diary."

When did he write this? Geraldine wondered as she turned back to his memoirs. It must have been late at night. When she had gone on that six-month trip with him, she realized that he was a first-class insomniac. He must have used those quiet hours in the middle of the night to pour out his heart on paper. Me, there's nothing that burns me up more than when I wake up at three o'clock in the morning and can't get back to sleep, she thought. I get too aggravated to get anything done.

At nearly midnight, using the magnifying glass as a

bookmark, she closed the cover and carried the heavy volume into the bedroom. She placed it on the night table next to her bed. I hope it's in there, she thought. I hope I hope I hope.

As she drifted off to sleep she reassured herself that from what she had read so far, Pop-Pop had written about everything. So surely he had written about *that*.

I'M SO TIRED I may just pass out with my clothes on," Kit said as Regan unlocked the door to their room.

"I thought your escort for the evening would have left you starry-eyed," Regan said.

"Mr. Search and Retrieve," Kit answered as she walked in the room and flopped down on the cot that had been left for her. "I don't think so. It figures you got the guy who had something to offer. Like a drop-dead face."

"I didn't get him, Kit," Regan protested. "He's nice, that's it. If you ask me, he's a little too pretentious. And too much of a pretty boy. He's the type you can't trust in the long run."

"The short run works just fine for me," Kit said. She unzipped her jacket and pulled off her boots. "What do you want, you're only here for a week. Doesn't he want to go skiing with you tomorrow?"

"With us. Doesn't Derwood want to ski with you too?"

"It's a blur," Kit said. "When he got into computers

of the future I started dissociating. In layman's terms, day-dreaming."

"Trust me, I think he'll be with us."

"He told me he was a great skier," Kit said. "I just dread that ride up in the gondola. It can seem like a lot longer than fifteen minutes when you're trapped listening to the history of the microchip. Can you imagine the people who get stuck in the gondola with us? Halfway up they'll want to jump out."

"He's not that bad. Actually he was kind of cute," Regan said. "Stewart filled me in on his boarding school and kept asking me if I knew this one or if I knew that one. When I'd said no for the ninety-ninth time I was sure he would leave. But it didn't seem to bother him."

"He liked you," Kit said. "I could tell. When I was dissociating I was staring at him and drooling."

"Is dissociating your new word?"

"Huh?"

Regan shook her head, went into the bathroom and took her robe off the back of the door. She slipped it on and tied the belt around her waist.

"Get up, Kit. Don't fall asleep in your clothes," she called.

"I learned it from you. The one whose new pajamas were still in the wrapper after four years of college."

Regan laughed. "I've got a new term for you. Baloneyizing." She shut the door of the bathroom. In the next three minutes she washed her face, brushed her teeth, and took her calcium pills because she'd read so many articles about the urgent need to take preventive measures to fend off osteoporosis. When she finally came out of the bathroom. Kit's eyes were shut. She hadn't moved a muscle.

"Kit. Get up."

"Thank God I'm so tired," Kit said. "Otherwise I'd never get any sleep. This cot is a piece of—"

"It does remind me of the beds at Saint Polycarp's," Regan said. The furnishings and plumbing in the antiquated dormitories had left something to be desired. "I'll sleep on it tomorrow night."

"Don't worry about it. I'll manage. I have an appointment to see my chiropractor next week," Kit said as she dragged herself up and into the bathroom.

Regan got into bed and pulled the covers around her. I feel guilty, she thought as she looked over at Kit's sleeping area. Oh well. Not that guilty. Tomorrow I'll have to see if Louis can do better than that.

It had been a fun evening. They'd all gone to dinner together and then went dancing. Larry had introduced them to everyone in sight. He had definitely missed his calling. He was a great dentist but he should have been a traveling social director. It seemed as if there was no one he didn't know.

When she and Kit had gotten back, there had been no messages for them. Regan picked up the pad next to the bed and jotted down a few notes. Call Yvonne. She hadn't heard from her tonight and Regan did want to try and call Bessie. She hoped Yvonne had found her cousin's number. Another thought had occurred to Regan tonight when she was dancing. Get in touch with the reporter who wrote the newspaper article on Geraldine. Regan didn't know why but she just thought that it might help. He was doing a series on people from the town. He'd recognized *The Homecoming* as a Beasley. Maybe he had some insight into the robbery in Vail. It couldn't hurt. And maybe he could shed a little light on Geraldine. He might even know

Eben. Whatever. Regan made a notation and put down the pen.

Kit came barreling out of the bathroom. "I bet your mother would love Stewart. To think that he could provide all those cutesy little outfits for her future grandchildren."

"Don't tell her," Regan said. They were having dinner at Kendra's the next night. "No use getting her hopes up."

"Thank God my brother has three kids," Kit said. "Or my mother would be all over my case to keep the lineage going. She should know what a nerd magnet I am. Would she want nerdy genes in the family?"

Kit and Regan looked at each other. "Yes," they said in unison.

"Whatever it takes to get grandchildren," Regan commented.

Kit lifted up the blanket and eased herself into the narrow metallic berth. "My own little piece of heaven," she muttered. "I'll just curl up next to this safety bar and pretend it's Mr. Wonderful."

Regan turned out the light.

"The more I think about it," Kit said in the dark, "the more convinced I am that this guy is right for you. Third-generation family business. He lives in New York, and your mother would love to have you back there. He's from an old Massachusetts family . . ."

"And in the Social Register," Regan said wryly. "Don't forget that. He certainly won't let you. If he had mentioned that in passing one more time, I would have hit him."

"Delete. Erase. Do not save. Overwritten," Kit said.

Regan felt herself drifting off to sleep. From across the room she heard her best friend ask, "Regan, did you know that the new laptop computers have the capacity to . . ."

"Shut up, Kit," Regan said and fell fast asleep.

32

Tuesday, December 27

Eben leaned over toward Bessie. "Up and at 'em!"

"I wish I could kick you out of bed," Bessie hissed sleepily. "You were snoring so loud last night, I thought your mouth was a jackhammer in overdrive."

"Let him who is without sin cast the first stone," Eben said. "There were a few decidedly unladylike noises emanating from your side of the bed and you don't hear me complaining."

"No lady should have to put up with you."

There was a long pause. They both lay still, their limbs aching for freedom of movement. Finally, Eben said, "You know, we only have each other. We should try to make the best of it."

Bessie turned away from him as far as she could. She

could feel her hairdo slowly disintegrating. "Nobody knows I'm gone. They think I'm at my cousin's in Vail. I don't even know if she's home yet. I just left her a message. If she doesn't get back for a few days, no one will ever miss me."

Eben puffed out his cheeks and exhaled slowly. "Out of sight, out of mind."

"You're an idiot."

"I'm sorry, Bessie. I understand your feelings, but I've been here a couple days longer than you. You start to get philosophical about things."

"Who would have guessed that I'd end up in the sack with Socrates?" Bessie mumbled to herself.

"Go ahead, make fun," Eben whispered, "but your stress levels will go way up if you don't work toward some acceptance."

"I'm not about to accept." Bessie's voice rose and Eben shushed her.

"Don't let them hear you getting upset," he warned. "It's not a good idea, believe me."

In a tightly controlled voice, Bessie began again. "I'm not about to accept the fact that we're both dead meat. Because we are, you know. You don't think that they're going to let us out of here alive, now do you? Do you? We can both identify them."

Eben wished he could scratch the stubble on his face. He hadn't shaved in more than a week now. Normally that time off would have been a treat. Shaving was such a nuisance, but now he'd give anything for a sink of hot water, a little lather and a nice sharp razor. What he could do with that! And how about a shower? They'd have to let him have some bathroom privileges pretty soon. It was only human.

"Get a grip, Bessie," he said slowly. "We'll figure out something. As you know, I was a con in my time—"

"That's all they're talking about in town," Bessie interrupted.

"Thank you, Bessie." Eben sighed. "I'm ashamed to admit that I landed outside the law. . . ."

"On more than one occasion. Now everybody thinks that you're an ungrateful jerk who cheated Kendra and Sam Wood after they trusted you."

"But I didn't do it, now did I? What I was saying was that maybe I can call on all that experience distracting people. That was the key to getting all that jewelry, simple distraction. Most people are incredibly absentminded and you just have to take advantage of that." He lowered his voice. "Let's face it, that Willeen is no Einstein. Um-hmmm. Distract, distract, distract. Poof—your pocketbook is gone off the back of your chair in even the best restaurant. Poof—your favorite necklace is a memory."

"I don't think Willeen's purse or jewelry is going to do us much good, Eben," Bessie grunted.

"I'm not talking about that."

"Then what are you talking about?" Bessie's angry whisper was positively raspy. "We're tied up by two losers who are probably going to kill us. We've got to get out of here! Vamoose!"

"There's an old saying, Bessie. 'If you can keep your head when all about you are losing theirs and blaming it on you . . .'" He immediately shut up when he heard the door to the bedroom open.

"How was your first night together?" Willeen asked in a tired, hung-over voice.

"Willeen, you really have to let me take a shower," Eben said in a pathetic voice.

"Judd's in there now," she answered practically.

"Please," Bessie whined. "I'm downwind of him and it's not healthy. I would like to take a bath, but at least I had one yesterday."

Willeen scrunched her nose. "There aren't too many towels here. The ones we've been using are little scraggly things that could barely dry a flea. Some luxury vacation in Aspen, huh?"

Towels, Eben thought. I just bought a bunch of towels! Two bags' worth. One bag I'm ashamed to think I brought into Kendra's house to use in the suite so I wouldn't have to use her good ones. The others I never carried up to my apartment the other day. They're still in the trunk of the car! The car that's parked out back! Eben had bought them at his favorite store, the Mishmash, which was in Vail. He'd taken a ride down there on Friday to do some Christmas shopping. Not that I have that many people to shop for, he thought sadly, but he loved to putter around that establishment.

The Mishmash was one of those discount joints that sold a hodgepodge of items, everything from decorative plates with sketches of the Rockies and plastic dog heads on springs that are designed to bob around on the back dash of your car and drive the people riding in the vehicle behind you crazy to irregular sheets, towels, underwear and socks. Sometimes it took a while to pick through all the sorry-looking merchandise in the bin in the corner, but with patience he usually came away with at least half a dozen decent briefs and three or four pairs of socks. And this time, the green towels.

Aspen's boutiques had gotten so exclusive that you couldn't even find a store within the city limits that found the sale of everyday underwear worth their bother.

Aspenites had to have them express-mailed to them through a catalog company or go on a field trip to find them. That's progress for ya, Eben often thought.

"You'll never guess what, Willeen," he said excitedly.

"No, I probably won't," she agreed, rubbing her eyes.

"I have a whole bag of new towels in the trunk of my car. If you go get them, we'd be all set."

Willeen looked at him and scrunched up her face. "I don't know."

"Please," Bessie shrugged. "For my sake."

Willeen shrugged her shoulders. "What's the harm? I wouldn't mind using a new towel myself."

Eben and Bessie listened as the back door slammed and Willeen crunched across the yard to the garage where Eben's car was hidden. A few minutes later she was back.

"I guess you like the color green, huh?" Willeen commented. "Ya know, sometimes it's good to buy two different colors that complement each other."

"Since I never really had a permanent home," Eben said in a dejected voice, "I never learned the tricks of decorating."

"Enough of your dismal stories," Willeen said. "Let me talk to Judd."

When Judd came out of the shower, Willeen tugged at the flimsy towel wrapped around his waist. "Our guests would like to go under the sprinkler, as it were."

Judd grinned at her. "We'll let them take a shower. Hey, Eben," he yelled, "do you two want to take one together?"

"NO!" Bessie bellowed from the depths of her being.

Judd got a good laugh out of that one. "Come on. Isn't there any sexual tension in that room?"

"Absolutely not!" Bessie croaked.

Eben rolled his eyes at Bessie. "You didn't have to be so definite. Would you like to go in the shower first?"

"No, you're more desperate than I am."

They had to wait until Willeen took her shower, after which there was no hot water left. Eben and Bessie still took their turns, and after they had both spruced up, they were allowed to sit at the scarred Formica kitchen table. Under Judd's watchful eye they ate their cereal with plastic spoons. The air was chilly and what could have been a cozy farmhouse filled with inviting smells and crocheted doilies instead reminded Bessie of an abandoned flophouse. How did they end up with this place? she wondered.

Willeen was sitting on a broken-down love seat a few feet away, filing her nails. The sound drove Bessie crazy. It went right through her, like fingers on a blackboard. Bessie's nails were strictly no nonsense, clipped to the quick, kept short to make her housework easier. They required a minimum of fuss, the way Bessie liked most things.

Willeen bit down on a cuticle and it seemed to relay a thought to her brain. "Ya know, I wonder if that washer and dryer work. I have some laundry and I didn't use Eben's towels because I hate to use towels before they're washed. Other people's germs are on them."

But it's all right for us, Bessie thought.

Judd opened the kitchen cabinet under the sink and discovered an almost empty box of laundry detergent. "There's some soap here, Willeen. I got some things that need to be washed too."

"Goody gumdrops," Willeen said as she put down her nail file and headed into the bedroom.

Bessie and Eben were eating in silence, except for the snap, crackle and pop of their cereal. They both munched

slowly, savoring the time they were allowed to sit up and have a different view. For both of them, even the sight of the tacky furniture was better than staring at the four walls of the bedroom. Finally Judd grew impatient.

"Hurry up, you two," he ordered. Quickly they gulped the rest of their food, were allowed to use the bathroom once again, and then were escorted back to their holding area. Judd yelled to Willeen to give him a hand.

After Eben was secured, Willeen left the rest of it to Judd. She went back into their bedroom and gathered up his pants and socks and underwear and a few of her own unmentionables off the floor. The Mishmash bag, containing two leftover towels, was on the couch in the living room. As she passed by, she scooped it up and carried it with the rest of the laundry over to the prehistoric washing machine by the back door. She stuffed everything in, poured in what soap was left, and closed the lid. After a few minutes of pulling and yanking the two lone knobs, she was rewarded by the sound of water rushing in.

"Voi-lah," she said aloud. "What a glamorous life I lead."

From behind, Judd put his arms around her. "After we finish this job, we'll go someplace great."

"I hope so."

"What do you mean, you hope so?"

"If we don't pull this off . . ."

Judd put his hand over her mouth. "We are going to pull this off. No problems, no complications . . ." He tilted his head in the direction of the guest room. "And no witnesses to worry about."

REGAN WAS DREAMING that she was in an audience somewhere, watching a play. The actor was onstage knocking at an apartment door and no one was answering. He kept knocking.

"Nobody's home," Regan wanted to yell, but in the way of dreams, she couldn't form the words. Instead she squirmed, moving from side to side, and finally drifted into consciousness. "Hmmmm. What? Oh." She sat up in the bed. Kit was still out like a light. The knocking was for real, coming from a few feet away.

Regan pulled on her bathrobe and answered the door. Tripp was standing there with a breakfast tray.

"Did I wake you?" he asked.

"Yes," Kit called from the cot. "But I'll take some coffee and then go back to sleep."

Tripp grinned and came in, setting down the tray on the dresser. "Louis thought you guys might like an eye-opener. Juice and coffee."

"What time is it?" Regan asked him.

"Nine o'clock."

"Nine o'clock! I wanted to get up early anyway," Regan said. "There are a few things I wanted to do this morning."

Tripp poured coffee for both of them. Regan took hers and sat on the bed. "How are you doing today, Tripp?"

He shook his head woefully and pushed back the ash-blond hair falling over his forehead. "My old man already called me from his office this morning."

"Is that bad?" Kit asked, as she sipped the freshly squeezed orange juice.

"He wants me to fax him my résumé."

"Louis has a fax downstairs," Regan said. "I'm sure he'd let you use it."

"He might have a fax. But I don't have a résumé. He's sick of me being a ski bum."

"Sit down and talk to us for a few minutes," Regan urged.

"Yeah," Kit agreed. "If you have a couple of hours, I'll tell you my problems."

Tripp laughed and sat on the room's only chair.

"My cousin is home for Christmas and was over at my parents' house last night. He's just gotten a really good job on Wall Street and now my father's all bent out of shape. He wants to see the résumé that I'm supposed to have been working on." He sighed. "My cousin is such a nerd."

"I think I've met him," Kit said.

"What?"

"Never mind." Regan laughed. "We'll help you with your résumé if you want."

"But I have no experience doing anything but working in this kind of job in ski resorts."

"We'll call in Regan's mother," Kit said. "She writes fiction."

Regan grabbed the pad next to the bed. "Tripp, what's your full name?"

He hesitated. "Are you ready for this? It's Tobias Lancelot Wooleysworth the Third."

Regan stared at him. "That's pretty heavy."

"You think my old man would have shown a little mercy," Tripp said. "But misery loves company. He'd been saddled with that name since birth, so why not old sonny boy? At least I'm a third, so they called me Tripp."

"Very preppy. Where are you from?" Kit asked.

"Connecticut."

"Me too. I'm from Hartford. And you?"

"Greenwich. But my parents are getting ready to retire to Florida. My father wants me to be 'settled' before they move. I told him I'm twenty-five years old, leave me alone."

Regan wrote his name on the top of the pad. "That name will impress the personnel department of any major corporation. Or at least raise their curiosity. It sounds like you come from somewhere. I should introduce you to the guy I met last night. He'd kill to have a name like that."

"So what do I put on the résumé after my name?"

"The schools you attended."

"I went to boarding school in Switzerland for a couple of years, then to Stanford," Tripp offered.

"Sounds great. Then, after listing your education, you just have to embellish the wonderful experiences you've had," Regan said with enthusiasm. "Like right now you're part of an international management team getting this restaurant off the ground."

"International?" Tripp asked.

"Louis's mother came from France."

"Cool." Tripp pointed to the canvas of Louis XVIII. "Speaking of France, what are you going to do about getting that cat framed?"

"I've got to find out this morning where to take him."

"If Louis lets me out, I'll help you carry it."

"Thanks, Tripp. I'm sure he'll let you. I'll get dressed and come downstairs."

Tripp got up. "I'd better head down. Louis is going to be looking for me. Thanks for your help. Maybe you two should do an infomercial on motivation or something."

Kit's head was buried in her pillow. "I don't particularly feel like a role model for motivation at the moment."

"Seriously, Tripp, when we get some time I'll help you with the résumé if you want," Regan said.

"Being a private investigator, she can spot lies," Kit said. "So she'll make it seem as truthful as possible."

"Anything to keep my father off my back," Tripp said and closed the door behind him.

"He's cute," Kit said. "Other than the fact that he's six years younger and has no clue what he wants to do with the rest of his life, I'd go out with him."

"Maybe you can teach him how to use the computer," Regan suggested.

"Now it's your turn to shut up."

Regan got up and stretched. "It's terrible to be that age and so unsettled."

"Not like us old broads, huh."

"You said it." Regan told Kit of her plans for the morning. "So why don't you take it easy? I'll come back to get you and we can go meet those guys at Bonnie's for lunch."

"I'm counting the minutes."

O N TUESDAY MORNING, Ida was so excited she could hardly stand it. She'd never been inside a celebrity's home before. And to think she was getting two for the price of one! Last night Ida had phoned her best friend Dolores back in Ohio and told her to go over to her house and get Nora Regan Reilly's books and send them out to be autographed. Priority Mail. It was worth the expense.

Ida checked her watch and hurried down the street. It was nine fifty-eight. She'd be working at the cleaner's from ten until two, and then was due at the Woods' house at three. At precisely ten she pulled open the door and scurried into the dry-cleaning shop. "Hello, Max."

Her boss looked up from the cash register. "Good morning, Ida. How are you feeling today?"

"Thankful to be alive," Ida said. "Thankful that the Good Lord allowed me to wake up this morning and still be breathing."

"That always helps," Max said as he unwrapped a packet

of quarters and watched them cascade into the drawer. He was a young man in his early thirties. Tall and skinny with gray hair, he was given to short sentences and what seemed like shorter conversations. Still waters hopefully run deep, Ida often thought.

"Today should be busy. Two days after Christmas and everyone's dirty clothes are piling up. And of course people drink too much over the holidays and get careless. Then they have to get their outfits ready for New Year's Eve . . ." Ida took off her ski jacket and hung it over the hook that was marked IDA.

"Good for business," Max said. "A few people were already in this morning. You can tag their clothes."

Ida adjusted her glasses, walked over to her work station, and reached into the bin of dirty clothes. She pulled out a man's suit and checked the pockets for any abandoned personal items and was disappointed to find there were none. Reaching for a set of tags, she tried to make her next remark sound casual. "Were any movie stars in here this morning?"

Max didn't even look up from his hard work arranging the money drawer. "Nope."

"Um-hmmmm," Ida said as she stapled the tags onto the jacket and pants. This suit looks expensive, she thought and dropped it into the second bin. She looked up at the big clock on the wall. Three minutes past ten. My God, she thought, this is going to be the longest day of my life. She could see that the hotels had dumped off their loads of cleaning and they all needed to be tagged. With the prices that Max insisted on charging just because it was Aspen and he could get away with it, Ida thought it would be cheaper to buy new clothes than send your old ones out for a few spins in a vat of chemicals.

Max slammed the register drawer shut with an air of authority and announced to Ida, "I'll be in the back."

Ida sighed and bent over the big white basket of soiled garments. She reached for a bundle and hoisted it onto her work area. The worst part of the hotels providing the cleaning service, she thought, is that many of the celebrities never needed to bring in their dirty clothes themselves, unless it was an emergency and they'd missed the morning pickup. Heck, Ida had taken this job so she'd meet people, and lately the only things that stared her in the face were big piles of smelly laundry.

The bell over the front door tinkled and Ida looked up.

"Hear that, Ida?" Max shouted from the back where the pressers were already at work, pressing and singing along and dancing to whatever song was on the radio. Max was at his work station armed with a squirt bottle, ready to attack any stained clothing with the zeal of a revivalist.

Deliberately Ida ignored him. Of course she heard it, she was standing right in front. Sometimes she worried that inhaling all those chemical fumes all year long was making him a little bananas.

"May I help you?" Ida said sweetly to a beautiful young woman with dark shiny hair wearing an expensive fur-lined jacket.

The woman handed her a piece of white material with spaghetti straps. "Someone spilled red wine on me last night. Can you get it out?"

"Of course we can," Max said, suddenly breathing down Ida's back. "Write out the ticket, Ida."

Ida turned to him and said wryly, "I wish I'd have thought of that." She licked her finger and pulled the top slip from a neat pile on the check-in counter. Next she

picked up the white garment. "Where's the rest of it, dear?"

The customer stared at her with a blank expression. "That's it."

"Sexy," Ida murmured. Hard to believe it's a dress, she thought as she wrote down the customer's name. It must stretch out more than a rubber band. I should only charge her for a necktie. "Here we go," Ida said, smiling, handing over the pink customer copy. "Tomorrow okay?"

"Sure. See you then."

Once again Ida checked the clock on the wall. I shouldn't wish my life away, she thought. But today I just can't help it.

After what seemed like an eternity, the hands of the clock finally rested on twelve and two. It was time for her to leave, to begin her new job rubbing shoulders with the rich and famous.

35

AFTER TAKING A hot shower, Regan felt ready to take on the day. She went downstairs to Louis's office and found him on the phone.

"Hi, darling," he whispered and then spoke into the mouthpiece. "This party is going to be so fabulous. Everybody's coming . . . Who? . . . I said everybody. We're getting extensive media coverage. It's the hottest ticket in town. . . . I'll fax you a press release." He hung up the phone and rolled his eyes. "I have national publications coming and the society editor of the *Ajax Bulldog* is telling me they have a lot of invitations for that night and they'll see if they can make it. Oh please . . ." He opened his desk drawer and removed his bottle of Tums. "I'm eating these things like candy."

"Those are what Eben had in his medicine cabinet."

"Don't mention him," Louis cautioned. "It's Tuesday and I'm still in business. There are only two more days where he can ruin me. How was the cot?"

"Kit said she was so tired last night she would have slept on a bed of nails, but on a normal night . . ."

"I'll see what else I can find. We're all booked up. Every bed in the house is taken. Are you going skiing?"

"Later. Now Louis, do you know the guy who wrote that article about Geraldine?"

"I've met him a couple of times. Why?"

"I don't know. I'd just like to talk to him about the paintings."

"Don't stir up any trouble!"

"I'm not going to. From the article it appears that he knows a lot about art. I think it could help. He might have some interesting insights about what's gone on, and about the painting in Vail too. Could you call him for me?"

Louis put his hand over his heart. "Regan, the last thing I need is any more negative publicity."

"What about the old adage: 'I don't care what you say about me as long as you spell my name right'?"

"After Thursday they can say whatever they want," Louis said as he begrudgingly picked up the phone and called over to the *Aspen Globe*. "Ted Weems, please . . . Oh . . . Well, this is Louis Altide at the Silver Mine . . . Could I get his home number? . . . I have a private investigator who wants to talk to him about the series he's doing . . ." Louis winked at Regan, hung up, and dialed Ted's number.

Regan sat there in awe as Louis pulled off a phone call that would have made a drama teacher's heart sing. He sounded so confident, so convincing, so full of admiration for Regan, so determined to cooperate with the authorities and get to the bottom of what looked like Eben's crime

spree. Finally he dropped the phone back into its cradle. "That was easier than I thought. He said to come on over to his apartment right now. It's not far from here." Louis wrote down the address and handed it to Regan. "He has to go out to do an interview in a little while."

"Louis, this is great."

"Now I've paid you back for yesterday."

"Of course, doll. You've made my life worth living. I'll leave now," Regan said, standing up. "Oh, I want to quickly call Yvonne Grant and see if she found Bessie's number."

"Here," Louis said, handing her the phone. "And then get out of here. You're making me nervous."

"I thought you liked having me here," Regan said in mock protest.

Louis came around the desk and gave her a kiss on the cheek. "You can come here anytime."

Yvonne answered the phone and told Regan that she couldn't find Bessie's cousin's number in Vail. "I thought we had it written down on a piece of paper in a drawer in the kitchen." Her laugh could not conceal a touch of annoyance. "Since I'm not too familiar with the kitchen ... Bessie is in charge of everything around here and I don't know where she would have left it. She's due back on Thursday. Can you wait until then?"

Regan was disappointed but kept it out of her voice. "Sure. But if you hear from her, ask her to call me at Louis's."

"Okay. You'll be at Kendra's for dinner?" Yvonne asked.

"Yes."

"We'll see you there."

"Great. See you later," Regan said and hung up. "Kit

and I are going to Kendra's for dinner tonight. Yvonne's going to be there too. Wanna come?"

Louis didn't even have to answer. He just reached for his bottle of Tums at the very thought as Regan grabbed her coat and hurried out the door.

36

T ED WEEMS ANSWERED the door and ushered Regan in. He lived in the area behind the Ritz Carlton where condos were modern and had their own balconies. The living room was light and bright, with a high ceiling and pine floors. It was filled with papers and books, and a computer was blinking in the corner. The place reminded Regan of her mother's office at home.

"I'm sorry," he said. "I've been working all morning and I didn't expect company."

"Thanks for taking the time to see me," Regan said earnestly. "I appreciate it."

He took her coat and then looked as if he didn't know what to do with it. Finally he threw it on a chair. "Coffee?"

"I'd love some."

"How do you take it?"

"Just some milk."

"I don't keep any milk in the house."

So why did you ask? Regan thought. "Black would be fine," she replied.

When he retreated into the kitchen, Regan glanced around. One wall of the living room was taken up by a floor-to-ceiling bookcase. A quick look at one of the shelves revealed an eclectic collection of history and art books. Comfortable armchairs and an overstuffed couch were facing the fireplace on the opposite wall. A great place, Regan thought, to curl up on a snowy day and read.

"Here you go," Ted said as he came back into the room carrying two mugs. Regan studied him as he pushed a newspaper out of the way and set the cups down on the coffee table. He was about forty, had dark hair flecked with gray, a thin intense face, and wore wire-rimmed granny glasses. Clad in blue corduroy pants, a white shirt and an old gray sweater, he did not look like the skiing type. Regan hoped that he wasn't one of those intellectuals who disdain ordinary conversation. She decided to start out by taking the middle road.

"It must be great to live in Aspen," she said, following his lead and sitting down in one of the armchairs.

Ted crossed his legs and wiggled his L.L. Bean duckboot. "Well, I'm here part of the time. I also have a rent-controlled studio apartment in New York. That's where I started out."

"A place here and a place there. That's not bad."

"I've always loved the West and its history. I thought it would be great to live here, but I never wanted to give up the city. Luckily, I can now afford both."

"And being a writer you can work wherever you happen to be," Regan said.

"Well, you have to be where the story is," Ted informed her. "My series on the descendants of the Aspen settlers

who live in Aspen now couldn't be done in Poughkeepsie."
He laughed and his eyes darted around the room. "I write
what I want to write," he continued. "And I'm syndicated.
That series is being carried by many, *many* newspapers
around the country."

Regan raised her eyebrows. "I didn't realize that. So a
lot of people from all over have been reading about Geraldine and her Beasley painting."

Ted smiled proudly. "I've gotten numerous phone calls
about the articles. Old friends. Relatives. People who wonder if maybe I have a spare room they can stay in if they
want to come out and ski."

Regan smiled. "Do you?"

He waved his hand at her. "I try and fend that off as
much as possible. What I really like to do is work. If I
had people in and out of here all winter long I'd never
get anything done. I deliberately bought a one-bedroom
condominium so I'd have no room for guests."

What a pal, Regan thought. "You spend a lot of time
working?" she asked.

"I'm doing this series. I do features. I've been working
on a history of the mining towns in Colorado. And I've
been writing about western art."

"So it's pretty interesting to talk to these people in
Aspen, then?"

Ted laughed. "Sure. I enjoyed talking to Geraldine. She
was a killer talking all about her grandfather. I asked her
to show me around and when I came across that painting,
I nearly died."

Regan leaned forward. "Tell me about that painting.
How did you know it was a Beasley?"

Ted's eyes glinted. "I've been doing a study of Beasley

and I planned on doing a story about him. He was . ." Ted paused for emphasis, "*fascinating.*"

Regan nodded, waiting for more. She didn't have to worry.

"Beasley was a tragic figure. He went around the mining towns in the 1880s and painted these masterpieces, then died when he was only twenty-eight. Like most great artists, he wasn't appreciated until years after he passed on. From his notations, he'd made twelve canvases. Ten are in museums in Colorado, where they belong, I might add. They should be shared by all." He stared intently at Regan. "I mean, after all, does the *Mona Lisa* belong in someone's living room?"

"No," Regan said dutifully.

"You're absolutely right. It does not." He pointed to the mountains outside the condo. "Does anyone have the right to hog these mountains? Keep them to themselves for no one else to enjoy?"

"No."

"You're absolutely right again. Ten Beasleys are on display. An eleventh was owned by a connoisseur in Vail, and look what happened to him. Those of us who are knowledgeable about Beasley were surprised he didn't paint Aspen. Then we thought maybe the missing twelfth was done in Aspen. After all, Aspen was called the 'richest five acres on earth' back then. If it was Beasley's intention to capture the spirit of the times, he certainly would have come here. And then"—he smiled beatifically—"the twelfth was discovered in the barn of longtime Aspen resident Geraldine Spoonfellow."

"You must be pretty proud of that," Regan said.

"I am. You can imagine my shock and excitement. The minute I laid eyes on it, I knew that it was special. I could

feel the mountain air, the sense of place, the authority of his brush stroke. I was transformed. *Astonished.* I got tears in my eyes, and so did Geraldine."

"She did too?" Regan asked.

"I think she did because it was her grandfather. She didn't really want to talk about the painting. She just wanted to cover it up. It was kind of strange. She didn't know what she had, hidden as it was behind an old wagon wheel. *Oh God!*" He sipped his coffee to ease the exasperation.

"It sounds like you could have bought it from her yourself for a pittance," Regan said.

He almost looked offended. "I'm not like that. That painting belongs in a museum. It's one of our greatest historical resources. I immediately got the ball rolling with the Rescue Aspen's Past Association. And let me tell you something, they're not finished with her yet."

"What do you mean?"

"She owns a lot of property around here and has no one to leave it to."

"I didn't realize she had much money," Regan said.

"She hasn't replaced a lampshade in fifty years. Her car is vintage. She shops by catalog. The vault at the bank has more than just Geraldine's painting. It's got a lot of her money too. She's a fascinating character, just *fascinating.*"

"What interests me," Regan said, "is that a lot of people were reading about Geraldine and her Beasley in your article."

"And my follow-up article."

"Follow-up article?" Regan asked.

"Actually it was an addendum. Do you know what that is?"

"I picked up the meaning somewhere along the way."

"Good. About a month ago I did an article about Geral-

dine donating the painting to the association and the plans for the museum. I said that this was the missing Beasley and it was headed where it belonged, to the new museum in Aspen, that there was going to be a big benefit party, blah blah blah. Louis was furious I didn't name his restaurant. Anyway, in it I did name the owner of the Beasley in Vail." He rolled his eyes. "Maybe I shouldn't have done that because afterward he started getting calls from a lot of museums and collectors. The people who contacted him last week and made the appointment to see him used the name of one of the most reliable art dealers in Europe when they called. They were talking about paying five million dollars for it! Of course it was all a setup."

Regan frowned. "I wonder if they're now after the Aspen Beasley. It's going to be on exhibit Thursday night. It's the only one left not under lock and key at a museum. Who knows what could happen?"

"I see what you're saying. I *do* see what you're saying." Ted's eyes widened, which made his face appear owlish. He started to laugh. "Don't worry. The museum guard will be there. His nickname is Barney Fife."

Regan chuckled.

"So why did you want to see me?" he suddenly asked.

Mildly taken aback, Regan cleared her throat. "As you know, I'm a private investigator. I had met Eben Bean, who is a suspect in the art thefts here in Aspen. Now they're saying he might have something to do with the theft in Vail. He just doesn't seem like the type. . . ."

"Totally different MOs," Ted interrupted. "My sources say the job in Vail was sophisticated. That it was an art ring working. Of course we all know now that Eben Bean was an accomplished jewel thief. Maybe his whole friendly bit was just a facade. If it was Eben in that Santa suit, then

he obviously knew how to catch people when they're at their most vulnerable. Who's afraid to let Santa use their toilet, *for God's sake*?"

"I just don't think it was a facade," Regan said. "Yesterday I visited Geraldine Spoonfellow. She is very upset about the robberies here in town and really believes it was Eben. I think that even if Eben has something to do with what's gone on, he's not acting alone. Or maybe there are two sets of thieves."

"I don't know." Ted shook his head. "I just don't know."

He leaned back, recrossed his legs and rubbed his chin. "So Geraldine has no patience for Eben, huh?" Suddenly he checked his watch. "Oh my God! I have an appointment to interview another old-timer, an Aspen descendant who is moving back to town. He got in touch with *me*. You'd be amazed how people love to read about themselves in the paper. He said he'd seen my article about Geraldine Spoonfellow and knew her way back when."

Regan's eyes brightened. "Really?"

"Would you like to come along?" Ted asked. "He sounds like a talker."

This guy is full of surprises, Regan thought. "I'd love to," she said and meant it. She was most anxious to hear about Geraldine Spoonfellow as a young girl.

he obviously knew how to reach people when they're at their most vulnerable. Who's afraid to let Santa see that smile for their family?

"Omigosh, I think it was reader," Regan said. "Once day I visited Geraldine Spoonfellow. She is very upset about the robberies here in town and really believes it was Ebel. I think, just even if Ebel has something to do with what's going on, he's not acting alone. Or, maybe there are two sets of thieves."

"I don't know," Ted shook his head. I just don't know."

He leaned back, crossed his legs and rubbed his chin. Geraldine has no patience for Ebel, huh? "Suddenly he looked at his watch. "Oh my God! I have an appointment to interview a number of people at an Aspen club and who is moving back to town. He got in touch with me and I'd

37

REGAN CONSIDERED HERSELF a fast walker until she tried to match the stride of Ted Weems. He practically galloped down the block. In just two steps, his long legs covered a lot of sidewalk. They passed the ice-skating rink, the bus stop, and a row of designer boutiques in what seemed like seconds. Regan felt like a small child being dragged along by an impatient parent.

The small brick and wood buildings they passed were so picturesque and storybook-perfect that the place almost didn't seem real. The little village of Aspen sometimes seemed as if it belonged on a movie lot; you had the feeling that if you opened the door of a building, there'd be nothing on the other side.

As they hurried along, Ted explained how the connection had been made. "Angus Ludwig wrote to me from California, where he's been living for the past fifty-five years, and told me how much he'd enjoyed the articles. He mentioned that he knew Geraldine Spoonfellow when they

were both young. He said he'd be here at Christmastime because he wanted to move back and would be looking for a place to live. His grandsons love to ski and he thought if he bought a place in Aspen he'd be sure to see them plenty. I thought it would make a great story—someone who grew up here coming back to live when he's eighty years old."

"Wow!" Regan said. "He's eighty?"

"He sounds like he's about twenty."

They reached the Hotel Jerome, the grand old hotel that had been restored in recent years and was now an elegant testament to Victorian Aspen.

The living room off the foyer was decorated with oriental rugs, traditional couches and chairs, and glass coffee tables supported by stands built of antlers. There are a *lot* of antlers in this town, Regan thought. I'd hate to be a moose around here. A large Christmas tree dominated the corner, and moose heads, mounted on the rose wallpaper, stared out in different directions.

It was eleven o'clock and they went immediately to the nearly empty dining room where the tables were set with pink tablecloths and fresh flowers. A long bar ran along one wall, and draped windows that reached high up to the ceiling covered another.

Angus Ludwig stood up from his chair and waved them over.

"You guessed it. I'm Angus, the oldest dude in the room," he said, chuckling. "Sit down, have some coffee and a doughnut or whatever it is they serve here."

Regan smiled at him. He had a full head of white hair, a rugged face, and a hearty demeanor. He was wearing a rust-colored corduroy jacket, a white shirt, a string tie and blue jeans.

"I brought someone with me, if that's okay," Ted said.

"The more the merrier."

Introductions were made and Regan and Ted sat down and ordered coffee and Danish. Ted pulled out his miniature recorder and Regan smiled, thinking of Larry.

"Mind if I record this?" Ted asked.

"Not at all." Angus beamed. "Am I speaking loud enough?"

"Yes," Ted said, searching in his bag for his notebook. "I'd like to take a few notes as well."

"Are you from around here, young lady?" Angus asked Regan.

"No. I live in Los Angeles. I'm just out here for the week."

"A California girl, huh?"

"By way of New Jersey," Regan said.

Angus's smile was broad. "I'm a San Francisco boy by way of Aspen. I guess that's why we're here today."

Ted cleared his throat as if to take control of the conversation. "Regan visited Geraldine Spoonfellow the other day."

"Well, I'll be," Angus said, turning to Regan and putting his hand over hers. "How is Geraldine?"

"She seems fine," Regan said, commenting only on her state when they left, not arrived, at her house. "You knew her?"

Angus leaned back in his chair. "We both grew up here. When I was eighteen I went to college back East. She must have been thirteen when I left. I wasn't back much at all, taking summer jobs in different cities because Aspen was so quiet then. I came back to live at Christmas when I was twenty-four years old. It was 1938, and things were starting to happen here. Ski races and the like." He paused, a

faraway look in his china-blue eyes. "It was a beautiful day, everyone in the Christmas spirit, and there I was, sitting in the barber's chair when she walked by the shop. The prettiest nineteen-year-old you ever saw! Geraldine Spoonfellow was all grown up! I wanted to run out in the street but my hair was all wet and I thought"—he raised his eyebrows—"it wouldn't make too good of an impression anyway. So I"—he paused and looked at Ted—"is the microphone picking all this up?"

"Yes, sir."

Angus leaned back and crossed his legs. Regan hoped that Ted had brought enough tape.

". . . I went over to her grandpa's saloon right after my hair was cut to see if she had stopped by. Her grandfather was there but no Geraldine. I asked him if maybe I could call her for a date."

"What did he say?" Regan asked and then realized she should maybe let Ted do the questioning.

"He didn't say no but he didn't encourage it either. He said that they had just come back from a vacation and it had been a long journey home by train. They wanted to get back to be with the family for Christmas and were both a little tired. He said maybe another time. I was hoping I'd run into her around town, and sure enough, at church I saw her, looking like an angel. But she looked so sad."

"Did you ever go out with her?" Ted asked.

"No. I just stared at her across the pews of that church. I must have looked like a lovesick cow. There was a New Year's hayride I wanted to take her to, but she wouldn't give me a tumble. Funny part is, I could tell she kind of liked me. But she just couldn't be bothered when I went up to her after the recessional hymn and everyone was walking out. Here it was Christmas and she was a pretty

young girl and I was a handsome rascal." He made a face. "I was, you know! But she wasn't interested. From what I read in Ted's articles, I guess she never got interested in anybody."

"She told me she had a boyfriend last year," Regan said.

"She did?" Angus sounded indignant and then quickly tried to cover his reaction. "A few months after that I had to go away on a business trip to California. That's when I met my Emily and I never came back to Aspen to live again. We got married, I went into Emily's father's business, my folks retired to Florida, I enlisted in the service, and all of a sudden Aspen was a memory. Until now."

"Geraldine is donating a valuable painting to the museum. It's called *The Homecoming*," Ted said.

"I remember that painting." Angus's fist rapped the table.

"You do?" Regan and Ted said together.

"Heck yeah. That was hanging behind the bar in Mr. Spoonfellow's saloon. The day I went in there panting after Geraldine, her old Pop-Pop was taking it down to make room for a little Christmas tree on the counter. He must have gotten ideas on decorating from his trip to New York. You know something? He never did end up putting that painting back up before I left town a few months later. Now here it is, famous as famous can be. I should have tried to buy it from him back then!"

"Now," Ted said, looking down at his notebook, "would you say that you had a longing to come back to your roots?"

"You could say that if you wanted to," Angus replied. "The fact of the matter is that after Emily died last year,

I felt lonesome. My kids were raised and were scattered all over. I didn't want to be a burden to any of them, but I knew I wanted to move somewhere else. There were too many memories where I was. So one day in the paper I read your article"—he slapped Ted on the back—"and it gave me a good kick in the pants. Why not go back? I said to myself. This place is where all the action is now! It's got the advantages of a small town with all the activity of a big city. I always missed the snow and the mountains. Emily always said she wasn't a cold-weather person, so we never came back. But my grandsons are such good skiers, I figured why not see what this place has to offer? I'm going to be looking at a few houses this week. It's expensive around here! But there's a house outside of town that needs a little fixing up. The lady at the real estate office thinks it might be just fine for someone like me. I like to tinker around with a house anyway."

Ted looked alarmed. "So it's not definite that you're moving back?"

"Are you kidding? After being here for one day I feel alive again. I've been so blue since Emily died. She had been sick for a while, but once she was gone there was this great big void and I didn't know how to fill it. When I stepped off that plane the other day, I just felt I was home again."

By now, Ted was scribbling madly. "Perfect! Perfect!"

Regan couldn't resist a question. "Do you think you'll call Geraldine while you're here?"

Angus ran his fingers through his thick white hair. "It's kind of hard when you remember that somebody wouldn't give you the time of day. And that's when I was good-looking!"

Regan laughed. "You're still good-looking! And that was a long time ago."

"Well, I don't know. But I will tell you something . . ." He pulled a ticket to Louis's party out of his pocket. "I'm going to do my best to get reacquainted."

38

WHEN REGAN FINALLY got back to the room, Kit was just about ready.

"Perfect timing," Kit said. "Tripp brought me up the newspaper to read. I lounged in your bed, caught up on current events, dozed and finally got together the strength to take a shower. How was your morning?"

"Interesting," Regan said as she pulled her ski pants out of the drawer. She told Kit about Ted and the meeting with Angus.

"I'll tell you one thing," Kit said as she combed her hair. "I want you to strangle me if I go mooning after the Pledge man decades from now. I'll just allow myself to be miserable for the next month or so."

"He's not mooning after her. This is different," Regan insisted. "He didn't come back here for her. He came back because he grew up here. They had never gone out, so it's not the same." She was now digging out her ski socks.

"He remembers the *Homecoming* painting hanging behind the bar of the Spoonfellow saloon."

"I wonder why Geraldine never went out with him," Kit mused.

"Me too," Regan said. "It could be that she just plain old wasn't interested, but there's something about it that just doesn't sound right."

"Hmmm," Kit said as she studied her appearance in the mirror. "It couldn't have been that he bored her to death with talk of computers. They weren't even invented yet."

Regan laughed. "There's always something boring to talk about. Let's get out of here. The guys must already be up on the mountain."

On the way out they passed Tripp at the desk.

"Hey, Regan," he said. "I called around to a few of the art galleries in town. I got one of them to say they'd come by and pick up the Louis painting. You have to stop by there tomorrow to pick out a frame."

"That's great!" Regan said. "Thanks a lot. They can get it done by Thursday?"

"They'll deliver it Thursday."

"Tripp, you do good work."

"Would you mind putting that in writing for my father?" he asked.

"We'll figure out a way to get it on your résumé," Regan said as she and Kit headed out the door.

Kit looked at her watch. "We're just on schedule. Everybody else has been out skiing since the lifts opened and we'll get to the mountain in time for a late lunch."

They took the gondola to the top of Aspen Mountain and then skied down to the midway point, where Bonnie's was nestled into the hill. A colorful array of skis and poles was propped up outside the restaurant, waiting in the snow

for their owners to reclaim them after they'd had enough food and socializing.

"Everyone here is so trusting," Kit said. "Don't a lot of skis get stolen?"

"What we should do is take one of your skis and one of mine and put the two mismatched sets in different places," Regan said.

"That's my buddy," Kit said. "Foiling those criminals at every turn."

It didn't take long to find Larry. He was decked out in all-black ski attire. His sunglasses were mirrored.

"Hi, Larry," Regan said, staring at her reflection.

"Hi, babe. We've got a table over there. Get your food and come on back outside." It sounded like the tone he might use to tell his patients to open wide.

"Isn't it a little chilly to eat at the outside tables?" Kit asked.

"You see more out here," Larry said. "These are the tables that fill up first. Don't worry. The sun keeps you warm."

Regan and Kit pushed their trays through the line, chose sandwiches and bottled water, and paid what could probably feed a family of four a nice turkey dinner. They were still getting used to walking in their ski boots.

"The bathroom is one flight down," Kit said.

"Grab the banister and walk sideways," Regan advised. "It's not worth it."

Outside, they walked over to the table where Stewart and Derwood were already eating.

Stewart wiped his mouth and patted the seat next to him. "Sit here, Regan," he said.

Larry's abandoned tray was next to Stewart. He was busy making the rounds of the picnic tables, looking for

old friends, new friends, anybody from the New York area who might need quality dental work.

"Larry should set up his dentist's chair in a gymnasium," Regan said as she sat down. "He'd be able to work off some of his excess energy in between patients."

Stewart laughed heartily. "The skiing has just been fabulous," he announced. "How many runs have you made today?"

"A half," Kit said and bit into her ham-and-cheese.

"You're joking," Stewart said.

"No, we're not," Regan replied. "I had some things to do this morning and Kit tried to get over her jet lag."

Stewart studied Regan. "What were you doing?"

Regan shrugged. "A few errands."

Derwood looked up from his leafy salad. "At the hotel where I'm staying you can actually hook up computer games to the TV set."

Kit was in the middle of taking a slug of water. She started to cough and some came out of her nose. Stewart winced while Derwood patted her on the back.

"Are you all right?" he asked.

"Never better," she answered.

"I was wondering," Stewart said, regaining his friendly expression, "where we should go for dinner tonight."

Regan glanced at Kit. "Tonight we're meeting my parents for dinner."

"Where?" Stewart asked.

"At Kendra Wood's house. That's where they're staying."

"Kendra's a beauty," Derwood mumbled.

It amused Regan that the remark seemed to annoy Kit.

"I'd love to meet her," Stewart said.

I don't know whether that's a hint, Regan thought, but

it would be best to just ignore it. "Maybe we can meet you guys later." She glanced around. "Hey, Stewart, do you produce skiwear for kids?"

"Not skiwear," he said and reached into his wallet. He unfolded an ad with two blond children modeling bright Christmas sweaters with matching pants. "We just ran this ad last month," he said proudly.

Regan and Kit clucked in admiration. "Those kids are really cute," Regan said.

Stewart smiled in gratitude. "They sure are."

When they had finished eating, they rounded up Larry and they all got back on their skis. When they pushed off, Derwood went barreling down and within ten seconds took a nasty spill. Kit skied over to where Regan had stopped.

"He told me he was a great skier," she whispered.

"Maybe on the computer," Regan said.

They made several runs and finally decided to head back to get ready for dinner. When they parted from the guys, Stewart put his arm on Regan's shoulder.

"We're going dancing later. I'd love it if you'd join us."

"We'll try," Regan promised.

As they walked back to the hotel, Kit sighed. "He's a hunk and he likes you. So what's the problem?"

"I don't know. There's something about him."

It was four o'clock and the sky was starting to darken. "We can get changed and grab a taxi to Kendra's," Regan said. She found herself hoping that just maybe Yvonne would have found Bessie's cousin's number and brought it with her to Kendra's.

AT TWO SHARP, Ida grabbed her coat and bolted out of the cleaner's.

"Where are you going, a fire?" Max called after her.

"Someplace even more exciting," Ida yelled back as the door closed behind her, leaving its Scotch-taped bells tinkling in her wake.

She hurried home to freshen up and at one minute of three found herself walking up the front path to Kendra Wood's home.

This looks like a famous person's house, she decided, noting its large size and the beautiful stone-and-log design of the exterior. It's the type you see on Robin Leach's television program.

She rang the bell and could hear the fancy chimes playing their own little melody through the house. How elaborate, Ida thought, when a simple ding-dong would do the trick. She pushed her glasses back against the bridge of her nose and blew out of her mouth, enjoying the sight of her warm

breath floating out into the cold air. That must be where they got the expression "You're full of hot air," she thought.

Suddenly the door was pulled open and standing in front of her was none other than one of her favorite actresses, Kendra Wood, looking as chic as expected, clad in a ski sweater and black stretch pants.

"Ida?" Kendra asked.

"That's what they call me," Ida joked and stepped into the foyer. "It's so nice to meet you. I've seen all your movies," she blurted, then remembered Daisy's warning not to talk too much.

"Well, that's good," Kendra said, taking Ida's coat, "although there are a few I'd rather forget."

"Oh, I know what you mean. There were a couple recently that just didn't measure up to your talent."

Kendra half-smiled as Ida stuffed her gloves into her coat pockets. "There we go. I understand that you're going to be appearing on Broadway soon."

"Yes," Kendra said. "I was just studying my script."

Ida's eyes widened. "Really! How exciting!"

"Let's hope it's exciting," Kendra said ruefully. "We think it's going to be a good show. Now come inside and meet everyone. They've collapsed after our first day of skiing. We went over to Snowmass today."

Ida followed her into the den where a roaring fire was blazing and Kendra's sons and husband and guests were lounging around reading.

"Ida, I'd like you to meet . . ." Kendra introduced her to everyone.

"I love all your books. I've read every one of them," Ida informed Nora.

"Thank you," Nora said, getting up from the couch to shake her hand. "That's always nice to hear."

"I'm a funeral director," Luke offered.

Ida looked puzzled. "How lovely," she said.

"Don't mind him." Nora laughed.

"Ida, why don't I show you around the rest of the house and then we'll end up back in the kitchen?" Kendra suggested.

"Fine with me," Ida said, all of her senses drinking in every detail.

They walked down the long hallway and glanced into the master bedroom and the guest suite. "We all make our own beds, but when you have time, if you could just run the vacuum and clean the bathrooms, that would be great."

"Nothing like a little vacuuming to make a place feel fresh," Ida said. "That and a few squirts of cleanser in the bathroom and it's as good as new."

Kendra smiled at Ida. "We're so glad this worked out. I hope it won't be too much for you. I know you're also working at the cleaner's in town."

Are you kidding? Ida thought. You don't even have to pay me to do this! She waved her hand at Kendra. "Oh, it's only for one week. I like to work!"

"Good." Kendra laughed. "I like to work too."

Back in the kitchen, Kendra had laid out salad makings on the large butcher-block table. "We're having some guests for dinner, so if you could make a salad and heat up this spaghetti sauce, it should be pretty easy."

"You made a sauce?" Ida asked.

"Well, I guess my former caretaker made it. It was in the freezer. He actually was kind enough to leave us with a few things before taking off," Kendra said sarcastically.

"Now, honey," Sam called from the couch. "Don't think about Eben. Come back here and study your script."

"You'd never know, Sam," Luke murmured, "that you're one of the investors in the play."

"You go sit down," Ida urged Kendra. "I'll take care of everything."

Kendra returned to the couch and picked up her script while Ida busied herself washing lettuce and cutting up vegetables. It was a pleasant, relaxed time and everyone in the den was enjoying the quiet. I wish they'd talk more, Ida thought after a half hour of silence. The sauce was on the stove, the bread was all ready to be heated, and the salad was chilling in the refrigerator.

Ida cut up some cheese and put it out on a tray with crackers. Finally, when she could delay no longer, she went down to the bathrooms and gave them a quick once-over. When she got back to the kitchen, the group in the den was breaking up. The boys had gone to their room downstairs where there were video games, and the others were going to shower and dress.

Kendra, her script in hand, leaned on the kitchen counter. "Ida, if you could do some food shopping tomorrow, I'd appreciate it. Maybe we should make a quick list." She pulled a pad and pen out of a drawer.

"A grocery list in one hand, a Broadway script in the other," Ida chuckled.

"Right," Kendra said absentmindedly as she started to write down the items she knew they needed. When the list was complete, Kendra gave Ida some cash. "Let me give this to you now so I don't forget later."

After Kendra had retreated to her bedroom, Ida set the table in the dining room, which overlooked the front yard. There doesn't seem to be a bad view anywhere in this house, she thought.

At six o'clock the chimes sounded and Ida hurried to

answer the door. It turned out to be the Grants. Ida knew that they were the other couple who'd been robbed. Kendra came out to greet them. They all went into the den, and before you knew it the place had the feeling of a party going. Nora and Luke and Sam reappeared and the men made drinks. The chimes sounded again. This time when Ida answered it was the Reillys' daughter, Regan, and her friend Kit.

"I'm Ida," she informed them as she took their coats. "Here to pitch in for a few days."

Since Eben's not here to do it, Regan thought.

"It's nice to meet you, Ida. I'm Regan and this is my friend Kit." Ida nodded and hurried down the hall with their coats. Regan and Kit wandered into the den and greeted everyone.

"Kit, it's so good to see you," Nora said, kissing both of them and steering them over to the couches. They all settled in and Sam served drinks.

"Have you two been having fun?" Nora asked hopefully.

Kit's grin was like the Cheshire cat's. "There's a guy we met who really likes Regan. We're meeting him later to go dancing. He has his own company . . ."

Luke could see Nora's pupils dilate.

"What kind of company?" she asked.

"Children's clothes," Kit pronounced. "He manufactures the most adorable children's clothes. He even showed us an ad."

"He sounds wonderful," Nora said, her voice cracking.

"Be still, my heart," Luke muttered.

"Mom," Regan protested. "You've never even met him. You know nothing about him."

"And we all know what can happen with that," Sam grunted.

"It shows he likes children," Nora said.

"It shows that he likes the money he can make off their clothes," Regan said.

"What about you, Kit?" Luke drawled.

"I'll tell you," Regan said quickly. "Kit has someone after her. Mr. 'Everything you always wanted to know about computers and then were sorry you asked.' I think he and Kit make a cute couple."

Kendra laughed. "And what do you say, Kit?"

"He's a nice guy but much too boring."

"Sometimes you can learn to love those types. Just give him time," Yvonne suggested.

Lester acted bemused. "Are you trying to tell me something?"

"No, darling; it was love at first sight."

Of your checkbook, Regan thought. "Yvonne," she said, "I hate to bring it up, but did you by any chance come across Bessie's cousin's number?"

Yvonne looked at Lester. "We didn't know whether to say anything right now."

"What?" Regan asked.

"Have I got news for you!"

"What?" Kendra asked quickly.

"I didn't find the number, but I did get a call from the insurance investigator. Boy, are they on top of things. They want to talk to Bessie as soon as possible."

"Well," Regan said, "they usually question the help when there's a theft at home."

"For the second time," Lester said.

"What do you mean?" Regan asked.

"From what this guy tells us," Yvonne said, "at the last family home where Bessie worked, there was a major theft. She was questioned about it."

"When was this?" Regan asked.

"Twelve years ago," Lester said. "Great, isn't it?"

Sam burst out laughing. "Well, Lester, you and I better work on our hiring practices. We hired a jewel thief and you might have hired an art thief. Maybe the two of them got together."

Ida was so excited she couldn't help herself. "I won't steal anything," she blurted out as she stirred the spaghetti sauce.

Sam turned his head in Ida's direction. "That's good, Ida, because we were worried about you."

Yvonne laughed. "I don't think Bessie had anything to do with any crimes," she said. "But it is suspicious, and now I don't know how to reach her."

"Why would Bessie have called me?" Regan asked.

"Maybe she wanted to say good-bye," Luke said.

Regan made a face at her father. "Yvonne, did the insurance investigator say anything else?"

"They know that Eben was there at our house that night. They know that he worked for Kendra and Sam and now he's missing and so is their art. Bessie was working for us and was there the same night Eben was. They think they might be connected."

Regan thought aloud. "I know Bessie said she saw Eben last week when he came by to pick up the toys for the kids."

"Maybe they hatched their plan then." Luke took a sip of his drink.

"What is Bessie's usual day off?" Regan asked.

"It's flexible," Yvonne answered.

"What day was she off last week?"

"Friday."

"Where did she go?"

"I don't know. She left in the morning and got home in the evening. The next day we were so busy with getting ready for the party that she never mentioned where she'd been. We'd been skiing. I don't even know if she was in and out that day."

"Eben was shopping at some dumpy joint in Vail last Friday. Nora found the receipt for some store called the Mishmish or something . . ." Sam said.

"The Mishmash," Nora corrected him. "Like a good person, I gave the receipt to the police."

"Wherever. He was gone last Friday. She had off last Friday. A Beasley painting was stolen in Vail that day by a man and a woman. Now both Eben and Bessie are missing. I don't know . . ."

Regan shrugged. "Well, Bessie is not officially missing. We just don't have her phone number. I don't see those two together. If I had to pick an unlikely team, they'd be the first on the list. And she was so mad at him for tracking in all the mud last year. She was still so annoyed about it when I talked to her. Unless it was all an act . . ."

Ida was in the kitchen trying not to look as though she was hanging on every word. She was in total bliss. Reaching in the freezer to get some ice, she once again noticed the carefully marked containers of food. For someone who was going to leave, she thought, he had been very considerate about preparing a few dishes before he left. Most crooks would have brought them with them. These days everywhere you turn there's a microwave beeping. I have to say something, she thought.

Ida cleared her throat. "You know," she said, "Eben left a lot of food here. Chili, lemon chicken, his spaghetti sauce, which I tasted and it is out of this world . . ."

"See," Regan interrupted. "It isn't consistent. Why

would he take the trouble to prepare all the food? And then leave the bedroom a mess and not take all his things with him. It just doesn't make sense."

"Bessie is due back Thursday," Yvonne said. "I hope she makes it and can give us some answers."

"If she just comes back," Regan said, "that's the first good sign."

"Well, everyone," Ida crowed. "COME AND GET IT!"

Where's the cowbell? Kendra wondered.

40

DINNER WAS DELICIOUS. The one thing you could say for Ida was that she did know how to put a hot meal on the table. And everyone agreed that Eben had done a great job on the spaghetti sauce.

"I wonder what Eben was thinking when he made this," Kendra said.

"A little more onions, a little more garlic . . ." Sam said and bit into a piece of bread.

Over coffee Regan and Kit decided they would go snow-mobiling with Patrick and Greg the next day.

"Snowmobiling is a real adventure," Ida piped in. "My son-in-law, Buck, says that everyone goes away with a smile on their face."

"It would be fun to try it," Regan said.

"Will you ask the clothing fellow to join you, Regan?" Nora queried.

"She better not," Kit said. "Or I'll be stuck with the computer whiz."

"Mrs. Reilly," Patrick said playfully, "Regan and Kit already have dates."

"I always liked younger men." Regan laughed.

"Well, why don't you take our car back into town tonight so you can pick up the boys tomorrow?" Kendra suggested.

"That'd be great," Regan answered.

An hour later Regan and Kit were walking into the dance club. They could hear the music blaring as they paid the admission fee. Taking a few more steps inside, they saw Larry dancing by with the blonde with the long mane of hair to whom he had been talking last night. He waved at them, beaming like a Dutch uncle. "Stewart and Derwood are by the bar. They're waiting for you," he shouted above the music.

Regan waved back. "Thanks, Lar." As he danced away, she turned to Kit. "Yeah, Lar, it was nice seeing you."

"How did I ever get so lucky?" Kit asked.

"I don't know. But we may as well push our way through the crowd and see if we can find them."

The strobe lights were twirling and bouncing and flaring all over the place. As they made their way across the floor, the song being played inspired every dancer to let loose, with a few zealous types deciding to fling their partners this way and that, most of them obviously never having graced an Arthur Murray dance class.

When they reached the bar, Regan shouted in Kit's ear. "I think I have three surviving toes."

"My rib cage was cracked by somebody who didn't check their rearview mirror when they decided to do-si-do."

"We'll get you a heating pad. There they are." Regan pointed. Stewart and Derwood were leaning on the bar a few feet away and looked as if they were in a serious

discussion. Regan walked over and tapped Stewart on the shoulder. He turned around and smiled broadly.

"Hey, Regan," he said, putting his arm around her shoulders.

"Hi, Stewart."

"Let me get you a drink."

"Sure."

While Stewart signaled for the bartender, Regan turned and watched as Derwood whisked Kit off to the dance floor. That was quick, Regan thought. I bet Derwood knows that there's a slow song coming up.

"What will you have, Regan?" Stewart asked.

"White wine. Thanks."

A few minutes later he handed it over to her. He really is nice, Regan thought. So what is it that doesn't seem right?

"How was your dinner?" he asked.

"Fun. What did you do?"

"Derwood and I grabbed a bite to eat in town here. It would have been more fun if you were with us."

Regan smiled up at him. "Well . . . hey, do you have a ticket for the party Thursday night?"

"Wouldn't miss it. I hope we can all sit together."

"I'm sure we can arrange that. . . . Glad to have the week off?"

"Huh? Oh yeah, sure."

"You'll have to send me your catalog. A lot of my friends are starting to have kids. Some already do. I'm always looking for some cute outfits and I never know where to go. What size do you go up to anyway?"

"What size? Uh, size eight," he responded.

"Eight?" Regan sounded surprised. "I thought your clothes were for babies and toddlers."

"Well, that's most of the clothes we make," he said quickly. "Let's dance."

"Okay."

They squeezed their way over to Derwood and Kit, who were boogying their hearts out. Derwood was doing a variation on the twist, whereas Stewart preferred the old swivel-your-hips and snap-your-fingers method.

The foursome danced for a long time and then stopped to have drinks. After chatting at the bar for a while, everyone decided it was getting late and they all walked out together. Stewart and Derwood strolled down the block with them to Louis's place and bid them good night.

Inside Louis's, the lobby was quiet. As they trudged up the steps to their room, Regan was deep in thought.

"What's with you?" Kit asked as she got out her room key.

"I was just thinking. It was fun dancing with Stewart, but when I asked him about his business, he didn't want to talk about it. It was kind of weird."

"We should have switched places," Kit said. "If you wanted to talk business, I'm sure Derwood would have been much obliged. He probably would have preferred it to twisting the night away."

"I didn't want to talk business," Regan scoffed. "But when I brought it up, he seemed uncomfortable."

Inside the room was a different cot. A note lay on top of it. "Hope this is better." It was signed "Tripp."

"How nice," Kit said, immediately stretching out to test it. "This is better. I'll probably only wake up four times during the night."

"I say Tripp should forget getting out his résumé. He ought to stay on with Louis and help him run this place,"

Regan said. "He's really on top of everything. He could end up having his own inn out here someday."

"Don't mention that to Louis," Kit advised. "If this place makes it, he'll want it to be the only new one in town until the day he dies."

"You're right. We should try and have coffee with him in the morning before we leave to go snowmobiling. We hardly saw him today."

"Maybe we should have dinner here tomorrow night," Kit suggested.

"That's a good idea," Regan said. "He'll be a wreck. The party is so close now."

"Let's do it," Kit said and got up to get changed. She went into the bathroom and closed the door behind her.

Regan sat on the bed. I'm so anxious to talk to Bessie, she thought. I hope she gets home early on Thursday. Maybe that's why I can't just let loose with Stewart. I've got all these other problems on my mind. And then that painting on display here Thursday. Louis is right, she thought. I can't wait until the pressure's off.

41

EBEN AND BESSIE lay together in the slowly darkening bedroom, the sound of the buzzing washing machine muffled slightly by the bedroom wall.

"I can't believe we've been listening to that all day now," Eben said. "Do you think they'll make a TV movie about us if we get out of here alive?"

"I suppose you'd want Paul Newman to play you," Bessie huffed.

"I bet Elizabeth Taylor will be just begging to play Bessie Armbuckle," Eben responded in kind.

The sound of an approaching car up the driveway made them both stiffen.

"Here they come," Bessie said flatly. "Bonnie and Clyde."

"Keep the faith, old girl, keep the faith."

"You have a nerve to call me old."

"It's just an expression."

"You don't even know how old I am," Bessie said.

"That's true."

"According to the newspaper, you're fifty-six."

Eben winced. "I hate it when my age is bandied about."
He changed the subject. "I keep worrying about Regan
Reilly."

"Knowing you doesn't do anyone any good. You just
better hope that she keeps the faith." Bessie pursed her
lips. "Old boy."

They could hear the back door opening and Willeen's
voice whine. "What's that noise?"

"It's coming from the washer," Judd said.

"Now they'll turn that thing off," Eben whispered.

"Has this been buzzing all day?" Willeen opened the
lid and saw the green towels and Judd's pants all clumped
together in a pile of suds on one side of the washing
machine. The agitator looked as if it were being strangled
by Willeen's bras. They were wrapped in knots around its
base.

"I can't wait to get out of here," Willeen snapped as
she reached into the cold water to rearrange the load.

"Are you sure you're supposed to wash all that stuff
together?" Judd asked impatiently.

"What am I, your private laundress? There was only
enough soap for one load." Willeen dropped the lid and
within seconds a low groan from the bowels of the machine
gave way to the energetic spinning sound of the revolving
basin as it picked up speed. Short, sharp blasts of water
being sprayed in to break up the soapy residue were a
further assurance that the machine was functioning again.

"I tell you, Judd. Everybody we meet in Aspen is parking
their behinds in nice hotels and we're stuck here staying
in this dump. And these two . . ." She tilted her head in

the direction of the guest bedroom. "Are you sure you've got it all figured out?"

"I told you, I'm sure, damn it!" Judd snapped. "We've got two more nights before we're out of here. Please cooperate with me."

Willeen went into their bedroom and slammed the door.

In the next room, Eben felt his heart start to pound. He knew it was a bad sign when the people in on the plan started arguing. They're getting edgy, he thought, and we've only got two days to get out of here. He looked over at Bessie, whose hair was now falling out of her carefully pinned braids.

"Bessie," he whispered. "We're going to have to try and get one of your hairpins. Maybe I can use it to pick the lock on our handcuffs."

"They're not the type that just fall out," she whispered back. "It might not look it now, but they're in pretty tight."

"When they go out again, I'll try and get one with my teeth."

"What?" she whispered indignantly.

"This isn't kidding around," Eben said in a dead-serious voice. "It's time for us to do something, or we'll never get out of here alive."

Tears filled Bessie's eyes as she realized that he was right. "Okay, Eben." She turned her face into the pillow and felt a tear roll across the bridge of her nose. If I die, she thought, I'll be with my parents. It was the only comfort she could find in one of her darkest hours.

Aʟ FTER MIDNIGHT, AS he sat in bed, the Coyote watched with amusement as Judd and Willeen came in from their night of partying and pulled their clothes out of the dryer.

"What the hell is this?" Judd said, holding up his pants, which were covered with little green fuzzies. "Those cheap towels of Eben's shed all over everything."

"We wouldn't have had to use them if there were any decent towels in this joint," Willeen hissed.

"I have to get my tux pressed for Thursday night," Judd snapped as he futilely brushed away at his pants. "I'll bring these with it to the cleaner's tomorrow morning."

"Since you're asking, yes, you can bring my dress too," Willeen said sarcastically.

The Coyote laughed out loud. "You two are beginning to lose it," he said. "But you don't even know what more . . ." He stopped at the mention of his name.

". . . there's no way the Coyote could beat us to it again, is there, Judd?"

The Coyote continued laughing and finished his sentence. ". . . well, I guess you do know what you're going to lose." He snapped off the set and turned out the light, anxious himself for the next forty-eight hours to be over with.

43

GERALDINE SAT PROPPED up in her bed, with her pillows around her and her quilt pulled up under her chin. She liked to sleep in a cold bedroom and she had opened the window because she was trying to stay awake while she read Pop-Pop's diary.

Her eyes were exhausted. I've read all day, she thought, when I should have been out in the barn searching out more Spoonfellow family personal effects for the museum opening on New Year's Day. They promised to put out anything worthwhile as long as they got it before the doors opened on Sunday.

But nothing, Geraldine had decided that morning, nothing could be more important than seeing if Pop-Pop had written about *it.*

She decided to read just one more page before turning out the light. Not too much of interest on this page in the grand scheme of things, Geraldine thought. I know by now that Pop-Pop enjoyed his days on the turnip farm. He sure

did get carried away writing about it. She finished the page and sighed. Time to call it a night.

She turned the page to put in the bookmark when her name caught her eye and read the first line. She let out a bloodcurdling scream. "Yippee, yippee!" she yelled. Here it was!

No longer aware of a headache or the fact that her eyes felt almost blinded, she raced through the page with a haste that would have been the envy of a recent graduate of a speed-reading course. It was all there. From the moment it began until . . . until . . . Geraldine turned the page and swooned. Her newfound knowledge made her light-headed. "Oh dear Lord, dear Lord!" she cried as she read on. "I never knew!!!"

When she had collected her senses, she jumped out of bed and sprinted across the cold floor in her bare feet, heading for the kitchen, where she poured herself a tumblerful of Wild Turkey. It was now 1 A.M. East Coast time, she thought. No use trying to phone the investigator until the morning.

"But I want to!" she yelled into the air. "I don't want to waste another minute!"

She threw back her neck and swallowed the firewater. "Aaaaah," she sighed. "That might calm me down but I don't think so." She knew that this was going to be the longest night of her life, the hours between now and the civilized hour of 8 A.M. East Coast time, when she could pick up the phone.

Geraldine hurried back to bed and picked up the diary. My fatigue is gone, she thought. I'll never sleep tonight. Forget counting sheep. There aren't enough in Australia to make me tired.

All of a sudden the impact of what she had read overcame

her and she started to cry. Tears streamed down her face. "Please don't let it be too late, dear Lord," she sniffled. "At least let part of it be okay. Pop-Pop, if you're listening, thank you for being such a good man. And thank you for sending that nosy reporter who pulled your picture out from behind the wagon wheel. Otherwise I never would have started digging around the barn, otherwise known as the Spoonfellow junkyard. Amen."

Just then, Geraldine's bedside light blinked. "I knew you were listening," she whispered. *"Now help me out!"*

44

Wednesday, December 28

Regan and Kit sat with Louis in the dining room having breakfast. He had the help in a frenzy of brass polishing.

"How'd you sleep, Louis?" Regan asked.

"What's sleep?" he answered. "I lie awake and think, did I take care of this, did I take care of that? It's terrible." He took a sip of coffee and inspected his fingernails. "I just hope everything gets done before tomorrow night."

Kit swallowed the toast in her mouth. "What's left?"

"I don't know," he whined. "That's why I'm awake at night. It's everything and nothing."

Regan put down her coffee cup. "Louis, you've got the food?"

"Yes."

"The dinner is sold out?"

"Yes."

"The paintings of the local artists will be dropped by tomorrow?"

"Yes."

"The band is coming?"

"Yes."

"The program is printed up?"

"Yes."

"The media is coming?"

"Yes."

"So don't worry."

"Famous last words."

"Two days from now you'll be sitting here, having launched a successful restaurant. Just wait and see."

"I feel like the bride," Louis said, "knowing that everyone's going to find something wrong no matter how good the party is."

"There you go," Regan said. "If you know that some of that is going to happen anyway, then you can just relax. People are going to have a good time. Believe me."

"I hope so, Regan. I guess I should be happy we haven't heard any more from Geraldine. I wonder how she's doing."

"She's probably cleaning out her barn and getting ready for her presentation tomorrow night. She's going to make a speech, right?"

"Which is another worry. She's been known to ramble when she gets the floor at town meetings. Something tells me we're going to have to get out the hook." Louis sampled a tiny spoonful of his oatmeal.

"I can't wait to meet this Geraldine," Kit said.

"She's great," Regan said. "She's probably rehearsing her speech right now."

Bright and early, for the third time that week, Angus Ludwig sauntered into the Wonder Properties real estate office.

Ellen Gefke stood up to greet him. "Hello, Angus. I didn't expect to see you today. How are you?"

"Itchy. Itchier than a bad case of the chicken pox."

Ellen smiled. "Will a cup of coffee help?"

"We could give it a try."

Ellen thoroughly enjoyed her job as a Realtor in Aspen. Forty years old, she'd moved to Aspen after her divorce three years ago and had never been happier. Always an athletic outdoorsperson, she loved to ski and felt that she'd finally found a real home. That's why she so enjoyed finding the right home for her clients. "A place," she'd say, "where you know right away you belong."

At the coffee machine, she poured the steaming liquid into two mugs, handing one to Angus, knowing by now that he liked his black.

"Thanks, Ellen," he said. "I'll tell you why I'm here. I'm dying to get a look at that house you were telling me about, the fixer-upper."

Ellen shook her head and sat back down at her desk. "Angus, it's rented until Saturday. I'd be happy to show it to you then. We hate to pressure our rental tenants to let us in when they've paid good money to have a place of their own for a few weeks. They have a right to their privacy."

It was obvious that this didn't bother Angus. "Who are they, anyway?" he asked.

"I've never met them. The reservation was made through a company who sent a check. I sent them the keys and a map."

Angus sipped his coffee. "Hmmm. I'm feeling restless, Ellen. I get it in my bones about doing something and then I'm like a little kid at Christmas. Being back in Aspen makes me feel so happy. Why don't we just drive by the place? How does that sound? I'd love to at least get a look at it from the outside."

Ellen checked her watch. She pushed back her blond hair and stood up. "Okay, Angus. You twisted my arm. Let's go now because I have an appointment coming in a little later."

Angus smiled his most charming smile. "I knew I came to the right office! Something about your ad made me pick up the phone last week. Isn't there sometimes a feeling you get about somebody, like you've known them a long time when you've only just met? I like doing business with you . . ."

"Sure, sure," Ellen said. She came around her desk, walked to the back, and poked her head into a private office.

"I'm leaving. I'll be back in a little while."

In her car Angus regaled her with stories of the old Aspen. "Yup, this place has changed, but it still has that feeling of magic. You breathe in this air and your lungs never felt so good."

"That's why I like living here," Ellen said as she concentrated on the winding roads.

Angus continued undaunted. "I left here before Walter Paepcke and his wife Elizabeth came here from Chicago in the forties and really got this town going as both a skiing and a cultural center. From what everybody tells me, they both did a lot for this town."

"They sure did," Ellen said. "They started the Aspen Ski Corporation, the Aspen Music Festival, the Aspen Center for Environmental Studies. It's really thanks to them that Aspen is a National Historic District." They were several miles from downtown Aspen. She turned off the main road onto an unmarked narrow dirt road that twisted, turned and bumped for half a mile.

"Where in tarnation are we going?" Angus asked as he hung on to the dashboard.

"You told me you wanted privacy and a breathtaking view. That's what you're getting!"

Finally she stopped and pointed. Nestled at the foot of the mountain, down a long driveway, was a small Victorian farmhouse surrounded by tall evergreens. A car was visible in the driveway, which curved around toward the back of the house.

"There's a barn out back," she said. "The house needs work. But the possibilities are endless."

Angus breathed in and stared, imagining what he could do with the place. He could picture this location in every season. Sure, the house looked neglected, but with a coat

of paint outside and some TLC, this place could do me just fine, he thought. Just give me three months to get it shipshape.

"It looks like they're home," he said, hinting.

Ellen playfully smacked his hand. "Now, Angus, I told you, we can't do that."

Angus turned his piercing blue eyes on her. His white hair looked crisp in the sunlight. With mock indignation he said, "I thought you told me everybody was friendly around here."

Inside the house, Willeen and Judd were about to freak out.

"Who's that?" Willeen asked. "What are they doing, Judd?"

"How am I supposed to know?" he answered sharply. "I know they want to sell this place, but according to the contract they're not allowed to show it while we're here."

Bessie and Eben had been having their cereal when the car stopped at the end of the driveway and could be seen through the living-room window. In a panic, Willeen and Judd hurried them back to their room. Judd took two scarves and tied them around their mouths. "Don't try anything," he warned.

"They're opening the car door," Willeen practically screamed. "I'm going out there and tell them the place is a mess."

"Damn it!" Judd yelled. "I didn't want anyone to know who we were. All right, go out there and get them out of here."

Willeen pulled on her jacket and boots and ran out the front door, which they'd never used. She trudged through

the yard and down to the car. "Hi," she said in her sweetest voice. "Can I help you?"

Angus shook her hand. "Angus Ludwig. We didn't want to bother you. I'm thinking of buying a place out here."

"And I'm Ellen Gefke, the real estate agent for the house," Ellen explained quickly. "Mr. Ludwig wanted me to drive him around. He was just stretching his legs. We don't want to disturb you."

"I'd invite you in," Willeen said halfheartedly, "but we had some friends over last night and I must admit we haven't cleaned up yet."

"I don't mind—" Angus started to say.

"We totally understand," Ellen cut in. "We'll look at the house after you leave."

"Good enough. Nice meetin' ya," Willeen said, pulling on a strand of her hair. She walked back up to the house, turning every few steps and waving, making sure that they were on their way.

Back inside, she dropped her coat on the couch and plopped down on top of it. "Judd, this is getting very dangerous."

46

WILD WITH IMPATIENCE, Geraldine waited for Marvin Winkle, the investigator, to return her call. He called himself "the private eye who never winks nor blinks until he's solved your problem." Never *thinks*, either, Geraldine muttered to herself as she once again checked the clock on the wall. Never thinks to check his answering machine. If there was anything she hated, it was that lie that everybody leaves on their machine saying they'll call you right back. Hogwash. It had been three hours now since she'd made the call at 6 A.M. Aspen time.

Suppose the loafer was taking time off during the holidays? The last time she had talked to him had been six weeks ago. The report had been no progress, but his bill had come in right on the button. Well, now he could start earning his money.

Geraldine was afraid to go out to the barn for fear she'd miss the call. Instead she sat at the kitchen table and read more of the diary. A smile played over her lips when she

came to the part where Angus Ludwig asked Pop-Pop if he could court her. He was a handsome rascal, she thought, but I was in no frame of mind to see anybody. Oh well. Everything in its season. In other words, my timing really stunk on that one. Would that damn phone never ring? At that moment it did.

An instant later she was shouting into the phone, "I was about to nickname you Rip Van Winkle." In a loud, excited voice she filled Winkle's vibrating eardrums with the news of her discovery.

"That's wonderful, Ms. Spoonfellow," he bubbled enthusiastically. "Fantastic. Amazing. Overwhelming. It's going to make the whole thing a lot easier."

"Enough drivel!" Geraldine barked at him. "Get to work!" She slammed down the phone and stared at Pop-Pop's handwriting on the crinkly pages. I've got to get my speech ready for tomorrow night, she thought. A lightbulb went off in her head. For the unveiling of Pop-Pop's portrait, I'll read excerpts from Pop-Pop's diary. But with so many selections to choose from, I'll never know when to stop.

47

Rᴇɢᴀɴ ᴀɴᴅ ᴋɪᴛ hurried over to the framer's. His office was in the back of a gallery that was filled with large paintings, many with a western theme. The floors were shiny and a hushed, reverential tone prevailed.

Eddie, a grizzled man in his fifties, with long gray hair and sinewy hands, greeted them with a nod of the head.

"This painting of King Louis the Eighteenth should have a thorough cleaning. It was filthy when it came in here! We've been wiping it down with a cloth dampened with turpentine and have gotten a lot of the dirt off, but it's just a start. At least now you can see his face."

"He does look good with a clean face," Regan commented. "The colors are so much sharper."

"Yay-uh," Eddie said, staring at the portrait. "This painting needs to be restored properly, but we'll have it looking good for the party tomorrow night. It's a real dandy."

"It's beautiful," Kit murmured. "Hey, Regan, is there a Queen Kit portrait you'll buy for me?"

"I'll look for it when you're on the verge of a nervous breakdown," Regan said.

"I'm almost there."

Eddie didn't seem to register their conversation, so intent was he on pulling out his frame selection for their perusal. "Yay-uh," he said, "this gold frame here is real pretty. Do you like it?"

Regan studied the gold leaf. "It's definitely regal, which is what we need. What do you think, Kit?"

"Go for it."

"It looks good to us," Regan said.

Eddie took the pencil off the back of his ear and started making notations on an invoice. Regan had once tried storing a pencil over her ear while she worked, but it kept falling off. "We had a specialist come in and take care of the Beasley painting," he said, putting the pencil back. "I wonder what else Ms. Spoonfellow has up in that barn of hers."

"I don't know," Regan said, "but I'm dying to see *The Homecoming*. I've heard so much about it."

"That's a dandy too."

Regan paid him for the order. When he handed her the receipt he said, "We'll deliver this to Louis's restaurant tomorrow afternoon. This painting is perfect for someone named Louis."

"Thanks," Regan said. "If the party is a success, he'll be the King of Aspen."

"No reason it shouldn't be," Eddie said.

I hope you're right, Regan thought.

48

I$_T$ WAS A wonderful day for snowmobiling. Ida's son-in-law Buck led them on a tour through the snowmobile trails in the mountains. They stopped at a tiny wood shack where instant hot chocolate was served in paper cups. Mini-marshmallows were an added bonus. The whole group huddled inside, stomping their feet to get warm.

"It makes you feel like a pioneer, huh?" Kit muttered. "My feet are freezing."

"Think of how good it'll feel when they're warm again," Regan suggested.

"I have an extra pair of heavy socks on. Do you want to borrow them?" Patrick offered.

"How come no one I've ever dated would have done that?" Kit asked rhetorically, smiling at Patrick. "I'll take you up on your offer, and if I'm still available when you're twenty-one, or eighteen, or whatever the legal age is, let's get married."

Greg smiled. "He's got a girlfriend."

"That's okay," Kit said, pulling off her boots. "As long as he isn't gaga over computers."

Regan laughed and stepped outside with her cocoa. She walked over to her snowmobile and sat down. Silence reigned. There were no signs of movement anywhere, no signs of modern life. The snow-covered mountains surrounding her were quiet and peaceful, probably looking pretty much the same as they did on December 28 a hundred years ago. Moments like these, Regan thought, taking in the beauty and the awesome scope of nature, are a cause for real wonder. Like the wonder of where the hell Eben disappeared to. The world is so vast, she thought, swallowing a runny marshmallow. He could be anywhere.

She finished her drink and got up to throw the cup in the trash by the shack. She smiled at the little sign that said, DON'T WORRY, WE RECYCLE. You wouldn't have seen that sign here a hundred years ago.

The others came out of the shack, Kit buoyed by the newfound warmth in her toes.

"Thanks to Patrick, I've fended off frostbite," she said happily.

"You've got to learn how to dress in the cold weather," Buck advised.

"I can't wait to go socks-shopping," Kit said. "It's funny how the little things in life give me such pleasure these days."

"We'll make a day of it," Regan said. "Lunch and socks."

They all got back on their snowmobiles and revved the engines. It was now three o'clock. They fell in line and

headed back down the path. Regan was glad they were on the last leg of their adventure. She was dying for Bessie to get back. She couldn't wait to talk to her. Why had she called her and never called back?

headed back down the path. Regan was glad they were on the last day of their adventure. She was dying for Ihesie to get back. She couldn't wait to talk to her. Why had she called her and never called back?

IDA WAS PULLING a load of wash out of the dryer when she heard the car pull up. "Oh dear," she said to herself. "I don't want to be stuck here in the laundry room folding towels while they're all talking." Quickly she scooped them up in her arms and brought them out to the butcher-block table in the kitchen.

Kendra and Nora were heating up apple cider. The two couples were just back from skiing.

Such excitement, Ida thought, when the boys came through the door, followed by Kit and Regan. Hellos were exchanged while Ida helped Kendra get out cups for everyone.

"How was it?" Kendra asked.

"Cool," Greg answered. "We should get some snowmobiles for around here."

"Snowmobiles you'll use about two weeks a year," Kendra said wryly.

Sam came into the kitchen. "If Eben comes back, he'll get plenty of use out of them."

"Will you stop!" Kendra laughed.

"Never," Sam said. He pulled a bottle of whiskey out of the cabinet. "How about an apple smasher?"

"Don't be rude," Kendra said.

"It's the name of a drink, my dear," Sam protested.

Kendra turned to place the mugs on the table and got a good look at the laundry. Green nublets from the lone green towel were liberally sprinkled all over the luxurious pastel towels that were color-coded to the bathrooms. "Where on earth did that green towel come from?"

Nora looked at the pile. "My darling husband is the guilty one," she said. "He used it."

"What did I do?" Luke asked, appearing in the doorway.

"You used a towel, Mr. Reilly." Kit laughed.

"We're not blaming you for anything, Luke," Kendra said. "But where on earth did it come from?"

"It was in our bathroom," Luke said, his eyes amused. "I figured a towel is a towel. My wife was surprised that I chose it. I must say I wasn't paying much attention. I just reached in the closet and grabbed it."

"Luke," Nora said. "These other fluffy towels were all lined up, and you picked . . ."

". . . this rag," Kendra said, holding it up.

Sam looked sympathetically at Luke. "Us men never get a break, do we, Luke?"

"Absolutely not," Luke agreed. "I thought the other towels were too good to use. And now look at them."

Ida started to get nervous. "I'm sorry, Kendra, I didn't mean for it to be washed with the light towels. I did a dark load first and then I put most of it in the dryer when the phone rang. When I came back I wasn't thinking and I thought I'd unloaded it all and I started throwing in the light towels to be washed."

"Don't worry about it," Kendra said immediately.

"A red sock played hide-and-seek with me in the wash once. Then I threw in bleach and some white blouses," Regan said. "I was just glad I liked the color pink."

Ida smiled at Regan. "That's terrible," she said.

"It must have been one of our friend Eben's towels," Kendra said. "As a matter of fact"—her fingers moved along the towel to the inside corner, where she found a cardboard store tag was still stapled—"he must have just bought it."

"What does the tag say?" Nora asked.

"The Ritz."

"The Ritz?" Nora said.

"Just kidding," Kendra said. She squinted. "I can just about make it out. The name of the store is the Mishmash. Ninety-nine cents," she pronounced in her most dramatic tone. "Yes, indeed. The Mishmash."

"That's the store I found the receipt for," Nora said. "The Mishmash in Vail. I remember it said towels and socks and underwear. I told Luke the other day it must have been one of his towels."

"If he left his socks around, I'll take them," Kit offered.

Patrick and Greg laughed while Regan explained the joke to the others.

"Well, if the socks are anything like the towels, I don't think you're missing out on anything, Kit," Kendra said. "And I don't think you could find rags like these in Aspen. One more thought-provoking gift from our good friend Eben."

"According to the slip, he bought about a dozen," Nora stated. She picked up an apricot hand towel and examined it.

"I wonder where the rest of them are," Kendra said.

"Did he stick them in other nooks and crannies of the house?"

"You know, it's funny," Ida said as she shook an apricot washcloth with great gusto. "I had a man come in this morning with these green nublets sticking to his cream-colored corduroy pants. He said his wife had washed them with some green towels and what a mess! The towels shed all over. So I said, 'Where did you get towels like that? You should take them back.' He said they were staying somewhere. They weren't their own towels. He also brought in his tux and her formal dress to be pressed."

"The same thing happened?" Regan asked.

"Isn't that strange?" Ida said, as she folded the washcloth.

"I think it is," Regan said. "I wonder where they're staying around here that supplies them with such lousy towels. And has a washing machine."

The phone rang and Greg grabbed it. "Mom, it's for you."

"Hello," Kendra said. "Oh my God, you're kidding!"

Everyone fell silent. "What?" Nora whispered.

Kendra put her hand over the phone. "It's Yvonne. Bessie's cousin just called from Vail. She was in Denver for a couple of days and came home and got Bessie's message that she was coming down." Kendra paused. "She never made it."

50

K IT HELD THE phone and waited as Regan stepped
out of the bathroom in her terry-cloth robe. She recognized
the distracted look on Regan's face. She knew she could
say almost anything to her right now and it probably
wouldn't even register.

"Heathcliff is on the phone," Kit whispered.

"What does he want?" Regan asked absently as she
opened a drawer and pulled out a wine-colored sweater.

"It's actually a wrong number. He's looking for someone
named Catherine."

"Oh." Regan unwrapped the towel from her head,
picked up a comb from the dresser, and caught Kit's reflection in the mirror, twirling the telephone wire. She suddenly
snapped into the present. "Kit, what are you doing?"

"Well, join the ranks of the living. Stewart is on the
line. He and Derwood want to join us for dinner."

Regan raised her eyebrows and smiled. "I was having
deep thoughts."

"I know. Here." Kit handed her the receiver.

Regan took it from her and sat on the bed. "Hi, Stewart," she said. ". . . snowmobiling was fun . . . actually my parents and Kendra and her husband are coming over here to Louis's for dinner . . . do you and Derwood want to join us?"

"Is the Pope Catholic?" Kit muttered.

Regan leaned back against the pillow and smiled. "Louis is getting geared up for the party tomorrow night. I think everyone wants to make it an early night tonight . . . okay, we'll see you around eight."

Regan hung up the phone and it immediately rang again. "Maybe Derwood just wants to hear the sound of your voice. Hello. Oh hi, Larry. We were snowmobiling today . . . thanks for the invitation? Who could ever find you? You're always so busy here." Regan smiled at Kit as she listened to Larry telling her he had no specific plans for the evening. "Well, why don't you come over?" she said, telling him about the dinner. "Yes, Larry, Kendra already has a good dentist. See you at eight. Good-bye."

"Kendra will have a whole fan club tonight," Kit said.

"That's good," Regan said. "Because I know I'm not going to be such great company. I can't stop thinking about Bessie. I can't believe that she and Eben are in cahoots. It just doesn't make sense. And why would she have tried to call me?"

"I don't know, Regan," Kit said. "And now her poor cousin is a wreck. That's Bessie's only relative, right?"

"Yes." Regan sighed. "I feel so helpless. I want to do something and I don't know what."

Kit nodded sympathetically. "Before you go back into your trance, let's get ready and go find Louis. Wait until he hears that Bessie is missing."

"As far as I know, he didn't recommend Bessie for her job. But I'm still sure he won't want anyone to tell Geraldine. She might decide to blame him for this too."

"For a party that is so anticipated, I think a lot of people will be happy to have it over with," Kit said as she pulled a pair of jeans out of her suitcase.

"You can say that again."

"For a party that is so anticipated . . ."

"Kit!" Regan went back into the bathroom and switched on the hair dryer. The whirring noise around her ear seemed to blow new ideas into her brain. For the next ten minutes Regan decided what she would do bright and early tomorrow morning. Call the Mishmash and see what they remember about Eben and the green towels. Visit Ida at the cleaner's and see if the green-nublets man came to pick up his clothes yet. It might be ridiculous but it was something.

Dressed in their ski sweaters and jeans and boots, Regan and Kit descended the stairs to the lobby below. It was lively and festive. The room sparkled with lights and candles and a roaring fire. Glasses were tinkling, people were laughing and Christmas carols were playing over the stereo.

Tomorrow night this place will really be something, Regan reflected.

THE TABLE WAS a lively one. Everyone looked very sporty. Kendra was wearing a bright green sweater that not only complemented her eyes but also reminded Regan of the green towels. The restaurant was bustling. Tripp took their drink orders.

Larry had managed to get the seat between Kendra and Nora and before long had his arms around the backs of both of their chairs.

"Hey, Larry," Regan said. "It looks like a good photo opportunity for the dentist to the stars."

Kit snapped her fingers. "And to think I didn't bring my camera."

Larry squeezed Nora's shoulder. "Will you please tell them to stop picking on me?"

Nora averted her gaze, which had been steadfast on the very handsome face of the very eligible Stewart.

"Huh?" she said.

"Your daughter and Kit are both mean to me."

"And they're not even your patients." Nora laughed.

"I know. What did I ever do to them?"

Derwood cleared his throat. "Kendra and Sam have been telling Kit and me about the play they're opening in New York. It's all so exciting."

"You seem to know a lot about the theater," Kendra said.

"I enjoy Broadway," Derwood replied. "I'll have to come to New York for your opening in February."

"We can all go," Nora said enthusiastically. "Regan can come in from California, Kit will come in from Hartford. Stewart, will you be able to make it?" she asked hopefully.

"Of course, Mrs. Reilly."

"Call me Nora."

Why not Mom? Regan thought.

"It will be such a good time," Nora continued. "You can bring me samples of your children's clothes. I'd love to order some."

"For what?" Regan asked. "Or should I say whom?"

"Lauren Dooley's daughter is expecting a baby in the spring," Nora said, with a "so there" expression. "It's her first grandchild," she added. "It must be so exciting."

"I bet." Regan smiled and glanced at Luke, who raised his eyebrows at her and grinned back.

"Say, Larry," Regan said, changing the subject, "what happened to that woman you were dancing with last night? She looked pretty cute."

Larry crossed his legs and sighed. "Let me tell you something, Regan. Beauty fades. But dumb is forever."

As everyone chuckled, Regan said, "You've made me misty-eyed with that advice. Your sensitivity is so far-reaching."

"I'm glad to know that you're looking for all the right qualities," Kit added.

"A heartening thought," Sam agreed, thinking back on his experiences as a single.

"I'll settle down one of these days," Larry said, clearly enjoying the attention of the entire table now.

Regan smirked. "When the cows come home."

To Larry's dismay, Tripp came over with the tray of drinks and distracted everyone from Larry's favorite subject: Larry.

"Mom," Regan said as Tripp distributed the drinks, "Tripp here is writing his résumé. We told him you'd help."

In her motherly way, Nora asked, "Tripp, what kind of job do you want?"

He smiled. "What I'd really like to do is stay here in Aspen and ski for a few more years." He placed Nora's white wine in front of her. "I'm the proverbial ski bum."

"Have you taken any computer courses?" Derwood chirped. "No matter what you end up doing, they're always helpful."

Regan didn't dare look at Kit.

"You're right, Derwood," Kendra said. "Our sons know way more than I do."

"Well," Nora said cheerfully, "if you need any help, give a shout. I've done everything from writing ads for Luke's homes . . ."

"What did they say?" Stewart asked, incredulous.

"Don't ask," Regan said. "Believe me, you don't want to know. I've been around for a few of the brainstorming sessions."

"My husband gets some funny ideas," Nora explained. Luke gestured dramatically with his hands. "All I

wanted to do was place an ad that reminded people that they could charge funerals."

"Tell them the rest of it, Dad."

"And therefore they could earn a lot of frequent-flier miles. My wife thought it showed a lack of sensitivity."

Tripp laughed and served Luke the last drink on the tray. "Makes sense to me," he said.

"Thank you," Luke said, nodding his head.

"I'll be back in a few minutes with the menus."

They all raised a toast to their health, wealth and wisdom in the coming year, clinking glasses with every other person at the table.

"I hope I see you next year," Stewart said quietly to Regan while everyone fell silent to take that first sip.

"Mmmm," Regan agreed.

Now that they had their drinks, Louis must have felt it was safe to emerge from the cocoon-like atmosphere of his office. He walked over to the table with all the confidence he could muster.

When he said hello his voice squeaked.

"Hi, Kendra. You're not still mad at me, are you?" he asked shyly.

"No, I just want to kill you," she joked. "I guess you know that the Grants' housekeeper is among the missing."

Louis's face blanched. "Yes. Regan mentioned it to me before you got here tonight. I can't believe it. But I don't think Eben had anything to do with it."

Louis's words sounded to Regan like a prayer. She sat back in her chair. I never thought of the fact that Eben could be responsible for Bessie's disappearance, she mused. I figured, if anything, they were in it together. Bessie was supposedly headed for Vail. What if Eben had intercepted her?

Kendra was talking now. She waved her hand. "Eben's been gone since Christmas Eve. He wouldn't dare show his face in this town again. Even if he wanted to shut someone up."

I hope not, Regan thought. Let's just get through tomorrow night before everyone in town starts spreading around the theory of Eben's not only being a thief, but also a kidnapper. Regan shuddered. Or possibly even worse.

Across the room, Willeen and Judd sat at a table for two against the wall. They were already there when Larry and his gang came into the dining room. They quickly waved hello and turned back to each other.

"Did you check out the staircase to the basement by the ladies' room?" Judd asked.

Willeen fished the orange slice out of her drink and popped it in her mouth. "Yeah."

"You're sure you know your way for tomorrow night then?"

"Yeah." Her mouth puckered as she pulled out the remains of the orange slice.

Tripp came over to the table and tried not to look disgusted when he removed the lipstick-covered orange peel from the crisp white linen tablecloth.

"Are you two ready to order?" he asked in that falsely cheerful voice that waiters use when they hate their customers.

"Not yet," Judd said. "We're just enjoying the scenery for a while."

When Tripp walked away, he added, "We need to study this place good before your big party."

AFTER JUDD AND Willeen had left for dinner, Eben attempted to grab one of Bessie's heavy, old-fashioned hairpins with his teeth, but he ended up leaving bite marks in her head. Finally they decided to try wiggling their bodies into a position where Eben could try to pluck a hairpin with his hands. It wasn't easy with their hands cuffed behind them and their legs shackled to the bed. Bessie moved her body as far as she could toward the foot of the bed. Eben faced the other way and reached back. He managed to remove a hairpin and then found her hands.

Eben was almost sure it wouldn't work, but their only chance was if he could release the catch of Bessie's handcuffs with the pin.

Willeen and Judd hadn't gone out until after dark. After that fellow came snooping around, they didn't want to take any chances that he might come back and peek in the windows. So when they left for dinner, all the lights were

out and the shades were drawn. Which meant no television either.

Time and time again Eben tried to use hairpin after hairpin to release the lock on Bessie's handcuffs. All to no avail. They had all bent when he tried to use them to pick the lock. "They just don't work," he grumbled in exasperation. But with numb fingers he kept trying. He knew that after tomorrow they wouldn't be here. By Friday they probably wouldn't be alive.

Several times he felt Bessie wince as the other end of the pin dug into her palm during his attempts to free her hands. "I'm sorry, Bessie," he said.

"It's okay," she answered. "We're on the same team."

Eben thought of all the safety catches he had released from bracelets and necklaces and wondered why the one time he really needed it, he couldn't jimmy the lock. It was useless.

Eben's hands ached. Finally he stopped. They lay there in the dark, both lost in their own thoughts. They even dozed a little and Eben woke with a start. "Let me try again, Bessie," he said.

"Okay," she answered wearily and let him take another pin from her head.

It felt like all the others, but Eben kept fiddling with it. Just as he felt movement in the lock and thought he heard a click, the sound of the car coming up the driveway cut through the stillness of the night.

"Damn it!" Eben muttered. "I thought I had it."

"Save the pins," Bessie urged. "We can try again tomorrow."

"I'll stick them in my back pocket."

Hurriedly they both felt around the mattress for any extra pins and Eben shoved them in his pocket.

The back door of the house opened. "I'll check on them," Willeen said. She walked across the living room and pushed open the door to the bedroom, which was slightly ajar. She then snapped on the light and walked into the room.

"Bathroom break," she announced and lifted up the blanket to unshackle Bessie's legs. "Come on, Judd," she yelled. "Give me a hand." She paused. "Why is this blanket so rumpled? Have you two been fooling around? Is that why your hair is so messy, Bessie?" Willeen started to laugh.

But when Judd unshackled Eben and he stood up, the sound of a hairpin falling to the floor made her stop.

Judd picked it up and held it out for examination.

"So that's what you've been doing!" Willeen screeched. She grabbed Bessie's hands and examined the slightly scratched cuffs. "Look at this, Judd!" she yelled. "These two were up to funny business."

"Eben, I'm going to frisk you," Judd said in a steely voice. Within seconds he had retrieved a handful of hairpins from Eben's pocket.

"Time for a new hairdo, lady," Willeen told Bessie as she roughly pulled each and every pin out of her head. With each yank, Bessie's hair slowly fell to the sides of her face.

"I'll tell you something, Judd. We're not stirring from this place until tomorrow night, when we're all packed and ready to go. Between that guy who wants to get a look at the inside here and these two . . . Thank God tomorrow is our last day."

It can't be our last day, Eben thought. It just can't. The same thought was swirling around inside Bessie's depinned head.

53

Thursday, December 29

AT NINE O'CLOCK the next morning, Regan was propped up on her bed with a cup of coffee in one hand and the phone in the other. She had just dialed the number of the Mishmash in Vail.

"Mishmash," a woman answered. Her voice was flat and nasal.

Regan cleared her throat. "Hello, my name is Regan Reilly."

"Good for you," the woman said.

"Good for me," Regan said. "Yes, that's right." She crossed her eyes at Kit, who was sprawled on the cot. "If you don't mind, I'd like to ask you a few questions."

"I don't mind. I'm not too busy now. Later in the day it gets busy and I'd hafta ask you to call back. Right now I'm just straightening the shelves, ya know?"

"Um-hmm," Regan agreed, then continued. "I'll get right to the point. A friend of mine is missing, and I think he was shopping in your store last week."

"Oh dear."

"I am a bit concerned," Regan said.

"Can you describe him at least? We get a lot of people in here, you know. We have such good bargains."

"I've heard," Regan said. "My friend's name is Eben Bean. He has——"

"Eben! The cops were in here the other day asking about him."

"Oh, they were."

"Yes, ma'am. Um-hmmm. Yup."

"What did you tell them?"

"They wanted to know if he was with anybody, that kind of thing. It wasn't much."

"Was he?"

"Was he what?"

"With anybody?"

"Nope. He spent a lot of time picking through a barrel and then he bought out all the green towels we had. They were irregular and we had a dozen of them. Eben loves a bargain."

"So you know him?"

"Oh yeah, uh-huh. I hope he's okay. I guess they think he might have stolen a fancy painting, huh? It doesn't make sense when you think he spent an hour that morning hunting for bargains in here."

"That's exactly what I was thinking," Regan said. "Did he come in there often?"

"Oh, maybe every month or so he'd take a ride down from Aspen and see what we got in. He really got a charge out of those towels for ninety-nine cents each."

"You say there were none left after Eben bought them?"

"He bought all the ones we had. I had just found them back in the stockroom, left over from the good Lord knows when. So I put them out and Eben scooped them up."

"Are you sure he bought a dozen?" Regan asked.

"Yup. I'm sure. He joked with me that when you buy a dozen doughnuts you get a thirteenth free, and I told him that I couldn't do that because he cleaned us out of all the green towels we had."

"Do you remember what he was wearing?"

"Oh, ya knooow," the woman said. "I think he had on his lumberjack coat and a cap. That's what he always wore. He seemed kind of excited about Christmas coming up and everything. I teased him because he hadn't shaved. It looked like he was even starting to grow a little beard and he told me it was because he was going to play Santa, and since his stubble comes in white now, he figured he'd let it fill in a little before the big night." She paused. "I hope he's okay," she said again.

"Me too," Regan said.

"I mean, he didn't seem like the type who would do anyone any harm."

"I know," Regan said. "So you haven't sold any of those green towels this year?"

"Nope."

"Do you know where they came from in the first place?"

"Who knows? Why are you asking so many questions about the green towels?"

"Just trying to track Eben down," Regan said casually. She did not want to start explaining about any possible connections or the fact that they shed. "I appreciate your help, miss . . . I'm sorry, what is your name?"

"Fannie."

"Thanks, Fannie, and if you think of anything else, would you give me a call?"

"I suppose I could do that."

Regan gave Fannie her number and hung up.

Kit's hands were resting behind her head on the pillow. "Well?"

"Miss Fannie says what I say. Why would Eben be shopping for a bargain an hour before he rips off a painting worth millions?"

"Some of the richest people in the world are the very ones who will chase a nickel down the block," Kit said practically. "You'd never know they had money."

"True. But this woman also said that Eben bought twelve towels. We only found six at Kendra's house. Why wouldn't Eben have taken them all with him?"

"I don't know."

"It sounds crazy, but I want to follow up with Ida about the guy who brought in the pants with the green nublets. It's the only lead I have to go on. Could those people for some reason have Eben's towels? If so, why? Is he with them?"

"What are you going to do?"

"Go over to the cleaner's this morning and see if Ida has a ticket for them with a name on it. Maybe they haven't picked their clothes up yet."

"Will you go skiing with me when you get back? If there's nothing else for you to do?"

"Of course. It'll be good to get out and move." Regan jumped out of bed. "I'll shower and get out of here right away. I don't want you stuck around here too long this morning. I imagine it would be wise to stay away from this place as much as possible today while Louis yells at everyone on the staff."

"I'll man the phones until you get back," Kit said. "Maybe Bessie will call with a ransom demand for Eben."

"That'd be a twist," Regan said. "God only knows where those two are. Here I am chasing down green towels to try and find out."

"Whatever it takes," Kit said and pulled the blanket up under her chin. "Maybe we should have Derwood feed all this information into one of his computers and see what it spits out."

"I think the computer would end up confused," Regan said. "I know I am."

54

REGAN WALKED INTO the dry cleaner's store where Ida was busy tagging articles of clothing. She looked up from a gravy-stained three-piece woman's pantsuit and a broad smile flashed across her face.

"Hello, Regan," she said excitedly. "Any news on Bessie? I was thinking about her all night."

"I haven't heard anything, Ida." Regan walked over to Ida's work counter and lowered her voice, even though there was no one else in the front of the store. "What I've been thinking about is that customer you told me about who brought in the pants with the green nublets on them."

Ida's eyes widened behind her glasses. "Oh?"

"It might be crazy, but I'd just like to see if you have a name and an address I could check out. I called the place where Eben got those towels and he bought up every one they had. Not that other people couldn't own green towels that shed, but I'd just like to follow through on this."

"Of course!" Ida said with enthusiasm. "Just like in the movies!"

Regan smiled. "Whatever. Who knows? Maybe those people found those towels."

Ida's face was positively radiant. Finally some excitement around here, she thought. "Let me see if I can help you." She pushed her glasses back against the bridge of her nose. "He wanted them for yesterday afternoon." She walked over to the ticket carousel. "I do remember that his name was Smith."

"Smith?" Regan said. At once she felt both excited and chilled. Excited that they might be on to something and chilled because Smith is the first name that comes to mind for most people when they don't want to give their real name. For whatever reason.

"Yes," Ida said. "That's why it's so easy to remember." Her index finger flew up and down the row of S tickets, which were filed by number. "I'll be darned," she breathed. "He must have picked it up." She reached down underneath the counter and pulled out the box of yesterday's tickets. As she filed through them, she felt like an actress in a thriller. I'm ready for my close-up, Mr. DeMille, she thought.

"Aha!" she finally said with not a little drama. "Here it is! He must have picked it up yesterday afternoon after I left."

Regan leaned over to take a look. "Is there an address on it?"

Ida felt crushed, afraid that her usefulness had just slipped away. "No, Regan, there isn't. Now I remember him mentioning something about not knowing the address or phone number of where he and his wife are staying."

"That's not surprising. Can I see the ticket?"

Ida handed it over. While Regan studied it, she tapped her fingers on the counter.

"There was an evening dress and tuxedo as well as his pants."

"Yes."

"I wonder if they're going to the party tonight. It's the biggest thing going on in town," Regan said. Complete with an expensive painting that will be on display, she thought.

Ida frowned, deep in thought. "I wish that other customer hadn't come in right after him. Otherwise I would have been able to chat with him longer. Not that he was the talky type, if you know what I mean. Oh! He did say that he needed it yesterday because he didn't know whether he'd be getting into town today and they needed the clothes for Thursday night! Which is tonight! I told him we'd do our best, I always say that, you know; we're supposed to act like we're doing them a big favor by getting it done quickly. Could there be any other big party he'd be going to tonight?"

Regan shook her head. "It would have to be a private party. If there were anything big going on, I'm sure my friend Louis would have mentioned it a million times by now. Ida, what did the dress look like?"

Ida stared up at the ad for martinizing on the wall. She then looked over to the rack of ties they had for sale by the door. She didn't think one of them had been sold in all the time she'd worked there. Adopting the pensive look she imagined actresses used when they were asked this kind of question in the movies, she took her time thinking. "It was black," she said finally.

"And?" Regan said quickly. "Isn't there anything else about it you can remember? Its style, length—something?"

"It was short and had a low-cut neck like almost every other dress in this town. It had some silver on it. I'm sorry, Regan; it's the kind of thing I'd recognize if I saw it again, but it's hard to describe."

Regan ran her fingers through her hair. Suppose those two were coming to the party tonight? What if Ida could pick out the dress? It was the only thing she had to go on. "Ida," she said, "I need your help."

Ida felt renewed. Her role in the drama wasn't over yet. "Yes?"

"Would you come to the party tonight as my guest and sit at our table? I need you to tell me if you spot that dress."

A surge of electricity jolted through Ida's body. "But Regan," she started to say, "those tickets are so expensive . . ."

"It doesn't matter. This is very important. Are you free tonight?"

Are you kidding? Ida thought. She could barely mouth the words. "Yes, I'm free."

Regan gave her the details and was walking out of the cleaner's when Ida called after her, "Do you mind if I bring my camera?"

"Not at all," Regan said. "But I need you to keep your eyes open."

Ida watched Regan Reilly walk down the block and out of sight. Slowly she floated back to the bin of dirty clothes and began to work like a demon. "Angela Lansbury, watch out!" she said to herself. Maybe there'll be a write-up in the local paper at home, she thought. Maybe I should wear my trench coat tonight. It was all just too exciting.

55

Back at the inn, preparations for the party were in full swing. Louis was in his office, answering phone calls, checking his list, only going out into the banquet room to yell at whatever employee happened to be within shouting distance. But he had to admit to himself that the place looked good.

The paintings of the local artists were being set up on easels all over the lobby and banquet room. The dining-room tables were cleared away to make way for a giant cocktail hour. Holiday decorations and flowers were in abundance and the stage of the banquet room was filled with poinsettias and greenery. A podium with a microphone was set at one side while two easels occupied center stage, ready and waiting for the Beasley and Pop-Pop paintings to be placed in their arms.

What gave Louis the biggest smile was when Regan and Kit appeared in his doorway and announced that the Louis painting had arrived and needed to be hung in a place of honor.

"Darlings," he said and jumped up. "Let's go see."

"I just got back," Regan said, leading them out to the lobby. "We're about to go out and do a little skiing. Tripp said they just dropped this off."

Louis XVIII was leaning against the wall by the fireplace, ensconced in a gold frame and looking perfectly regal.

"Look at the colors!" Louis exclaimed.

"It's called wiping off the dirt. You like?" Regan asked.

Louis hugged her. "Darling, I love it. Where should we put it?"

"How about over the fireplace?" Kit suggested.

"The hearth, as it were," Regan said. "The center of the home."

"Where it belongs," Kit added.

Tripp came over with a ladder and the supplies needed to nail Louis to the wall. They all deliberated over how high he should be placed. Finally it was done, and Tripp stepped down off the ladder to survey the effect.

"I'd say he looks pretty good."

Louis glowed. "Regan, I'm going to cry."

"Not now, Louis. You're only allowed to cry if tonight is a flop."

"Regan!" he protested.

Regan laughed. "Chop off my head, King Louis. Everything is going to be perfect. Don't worry. Now Kit and I are going to get out of here for a couple of hours and then we'll come back and get ready and have a pre-party drink with you."

"That sounds wonderful, Regan. Everything is going to work out fine tonight, isn't it?" He sounded like a pleading child.

"Of course, Louis," Regan said. When she and Kit

walked out the door, she added, "I only wish that was how I really felt."

Even an afternoon of great skiing did not relieve her nagging apprehension.

Eben and bessie listened to the sounds of Willeen and Judd packing up their things.

"I'm so scared, Eben," Bessie whispered.

"It ain't over till it's over," he replied with a tightness in his voice. He knew he was not being much of a comfort. When they heard Judd order Willeen to start putting Kendra's paintings in Eben's car, he really started to worry. Why are they doing that? he wondered. They'll never take my car with them. Every cop in the state must be on the lookout for it.

"I don't want to get to that party too early," they could hear Willeen saying in the living room.

"We have to get there early enough to get a good parking space," Judd answered. "If we don't make a quick getaway with that painting, then we're asking for trouble."

The sounds of the kitchen cabinets opening and closing filtered into the bedroom.

"It's all ready for when we get back," Willeen said.

"Be careful," Judd yelled.

Eben and Bessie froze as they heard him say, "That's chloroform in that bottle, dummy."

Across town, the Coyote turned on his set. While watching Judd and Willeen pack, he did a little of his own. He was about to dismantle his surveillance equipment in case he had to make a quick getaway tonight.

Mentally he reviewed his plans. After the painting disappeared, there'd be a lot of confusion. He would put it in the false bottom of the car where the other Beasley was now resting. There was no problem about parking the car only a few feet from the emergency exit door of the dining room.

Listening to Judd and Willeen was exhilarating—the moment of danger, and ultimately of triumph, was approaching.

"Bye-bye, folks," he said, turning off the set and pulling out the plug. "See you tonight."

"Judd, I've covered all the ___ ___
in his crate. He knew he was not ___ afraid of a coyote.
When they found Judd with Willeen to stand putting back
the paintings in Eben's crate. He really started to worry.
What are they doing now? he wondered. They'll never take
the car with them. Away over in the same house be on the
lookout for it.
"I don't want to get to the Twenty-one later," Willeen cried.
Eben, Willeen sobbing in the living room.
"We have to get there early enough to get a good parking
space, dummy, answered. If we don't make a quick getaway
with that painting, then we're asking for trouble.
The sounds of the drawer cabinets opening and closing
filtered from the bedroom.
"all right, ready for when we get back," Willeen said.

MARVIN WINKLE WAS on an airplane thousands and thousands of feet over the state of Illinois, enjoying a cocktail and anxious as a child on Christmas Eve. His every nerve was twittering with excitement. The bearer of good tidings, that's what I am, he thought.

It was all so unbelievable.

Just wait until Geraldine heard the news. He was sure that she wouldn't mind that, instead of phoning her, he'd quickly packed a bag and raced to the airport, rushing back inside his house just once to grab the short skis he had had since high school. Maybe after his good work was completed, Geraldine would urge him to stay on in Aspen. Being that it was Christmas week, and all the hotels were charging premium rates, he'd probably be invited to stay at the Spoonfellow estate.

He stared at the phone attached to the seat in front of him. It looked so inviting. Just slip in a credit card and call anywhere.

Should he splurge? Why not? The two Scotches were working their magic and Winkle was in the holiday spirit. Humming "Winter Wonderland," he reached under the seat in front of him and pulled out his worn black briefcase. Pushing the buttons on either side at the same moment always gave him a minor thrill. The pistol-like sound of the locks releasing, springing open and snapping to attention made him smile. Just for the fun of it he reattached them and fired them off another time. And then again.

His seatmate, with whom he had unsuccessfully tried to start a friendly conversation, glowered at him.

Winkle sighed and pulled out his wallet from the briefcase. He liked to keep it in there because he knew how pickpockets were everywhere, especially during the holiday season. He found himself briefly studying his Pennsylvania driver's license, which was a little frayed at the edges, and then pulled out his credit card.

With his briefcase resting on his lap, he slid the credit card into the phone apparatus and dialed his number. His machine picked up on the second ring, which meant there was a message. He punched in his secret code and waited while the electronic voice informed him he had one message.

Suddenly Geraldine Spoonfellow's voice was screaming at him, forty thousand feet in the air. Winkle tried to smile and hoped that his seatmate couldn't hear what her tape-recorded voice was saying.

"I'm going to get me another investigator if you're never there to take my calls. *Call me back!*" Winkle sat there looking out the window of the plane as the phone clicked in his ear.

He pushed the disconnect button, not wanting to be charged for an extra minute, and shrugged.

Oh well, he thought to himself. I don't want to call her now. I'll give her the good news at the party tonight. I'll go straight there when I land. She'll be so happy, she'll have all the publicity people taking pictures of them.

He jiggled the ice cubes in his glass. Who knows? After tonight I might be considered the next Sherlock Holmes.

58

GERALDINE STOOD IN front of the mirror, pinning a silver broach on her black high-necked taffeta dress. Normally she eschewed jewelry, but in honor of Pop-Pop she had decided that tonight was a night to wear silver. She'd had the dress for over twenty years, wearing it to the few formal events she attended.

Today she had written her speech. It meant tearing herself away from his diary, but the excitement of tonight had started to build in her stomach that afternoon. Finally Pop-Pop would be getting some of the recognition he deserved. Aspen would sit up and take notice of his contributions to this town, and she'd made sure to lay them out one by one. They hadn't told her how long she was supposed to talk, but they wouldn't dare try to stop her in the middle of her message to the people, she thought.

Applying a bit of lipstick, which for her was an occasion, Geraldine studied her reflection. It's hard to believe that

I'm seventy-five years old, she thought. I feel so much younger, but at the same time I think I've lived through three lifetimes of sadness. Not that there weren't good times too. But not having a family always made the holidays more difficult.

It's a good thing I'm a pain in the neck, she thought, or else I'd be sitting around here feeling sorry for myself. I'd rather be yelling at Rip Van Winkle than crying, she thought. Of course he hadn't called back yet. Where in tarnation was he, and what was he doing anyway?

Geraldine picked up her silver brush and smoothed a few wisps of hair into her bun. If only my brother Charles had gotten married and had children, she thought, at least I'd have somebody to spoil. And someone to share tonight with. Pop-Pop is being honored and I'm the only relative to soak in the adulation.

At least I can turn my energies to this town. I could get a fortune for that Beasley painting, but I don't need it. I've got plenty of money to last my lifetime. I guess I shouldn't complain. My life's work will be to keep the Spoonfellow name alive by helping with the new museum and donating all the junk in the barn to the cause. The parade on New Year's Day, led by Pop-Pop's painting, will be just the beginning.

Replacing the hairbrush on the dresser, she picked up a perfume bottle that had been resting on the same doily since her boyfriend died last year and smiled. I never bother with this stuff, but why not tonight, she thought. I gave up fussing over myself a long time ago, but tonight, well, tonight I just feel like it. She pulled on the neck of her dress, poking the bottle under the taffeta. She spritzed a few times and then misted her

wrists. Before putting it back, she sprayed all around her dress.

Checking her lipstick again, she smiled. I'm not dead yet, she thought. After all, who knows just what excitement tonight will bring?

WHEN MARVIN WINKLE arrived in Denver at 5 P.M., he was distraught to find that visibility in Aspen was dropping rapidly and there would be no more planes flying in there tonight. The airport was closed until morning and conditions changed.

Tomorrow wasn't good enough. Suppose the original Greek runner had taken a couple of days to get where he was going to announce "Victory, Victory"? He might have lived longer but there wouldn't be marathons run all over the world today.

"I need to get to Aspen tonight," he told the ticket agent.

She pointed with her well-manicured blood-red fingertip. "The car rentals are right over there."

There was a long line.

Winkle hurried over and pulled out his credit card. It's the second time I've used it in the space of a few hours, he thought. The last time, what did I get for it? Geraldine screaming at me. Let's hope I have better luck this time.

He calculated rapidly. It would take four hours to drive to Aspen. He waited on line for what seemed like forever and finally was taken care of. He completed the paperwork and was told to sit down and wait for the shuttle bus to the big parking lot full of rental cars. Everything was taking so much time!

He consoled himself, as he sat there waiting with his luggage and the short skis, which in the cold light of the terminal were a great embarrassment. Geraldine had told him that the highlight of her life would be to present her grandfather's picture to the museum. When she finished, he'd present her with a highlight that would even top that.

60

At NINE O'CLOCK it was obvious that the party was a great success. Louis was beaming happily as he listened to the compliments on the restaurant and the paintings. The Louis painting was widely admired, and he was hearing himself referred to as the King. He loved it. He had already posed for several pictures in front of the fireplace with celebrities and moguls and the elite of Aspen.

The reception area was filled with over six hundred people sipping cocktails and mingling and checking out the latest designer evening wear adorning many of the women in the room.

The most serious looker was Ida. Threading through the crowd, she was having the time of her life, pretending to admire every black dress she was caught staring at. Where, oh where is the one I held in my hands just yesterday morning? she thought. I've got to find it, I've just got to.

Slowly the assemblage was herded into the banquet room for the dinner, dancing and program.

At a well-placed table bordering the dance floor, Kendra, Sam, Luke, and Nora took their seats. Regan, wearing a black velvet dress, found Ida in the crowd and ushered her to the table.

"I want you to sit down for a few minutes," Regan told her. "You've been wandering around this party for too long."

"Don't worry, Regan. This is the best time I've had in years. I'm just getting frustrated that I haven't seen the dress or my customer!"

Kit and Regan had been standing in the cocktail area with Derwood and Stewart and flashes of Larry when Regan went to find Ida. Larry was making the best of every last moment of socializing.

"I hate to sit down at the table, Regan," he said. "I get antsy. That's why when I get married, it'll be a buffet reception."

"I can't wait," Regan had said. "I'll see you guys inside."

After Ida had sat down and started chatting with the group, Regan looked around the room. The band was playing music with a pulsating energy. Everyone looked great and the drinks were flowing. The party had that indefinable quality that made it a winner. Louis should be happy, Regan thought. So far so good.

Regan spotted Geraldine Spoonfellow at the table closest to the stage, in a place of honor with the Rescue Aspen's Past group. Her seat was closest to her grandfather's paintings, which were now both onstage. The Beasley was covered with a drop cloth with a blue-spruce decor, the symbol of Colorado. The other Pop-Pop, a portrait of a resplendent senior citizen with white goatee, string tie and a sternly

benevolent expression, was highlighted and impossible to ignore.

Regan hurried over to say hello. Geraldine shook her hand and seemed genuinely glad to see her. "Regan, the other day when you and Louis first came to the house, I didn't think we'd be together here tonight," she said warmly, covering Regan's hand with hers.

"I'm awfully glad we are, Geraldine," Regan said. "I can't wait to hear you speak."

Geraldine held up a notebook. "It's all in here."

From over Geraldine's shoulder, Regan could see a tall older man approaching. It was Angus Ludwig, the old-time resident she'd met when she visited him with the reporter. He was crisp and elegant in his tuxedo with a red cummerbund. "You look mighty sharp, sir," she said admiringly.

"Thank you, Regan. You look very sharp yourself. I just came over here to see if this pretty lady would like to share this dance with me. But I'm a little nervous, seeing as how she turned me down nearly sixty years ago. My feelings are still a little hurt."

Geraldine's head swiveled and she looked up at the man she hadn't laid eyes on since she was a young girl. Her mouth dropped and her heart raced. "Angus Ludwig," she whispered.

Simultaneously they both laughed and said, "You haven't changed a bit."

Angus took her hand in his. "My lady?"

Geraldine rose from her chair, never taking her eyes off him.

"If you'll excuse us, Regan . . ." Angus said.

"Of course," Regan replied and walked back toward

her table. Let's see, she thought, who might come back looking for me in fifty years? She couldn't think of anyone.

Kit was making a beeline for the bathroom from the cocktail area. Regan hurried to follow her. "Kit, wait up," she yelled.

Kit turned and smiled. She was wearing a bright red dress, her blond hair swept up in a chignon. "Regan, I feel like a louse," she said.

"Why?"

"Derwood just asked if he could come and visit me in Connecticut in a couple of weeks."

"What did you tell him?"

"I told him I was seeing someone and it was starting to get serious."

Regan paused. "Poor thing. He really seemed to like you."

"There's just no chemistry. He's nice, but I don't think it's there for us. I figured that was the best way of getting out of it."

"It is. It's just too bad that it had to happen tonight."

Kit's face looked pensive. Her eyes wandered and quickly they brightened. "Look, Regan. He doesn't waste any time. He's already out dancing with somebody else."

Regan turned and there was Derwood out on the floor, dancing his heart out with a very attractive blonde.

"I guess he likes you blondes," Regan said. "I never had a chance with him."

Kit laughed. "I feel better now. He is a nice guy. I still say you should go for his friend Stewart."

"Whatever." They pushed open the ladies' room door and went inside.

61

JUDD AND WILLEEN were randomly seated at a table for eight, which the other people at the table sourly observed might as well be in the kitchen. But it suited Judd and Willeen's purposes admirably. Only a scant twelve feet behind them was a discreet arrow that pointed to the rest rooms.

Claude, the master planner of the art ring, who had arranged the appointment for the supposed sale of the Beasley in Vail, had secured blueprints of Louis's inn. Willeen knew exactly where to go downstairs when the time came for the heist. When she supposedly went to the ladies' room last night, she had established that the box and the switch were exactly where they were supposed to be.

The fake handicapped sign in the window of their car had ensured privileged parking and privileged escape. To ensure that spot, they'd arrived in plenty of time for the seven-thirty cocktail hour, but instead of mingling had sat

in a quiet corner of the bar sipping club soda. Both of them were too keyed up even to attempt small talk.

At the dinner table, the woman seated to the right of Judd insisted on carrying on a steady stream of conversation. "I'm from Florida. My husband and I met in school. We love to give dinner parties. Isn't the salmon mousse delicious? I never eat soup. It fills me up too much. But look at my husband. He's really enjoying the cream of broccoli. I like the idea of dancing between courses. It sort of works off what you eat. My husband hates to dance. Do you like to dance?"

"No," Judd said shortly, wishing he could strangle her, as he studied from a distance the drop cloth with the treasure behind it that would soon be his.

Finally they were serving the filet mignon. He knew that when this course was finished the presentation would be made. He looked around with a glimmer of satisfaction and started to feel reassured. A lot of people had had enough to drink and were obviously feeling pretty relaxed. In the left wing of the stage he could make out the figure of an older man in a security uniform who, according to their sources, was a retired Aspen cop and now worked for the museum. He was in charge of guarding the painting during the evening. It had been dropped off by a security car earlier and was to be picked up by the same car and returned to the bank vault at the end of the evening. Or at least that was their plan, Judd thought.

The waiters started to clear the main-course plates. Judd watched as a man from the table situated front and center to the stage stood up and offered his arm to an elderly woman. The ceremony was about to begin.

He turned to Willeen and mouthed, "Now."

* * *

Ida obviously had taken her appointment as amateur sleuth seriously. Regan watched with gratitude as Ida wandered through the room between courses, stopping at various tables with a friendly hello for some of the clients from the cleaner's. She was also keeping a hawkeye on the dancing couples.

When she returned to the table each time, she gave Regan a shake of the head. "No luck so far. There are so many people here."

After the main course had been cleared, trumpets blared and the spotlight fell on Geraldine Spoonfellow, who was being escorted to the stage by the president of the Rescue Aspen's Past Association.

"The ceremonies are starting? Aren't they going to serve dessert and coffee? I guess they want to make sure everyone stays for the speeches," Ida commented. Then her gaze became fixed. "Regan," she said urgently. "You see that woman over there in the hallway? The one with the black-and-silver shoulder straps? That's the dress we pressed! I'm sure of it! I guess she's going to the rest room."

Regan stood up. Louis had just pulled up a chair at their table to hear the speeches. She was aware of his reproachful gaze as she murmured "Excuse me" and Geraldine's decisive voice resounded over the microphone. "My beloved grandfather, Burton Spoonfellow . . ."

The Coyote had also observed Willeen leaving the room. He noticed the glance she threw over her shoulder, establishing eye contact with Judd. He quietly slipped past the outside tables until he was at the entrance to the ballroom. The foyer leading to the rest rooms was on the right; on the left was the first emergency exit from the ballroom. It

was the one he would use after he was sure that Judd had successfully completed phase one of his plan to have the Beasley painting in his possession that night.

Willeen disappeared down the corridor. Not, he knew, to the ladies' room but down the dark narrow stairs that led to the basement and the master switch, which would plunge the entire restaurant into chaotic darkness. As he watched, Judd, on schedule, left his chair and began to make his way toward the stage just as Geraldine Spoonfellow was being announced. Then the Coyote frowned. Regan Reilly, always a nagging worry, was making her way swiftly from her privileged seat, weaving her way through the tables. He had no doubt that she was following Willeen. How much did she suspect?

He drew back so she would not notice him as she rushed down the corridor toward the ladies' room, where he knew she would not find Willeen. Maybe it didn't matter. Whatever instinct or knowledge had set her on Willeen's path wouldn't do any good now. As he watched he could make out that Judd was reaching both hands in his pockets. From one, he knew, he would extract a gas mask and night glasses; from the other, a gun that would send pellets of tear gas cascading through the air. Coupled with the plunge into darkness, the choking gas would terrorize and immobilize the unsuspecting guests. Judd, within an instant, would have the Beasley painting under his arm. He and Willeen would be in their car, which the Coyote had observed was so conveniently parked, and they'd race back to their house, where he'd be the unexpected guest.

Let the other guy do the dirty work, he thought. That was always best.

In a few seconds the lights would go out and he knew Judd would fire the pellet gun. Judd was at the bottom of

the right-hand stairs that led to the stage. He'd get away with it. The Coyote began to hurry toward the emergency exit door on the left-hand side just before the ballroom.

Marvin Winkle found it very unnerving to drive on the mountain roads to Aspen. And of course it had started to snow. He proceeded with great caution, afraid that he might slip off the road and into oblivion. Once again he thought of the marathon runner who in the moment of proclaiming victory had dropped dead.

As a result of his caution, it was one minute of eleven when he finally pulled up to the Silver Mine Inn. The parking lot was completely full. He knew Geraldine was scheduled to speak at eleven and he wanted to be there.

What difference? he thought as he double-parked, partially blocking a seedy station wagon. It was the nearest he could get to the hotel entrance without blocking the handicapped spots. It won't matter, he thought. I can be out before the rest of the crowd. I want to hear Geraldine speak and then I'll come and move it.

He hurried inside and reached the banquet hall in time to get one glimpse of Geraldine and hear her opening words. Then the lights went out and he began to cough.

The moment after the lights went out and gas pellets plunged through the air, the Coyote rushed outside to his car, catching sight of Judd clumsily running while carrying a bulky object. He and Willeen jumped into their car and took off.

The Coyote jumped in his to follow. Then he began to swear. Some fool had parked partially behind him. He began to twist and turn the wheel, inching back and forth until he could get around the heap that was blocking him.

But before he could get away and follow Judd's car, his passenger door opened.

"Tripp!" Regan yelled as she coughed and her eyes teared. She quickly slid in beside him. "You saw them too! Follow them!"

Only minutes earlier, Angus had sat beaming as he watched Geraldine being escorted up to the podium. A pretty girl had become a handsome woman. She'd invited him to sit at her table and the evening had flown as they talked about the old days. When he had joked with her about her turning him down when he wanted to come courting, she had patted his hand and he could have sworn her eyes had misted a bit.

"Well, maybe there were reasons you didn't know anything about," she'd said. She'd been very happy to hear that he was settling back in Aspen.

Angus leaned back, prepared to enjoy Geraldine's address. The historical-committee guy gave a nice introduction, one that Geraldine deserved. How many people would do what she'd done for this town? Then Angus frowned. That fellow who'd rented the cottage he was interested in buying was snaking his way up to the stage. In the bar Angus had recognized the wife, the one who'd acted so friendly but wouldn't give him a chance to glance through the house. Angus had gone over to say hello and she'd introduced them. He hoped this fellow wasn't one of those camera buffs who would start flashing lights in Geraldine's face while she talked. If he did, Angus would make sure he stopped it.

As Geraldine began to speak, the man who was the object of his attention reached both hands into his pockets.

What was he doing? Angus's eyes narrowed. What kind of crazy gadget was he putting on his face?

The lights went out and screams resounded through the room. A burst of staccato sounds came from where that man had been standing. In an instinctive movement Angus jumped up from his seat, rushed the few feet to the stage and hopped up. Reaching out, his arm found its way around a choking, coughing, furious Geraldine.

As Tripp grimly sped from the parking lot, choking, gasping people began pouring from the exits of the restaurant. With dismay Regan realized that her mother and father might be looking for her in the area of the rest rooms. But there was nothing she could do about it.

When they reached the road, there was no sign of the other vehicle, but Tripp turned right without stopping. She knew he could not have seen where the other car went. "Tripp," she said, holding on to the handle of the door, "how do you know where to go?"

"I served them in the restaurant last night. I know where they're staying."

Regan leaned back. "They told you?" she asked in disbelief. "That's the last thing I think they'd do. They might not even be going there now."

"Have you got a better idea?" Tripp snapped.

Shocked, Regan glanced at him and then dismissed his tone by thinking that he was upset about what had just happened. Tears were still streaming from her eyes from where the gas had stung. But now, in the faint light from the dashboard, she could see that his were clear and showed no sign of physical distress.

For the first time she noticed the phone on the seat between them. "Let me call the police!" she said. She

picked it up and opened the cover but before she could push the first button he grabbed it from her and threw it in the back of the station wagon. The back seat was down and she heard it land somewhere near the rear window. "It's broken," he growled.

Now it is for sure, Regan thought. Something was wrong with Tripp. A gnawing sense of danger made her stare straight ahead as he drove without hesitation. What would-be thief would talk loosely in front of a waiter? she thought. He must be in it with them! It made sense. He worked in the inn and could have told them where the master switch was. He had been outside when the tear gas exploded. He was driving so fast because he knew where to meet them. His car was piled with belongings. Her heart beating rapidly, she knew she couldn't let him realize she was on to him.

The snow was pelting down. It was hard to see more than a few feet ahead. She heard him swear under his breath.

"What's the matter?" she asked solicitously.

"I've missed a turn somewhere." He made a dangerously fast U-turn and the car began to fishtail. Everything was going wrong, he thought furiously as he righted it. That damn car blocking the way. Regan getting in with him. Well, that was her bad luck. He'd intended to steal the Beasley from Judd and Willeen's car when they went in the house to change. If they came out before he was finished, that was their problem. Now it was too late for that. He'd already lost at least five minutes, and with every passing second, the risk that they'd get away with the Beasley was getting greater.

From a road on the right he caught the flicker of approaching headlights. He jammed on his brakes as two

vehicles flew out onto the road and passed them going in the other direction. Tripp knew that Judd was driving one and Willeen the other.

The road was too narrow for a U-turn. He turned into the side road from which they had emerged, backed out, then followed the direction they had taken.

He smiled to himself. They were going ahead with their plan. At Observation Point, they would dispose of their unwanted guests. And so would he.

Angus clasped his hand over the mouth of the sputtering, choking Geraldine and led her into the fresh air outside. Others began streaming out behind them. He was in time to see Regan Reilly jump in a car that was just pulling away. As more people came stumbling out, he looked around. There had to be a cop coming soon and he was probably the only one who knew exactly where those thieves lived.

Everyone at Nora and Luke's table groped their way to the exits. Outside Nora said frantically, "Luke, Regan went to the rest room! She may still be in there!"

Luke turned, about to make his way through the solid mass of exiting people, then felt his hand clutched.

"She's not in there!" Ida said. "I was following her. I just got out when I saw her get into a car that was parked right there." She pointed to the space.

Angus, overhearing their conversation, turned. "Regan Reilly is your daughter? I saw her get into the car too. I think she and the driver are chasing whoever took that painting. And I know where he lives!"

Geraldine was suddenly recovered. "Then let's get in a

car and go!" she snapped. "No one's taking Pop-Pop's painting!"

Marvin Winkle, who had finally spotted Geraldine after he hurried outside in all the confusion, came up in time to hear the conversation. He pointed to his Rent-a-Wreck. "Miss Spoonfellow," he said. "Marvin Winkle. Always at your service."

Angus snatched the key from his hand. "I'll drive."

Geraldine jumped in the front seat.

"Come on, Luke," Nora said, pulling open the back door.

Winkle followed them in.

Angus was about to start the car when Ida opened the passenger door and burrowed in beside Geraldine.

Eben and Bessie had spent the seemingly interminable four hours since Willeen and Judd had left for the holiday gala quietly talking. Having both accepted that they probably wouldn't live until morning, they were exchanging confidences about their lives.

Eben even made Bessie laugh when he told her about some of the jobs he had pulled off.

"Since I never had any real parents, I guess no one ever steered me in the right direction."

"You never hurt anybody, did you?" Bessie asked.

"I never killed a fly. And I'm sure that anything I took was insured. If it wasn't, the people I took it from never missed it. Sometimes I think that I did it because I was mad. Everyone thought I was dumb. No one ever told me I was smart or cute. I wanted to get back at them. I feel real comfortable with you. You sound like you came from a nice family."

"I did. My mother and father were wonderful. That's

where I was luckier than you. You see, I never usually tell anybody because I loved my parents just as much as if I'd been born to them."

"What do you mean?" Eben asked.

"I was adopted."

"You were?!" Eben was just about to ask Bessie if she'd ever tried to find out where she came from when all thoughts in that direction left his mind. The faint sound of a car roaring up to the door made them both jump. They knew Willeen and Judd were back.

"So what the heck are you so nervous about?" Willeen snapped. "We got the painting."

"Yeah, we got it and I'm telling ya, I don't feel good. We've got to get out of here fast."

Willeen bit her lip. Every instinct told her that Judd was right. When she'd come up from throwing the master switch in the inn, she'd heard the door of the ladies' room open. Despite all the chaos and confusion after Judd fired the tear gas, she was sure someone had been trying to follow her out. She was sure it was Regan Reilly. When she glanced back at Judd, she'd noticed her get up and leave her table. Then, as they were pulling away, someone in the parking spot next to them had been trying to maneuver his station wagon to get around a parked car. With what was happening inside, who except her and Judd would have left the hotel without trying to help other people? Was it possible the Coyote had been in the next car? The thought sent cold chills through Willeen. She did not need Judd's urging to strip off her evening gown and jump into the ski sweater, slacks and boots that were laid out in the kitchen. Judd changed with her. An instant later their evening wear was in a suitcase and tossed in the car.

The bottle of chloroform and pads were on the kitchen table. They looked at each other.

"Now we get them out of here," Judd said.

Willeen picked up the bottle of chloroform and cotton pads and put them in her shoulder bag. With businesslike authority she trained the gun on Eben and Bessie as Judd released their leg shackles and herded them into Eben's car. Kendra Wood's paintings were already there. When the wreckage of the car was discovered, enough pieces of them should be intact to establish Eben as the art thief.

Outside, the air had turned bitterly cold. The sky was heavy and overcast. Not a single star was visible. Suddenly it began to snow.

When Bessie and Eben were seated, their hands firmly handcuffed behind them, Judd nodded to Willeen. She opened the bottle of chloroform, soaked the cotton pads, got in the front seat of the car and in one quick gesture held the soaking pads to their faces. They both tried to pull away. Swearing, Judd jumped into the car, dropped his gun on the front seat, and kneeling beside Willeen, he leaned back and grabbed Eben's face in a viselike grip. After that Bessie could no longer escape the pad that Willeen forced under her nostrils. They both slumped down unconscious, sliding toward the floor. Judd got out of the car and in the back door. Bending over them, he released their handcuffs.

"Get in our car and make sure you don't lose me," he snapped at Willeen. "We'll get rid of them at Observation Point."

Eben was coming to as Judd drove the car to Observation Point. Groggily he tried to raise his head as he felt the car stop and a rush of cold air. Where were they? What was

going on? Then he realized his hands were free. A moment later he felt movement as the car was slammed from behind. What was going on?

Through the headlights Regan could see a figure leap from the car that was stopped at the very edge of the observation area. Through the heavy snow she saw him run to the car that was parked behind it. An instant later he rammed the back of the car he had just gotten out of. With horror she saw the fence separate and the front wheels go over the edge. In the seat next to her Tripp was grinning.

Judd saw the approaching headlights as he leaped from Eben's car and into his own. They had been followed! He jammed on the accelerator, sending Eben's car flying forward, then backed up and started down the road to find it blocked by the station wagon. It was deliberately blocking the narrow path back down.

"You can't make it around him!" Willeen screamed.

"Watch me!" he snarled. His front wheels began to slip as he drove around the back of Tripp's wagon.

"You're going to kill us!" Willeen screamed. "Look at that drop!"

Frantically he reversed. The car spun out and slammed into the side of the mountain, its headlights shining back on Eben's car. Willeen's head banged into the glass. Judd's head hit the steering wheel. Dazed and bleeding, he heard the back door open.

"Don't turn around," a voice warned. "Don't reach for a gun. Once again I owe you my thanks."

Regan saw the gun in Tripp's hand in the same moment she realized that someone was in the back of the car whose

front wheels were dangling over the edge of the mountain. Acting instinctively, she threw open the door of the car, crouched down and ran toward the vehicle. She yanked open the back door and couldn't believe her eyes. She came face to face with a dazed Eben.

"Eben," she gasped, grabbing his hand and pulling his weight toward her.

"Bessie's here too," he said weakly.

"Get out, get out; I'll get her," Regan said, yanking him sideways. He fell to the ground. His weight had been stabilizing the car. The front end dipped dangerously.

"Get Bessie out of there," Eben moaned as he tried to struggle to his feet.

Regan tried to pull Bessie's arms but she was a dead weight. She felt the car begin to slip. As fast as she could, she got in the back of the car in a crouching position, put her arms around Bessie's back, and lifted her inert body. It took several tries but finally she had her head and shoulders hanging out the door of the car.

She could see Eben struggling to get to his feet and reaching toward them. He pulled Bessie's limp body forward, clear of the car, coming to rest on the ground beside him. Without their combined weight the car slid forward. As it pitched forward, Regan leaped out. It snapped through the remaining barrier and plunged over the side. Regan's right arm and leg were hanging over the side of the mountain. She was sliding downward, frantically trying to find something to grab on to when she felt a solid hand grasp her wrist.

"No skiing tonight, Regan," Eben said as he pulled her onto safe ground.

In the distance, Regan could hear the wail of approaching sirens. Then familiar voices were calling out to them.

* * *

It had not worked the way Tripp had expected. His cover was blown, but in fifteen minutes it wouldn't matter. The Beasley painting was in back of the car. He had taken the keys to Judd's car. Regan Reilly was still struggling to get that woman out of the car when he drove away. By the time anyone found them, his contingency plan would be in operation. The other car, locked in a barn with clothes, identification and a disguise, was only fifteen minutes away.

But as he rounded the curb he could see a caravan of vehicles approaching. Four of them had flashing domes. As he sped past them in the opposite direction, one of the police cars did a U-turn, and he knew he couldn't outrun it and his luck had finally run out.

"Regan!" Nora screamed. Everyone was running toward them.

"I'm okay," she yelled.

Winkle couldn't believe it. His car had led the chase. His car with the portable telephone that he'd decided to splurge on, which had summoned the police. They had all witnessed the vehicle going over the cliff. When Angus stopped his car, they had all jumped out and gone running up the hill. The Reillys' daughter, Regan, was on the ground with two other people.

The whole group was standing over them. A man with a short beard was shaking his head. The woman on the ground was stirring. Regan stood up. "Look who I found. I knew they were together. I want you all to meet the missing Eben Bean and Bessie Armbuckle."

Winkle felt as though he'd been electrocuted. "Eben Bean and Bessie Armbuckle!" he shouted. "You're the

reason I'm here tonight!" He turned to Geraldine, who was being protected from the cold by Angus. "Mama," he shouted. "May I introduce you to your missing twins?"

Geraldine looked at him dumbfounded. Then she looked down at Eben, who resembled Pop-Pop with his white beard. Bessie's loose hair hung around her face the way hers did when she didn't wear it up. She bent over and started to cry. For the first time in her life she was allowed to wrap her arms around her babies.

Fifty-six years after the birth, huddled in the swirling snow on a cold mountaintop in Aspen, Geraldine couldn't feel anything but the warmth of their bodies. She didn't think she would ever let go.

Back at the restaurant, the aftermath of the tear-gas attack and the theft of the Beasley had turned into a celebration. The place was still a shambles, and Louis's attack of nerves had almost killed him, but when Geraldine came walking through the door with Eben on one side, Bessie on the other, and Angus close at her heels, Louis wanted to cry. So he did. To think that Eben was Geraldine's son!

Most of the guests had left amid the hysteria. But the media hadn't. News crews and reporters were still swarming about. When the caravan from Observation Point got back, Louis had called upon his staff, minus Tripp, to prepare plates of scrambled eggs, muffins, pots of coffee, and, of course, to bring out the champagne. I'm not ruined after all, he thought. I might need to buy a lot of new dishes but I don't have to close the doors and go hide.

Geraldine sat at the head of a large banquet table, holding hands with her twins. Her eyes were constantly welling

with tears, at which point she'd briefly let go of their hands, reach in her pocket for her soggy handkerchief, give a quick dab, and then grab their hands again, this time even tighter.

"Don't cry, Mama," Eben said.

"I can't help it, baby," Geraldine said with a sniffle. "I never dreamed that I would live to see this happen. To think that I didn't know until I read Pop-Pop's diary that there were not one, but two of you out there. In those days they used to knock you out when you had a baby. Pop-Pop never wanted me to know that I had twins. He thought I'd feel twice as bad. He was such a good man. He was the one I turned to when I found out I was pregnant. My parents agreed to let him take me away so I could have my baby . . . babies . . ."—Geraldine dabbed her eyes again—"without being disgraced."

"Who was our daddy?" Eben asked softly.

Geraldine's spine straightened. "The biggest varmint and snake to pass through these parts, that's who your daddy was. His grandpa is in that painting with Pop-Pop. They'd been partners and then broke up. Pop-Pop became successful and his partner didn't, so the family left town. Years later the grandson came back and wooed me. My judgment wasn't too good and I ended up pregnant after the big barn dance. The minute he heard, he hit the dusty trails. Pop-Pop thought it was revenge. But at least I now have you . . ." Geraldine turned to Bessie. "I'm so happy you had a good family who took you in."

Bessie looked at her. "I did. But this is special. Even though I had a wonderful woman who I think of as my mother, may she rest in peace, I would still like to call you Mama."

Geraldine reached for her handkerchief once again. She

wiped her eyes and yelled to Louis, "Bring me a cup of that herbal tea of yours. I think I need it."

Louis smiled. "Coming right up!"

"Nora! Luke!" Kendra and Sam came running over as the whole group filtered back into the restaurant. "We didn't know what happened!"

"A little joyriding," Luke said, his arm around Nora.

"I'm telling you, Kendra, this happens every time we go somewhere." Nora smiled and shook her head.

"We knew you wanted to get your caretaker back, so we thought we'd help." The lines around Luke's eyes creased as he smiled.

Sam pointed over to the table where Geraldine, Eben, Bessie and Angus were all together, engrossed in conversation. "I don't know about that. Something tells me he might have better things to do now. . . ."

"Mama," Eben said, "do you think we could build a Jacuzzi up at the house?"

"Anything you want," Geraldine assured him.

"I'll help," Angus cried. "I'm a great fixer-upper."

Bessie hit him on the shoulder. "You can be our new daddy."

Angus smiled at Geraldine. "Never say never."

Stewart greeted Regan at the door. "Are you okay?" he asked with real concern.

"Yes," she said, looking up at him. He'd loosened the tie of his tuxedo and for the first time since she'd met him he looked rumpled. And worried.

"Your dress is wet from the snow," he said and took off his jacket, putting it around her shoulders.

"What happened to Kit? And Derwood?" she asked.

"They're around here somewhere."

"Stewart, let's walk to the back. I'd like to take a look at that ballroom."

"Sure."

They headed through the restaurant and paused at the french doors that led into what was now a disaster area. Tables were overturned, dishes were smashed, the podium was on its side on the stage. Only the portrait of Pop-Pop, still upright on its easel, was in place as he stared out at the wreckage before him. The camera crews had asked Louis not to clean up before they got some good shots of the room. He'd been more than happy to oblige.

"You'd never know from looking at this place that everything turned out all right," Regan said, holding Stewart's jacket closed around her. "Willeen and Judd and Tripp are all behind bars right now. I just can't believe I never suspected a thing about Tripp. He seemed like such a nice kid. Obviously my instincts weren't so sharp about him."

"What are your instincts about me?" Stewart asked as he put his hand on her arm.

Regan paused. "Aah. Aah," she started to mumble.

"I can tell you've been holding back. It seems like you don't trust me," Stewart said with a soulful look. "That's why I want to come out in the open with you."

Regan looked puzzled. "Come out in the open about what?"

"I don't own a children's company."

"You don't?" Wait till my mother hears that one, she thought. She'll go into a depression.

"No. But my uncle does, and I worked there a couple of summers in college."

Regan was silent for a moment. "Why did you lie to me?"

Stewart stared into her eyes. "I didn't want to. But I had to. You see, Regan"—he pushed his hair back from his forehead—"I'm Derwood's bodyguard and he doesn't want people to know it."

Regan's mouth fell open. "His bodyguard? Why does he need a bodyguard?"

"He needs protection because he just sold his computer business for two hundred million dollars. He's just a little nervous about kidnappers because the sale got a lot of publicity."

Regan gulped. Wait until Kit hears this one! She'll be a basket case. "I'm glad you told me, Stewart," Regan managed to say weakly as from the corner of her eyes she could see Kit and Derwood approaching.

"Regan!" Kit said. "Thank God you're back!" She peered into the abandoned ballroom. "It looks like a game of musical chairs really got out of hand, doesn't it?"

"Um-hmmm," Regan said.

Derwood smiled at Regan. "We were worried about you."

"Thanks, Derwood. Hey, we should join everyone at the table, but first I'm going to pop into the ladies' room."

"We'll meet you inside," Stewart said.

"Kit, would you come with me?" Regan asked.

"Why not? It looks like you could use some help with that dress."

When the door shut behind them, Regan turned to Kit, who was now smiling at herself in the mirror, fixing a few wisps of her hair that were springing from her chignon.

"Regan," Kit said as she smoothed the sides of her head, "I can't believe everything that's happened tonight.

When the lights went out and the tear gas went off, Kendra, Sam, Derwood, Stewart and I were all on the side of the table that made it hard to get out. People started running and panicking and I fell. But Derwood was so sweet. He scraped me off the floor. I'm telling you, maybe he isn't such a bad guy after all. I should really give him a chance. It was a stampede but he stopped to help me when I needed help and that counts for a lot." She shrugged. "And his arms felt so surprisingly strong around me as he led me outside." Kit looked at Regan. "So Stewart gave you his jacket. That's so romantic. I love it when a guy does that."

"Kit," Regan said, "I have something to tell you and I think you'd better sit down."

"Why?"

"The news might make you sway a little."

"Where should I sit?"

"Put the seat down on one of the toilets."

Kit looked alarmed as she hurried into a stall, let the toilet cover drop with a bang, sat down and crossed her legs. "Regan, what's wrong?"

"Kit, Stewart is Derwood's bodyguard."

"Bodyguard! That liar! Why didn't he tell you?" Kit paused for the briefest of seconds, a look of recognition and then fear crossing her face. "Why does Derwood need a bodyguard?"

Regan swallowed. "Derwood doesn't want people to treat him differently just because . . . just because . . . just because . . ."

"Just because *what*?"

"Just because he sold his computer company for . . . for . . . for . . ."

"HOW MUCH?" Kit screamed.

"Two . . . two . . ." Regan was having trouble forming the words.

"Two million dollars?" Kit asked with a pained expression.

Regan shook her head slowly. "No no no. Two HUNDRED million dollars."

The words sent a jolt of electricity through Kit's body that made her shoot up from the commode like a rocket. She pushed Regan out of the way, her high heels scraping across the bathroom floor so fast that Regan was sure she saw sparks, and raced out the door. "Derwood!" she called anxiously. "Honey, where are you?"

Louis was running around the restaurant making sure that the media were happy. He wanted to get everyone together for a toast, and *People* magazine wanted a group shot of everyone involved. But first he had to wait until certain interviews were finished.

Ida was in a corner being questioned by Jill Brooke of CNN.

"You wouldn't believe it," Ida beamed. Suddenly she scrunched up her face at Jill, who was holding out the microphone for her. "Shouldn't I look directly in the camera?"

"No," Jill said. "Pretend you're just talking to me."

"Oh, okay. As I was saying, I noticed the green nublets on that criminal's pants when I was working at the dry cleaner's here in Aspen. I just happened to mention it when I was at the home of Kendra Wood, the famous actress. To think if I had never said anything, Regan Reilly wouldn't have been on the lookout for the villains and they might have gotten away with it . . ."

* * *

Marvin Winkle straightened his tie as Cindy Adams of the *New York Post* sat down next to him for an interview.

"Now, Mr. Winkle," Cindy said, "this whole incident is filled with individual stories that could give every talk show on the air an exclusive. Tell me about your part in this drama."

Marvin smiled. "You know, Cindy," he said with a self-satisfied expression, "I get great pleasure from my job. I'd been hired by Geraldine just recently to find the baby she'd given up fifty-six years ago. She'd given birth in a private home near Pittsburgh. An agency handled the adoption, but Geraldine had no idea which one. Some of them aren't even in business anymore. It wasn't until she let me know the other day that twins had been born that I was able to do some sleuthing that tracked them both down. Well, let me tell you something, when I found out that her twins had both tried to find her, and they both spent time in Aspen, I ran out and bought an airplane ticket to come right out here and tell her in person. Without advance notice, those tickets are very expensive. Anyway, I thought I could track them down when I was here." He laughed. "It was my car that transported Geraldine to the reunion with her youngsters . . ."

Eben leaned over to Bessie. "You know something, Sis, when we were trapped in that bed, it somehow felt strangely familiar. I knew we'd been naked together at some time in our lives."

Geraldine swatted him on the side of the head, her eyes twinkling. "Don't be so fresh!"

Bessie laughed. "I've got to call my cousin and have

her come visit. She must be wondering what happened to me."

"The more the merrier," Geraldine said.

Ted Weems came hurrying into the restaurant. *"Oh my God!"* he was mumbling. *"My God! My God!"*

Louis hurried over to him. "What's wrong?"

Ted pointed to the Louis painting that was hanging over the fireplace. "That!" he said. "That!"

"What?" Louis asked. "Do you like it?"

Ted paused to catch his breath. "I was here for the party and spotted the painting across the room just as people were going in to dinner. Someone told me you had just gotten it from Geraldine Spoonfellow's barn. I ran home to check my art history books and call my sources in France. Have I got some exciting news for you! Wait until you hear this!" He dragged Louis over to the painting and pointed excitedly as he talked.

Louis called everyone over to the table. "I know there'll be lots more interviews, but I'd really like to make a toast."

With that the door swung open and Larry walked in.

"Here he is," Regan said. "Don't worry, Lar. Everyone is all right."

"Hey!" Larry protested. "I just got back from the emergency room. Somebody broke all his front teeth trying to escape from that disaster back there!"

"That'll pay for your trip." Regan smiled as she handed him a glass of champagne.

"He's probably the one who stepped on me," said Kit, who was now sitting with Derwood's jacket around her.

Louis tapped the table. "I want to make a toast to everyone and an announcement."

"Let's have the toast first," Luke said.

"To the most exciting opening in restaurant history . . ."

"Hear, hear," they all said and gladly sipped.

"And to the fact that the Beasley masterpiece was in very good company in Geraldine's barn. Early this evening, the eagle eye of our art historian and esteemed reporter, Ted Weems . . ."

Ted bowed and raised his glass.

". . . took a close look at the Louis painting. He got on the phone with Paris and through the markings he was able to describe, he has verified that the painting is by Antoine Francois Callet, a famous French artist who was a court portraitist under Louis the Sixteenth. As a matter of fact, Callet's portrait of Louis the Sixteenth is now hanging in Versailles."

A hum of excitement rippled through the room.

Louis made a grand gesture to the portrait over the fireplace. All eyes became fixed on the imposing figure of Louis XVIII.

"What we have here is one of Callet's last works, Louis the Eighteenth, who was painted on his Coronation Day in the early eighteen-hundreds. It's a lost masterpiece that disappeared from France many years ago. It's an important part of their culture and they desperately want it back. Geraldine, you are the rightful owner of it. When you gave it to Regan we had no idea of its value."

Geraldine jumped up. "No sirree. A deal is a deal. It's yours, Louis . . ."

I knew there was something I liked about that painting, Regan thought.

"You gave my boy Eben a chance by recommending him to Kendra and Sam. And he was a good caretaker, wasn't he, Kendra?"

When he wasn't sleeping in the guest room, Kendra thought, but she nodded yes.

"... and it wasn't easy for you when people like me were screaming at you for giving Eben that chance. So that painting, whatever it's worth, is yours. You do what you want with it."

The television cameras were whirring madly. The photographers were snapping pictures. Reporters were frantically taking notes. For one terrible moment, Louis wavered and then did what he had to do.

"The painting goes back to France," he announced grandly. "I think this whole group should plan a trip to Paris in springtime to deliver it. Nora, your books are popular in France. You've got to be with me when I present it."

Nora looked at Luke. "How about April in Paris?"

"Sounds good to me."

"I hope I'm invited," Ida threw in.

"Everyone's invited!" Louis said.

"Can you believe that two such priceless treasures were found from poking around in your barn?" Ted Weems asked Geraldine.

Geraldine put her arms around her twins. "I certainly can't. ..."

EPILOGUE

Tuesday, February 14

Regan's office was in an old building on Hollywood Boulevard, the kind with wide dingy hallways and black and white tile floors and what felt like the presence of the ghosts of tenants from a different era. Regan had chosen to work there because she felt it had a sense of history in the walls. And most important of all, no fluorescent lighting.

It was a sunny afternoon. Regan walked briskly into the building and took the creaky elevator up to the fourth floor where she had a view of the Hollywood Hills, even if her window was small. When she rounded the corner of the hallway, she could hear her phone ringing. Pulling her keys out of her purse, she unlocked the door, took the two steps to her desk and reached for the phone.

"Regan Reilly."

"Happy Valentine's Day."

"Hi, Kit." Regan smiled. She sat down in her swivel chair and leaned back. "How's it going?"

"Well . . ." Kit began. "No flowers yet. No candy. No cards."

"Who were you expecting to send them?"

"Nobody in particular. But I thought some poor soul might remember me. I can't believe Derwood never called."

"You hated him."

"Not for long."

"If it makes you feel any better, I haven't gotten any deliveries yet either."

"Los Angeles is three hours behind Hartford. You've still got time."

"Kit, I just got back from lunch. It's two o'clock. If I was going to get anything, I would have gotten it by now." Regan reached over and picked up the mail off the floor that had been dropped in the slot while she was out.

"The only thing good is that today is the end of the Bermuda Triangle. We're safe for the next ten months. Regan? Regan?"

Regan, who'd been shuffling through the mail, ripped open an envelope. "Hmmm? Just a second."

"Reilly, if I think you're bored talking to me, then I'm really dead."

"No, Kit!" Regan exclaimed. "You'll never guess what I have in front of me!"

"A card from Stewart."

"No! It's an invitation to Geraldine and Angus's wedding! With a special note from Geraldine!"

"Oh God, now I'm really depressed. What does it say?"

Dear Regan,

Life really couldn't be more wonderful. Angus and I have decided to seal our love after all these years and get married next month. At our age, we don't think long engagements are a great idea.

We certainly hope that you and your parents and Kit and Sam and Kendra will be able to make it. But I know that Kendra is doing so well in that play in New York, she probably won't be able to come. We'll have to send her pictures, I guess.

And can you believe it, thinking back to the first day I met you, that the reception will of course be at Louis's place? He's a real star here in Aspen now. Angus and I bring the twins down there several nights a week for dinner. Louis has a special table he keeps for us because it's so hard to get a reservation there!

Eben's fine. He loves working for Kendra and is so glad she let him keep the job and even gave him permission to live in the guest suite when they're not there. But he made me put a hot tub out back here so there'd be one for when he comes over! I must admit that Angus and I love soaking our bones in that gurgling water.

And Bessie loves her new apartment. I couldn't stand the thought of her going back to New York with the Grants. After all this time apart, I wanted us to be as close as possible and make the most of the rest of our lives together. So we got her a place in town and she's got a good job with the Rescue Aspen's Past Association, overseeing the room dedicated to Pop-Pop, her Great-Pop-Pop. I think she's a little bossy with them but I guess

she comes by it honestly. She was in charge of cleaning all the junk that came out of my barn for the museum. You should see the shine on those spittoons!

So, Regan, after all these years I have a family! How can I ever thank you for your part in saving my children? And Angus and I are so happy together. Who would have thought that at my age I would have found again this most wonderful man? It can happen! We really hope you'll be able to share with us our special day. The ski slopes will still be open too!

Let me hear from you.

Love,

Geraldine

Regan paused. There was silence on the other end of the phone. "Kit, are you still there?"

"Yes."

"What are you doing?"

"Arithmetic. Geraldine is getting married for the first time at seventy-five. If we follow in her footsteps, that means another forty-five years."

"It'll fly by."

"I don't think I can live through forty-five more Bermuda Triangles."

"Sure you can. I'll throw you a shower when you and Derwood are reunited in the year 2040."

"I'm looking forward to it."

The phone beeped in Regan's ear. "Hold on, Kit." Regan pressed the clicker. "Hello."

"Regan, it's Lar!"

"Hi, Larry! I'm talking to Kit on the other line. Can I call you back?"

"Sure. But tell Kit she has to come to Aspen for the World Cup Weekend in March. It's the first weekend. There'll be lots of guys I'll introduce you both to."

"That's the weekend Geraldine and Angus are getting married!"

"They are! What's the rush?"

"It's called love. I'll call you back." Regan got back to Kit. "That was Larry. He'll be out in Aspen the weekend of the wedding. It's the World Cup. You're going to come, aren't you?"

"Sure," Kit said. "Why not? After all, I think I'll make each minute of the next forty-five years count." She laughed. "Hey, Regan, do you think Geraldine will throw a bouquet?"

"Are you kidding? She'll fire it into the crowd." Regan laughed. "But don't stand next to Bessie!"

AND KUDOS FOR HER TWO PREVIOUS
REGAN REILLY MYSTERIES, *SNAGGED* AND
DECKED

"FAST, GLAMOROUS, INTRICATELY PLOTTED. . . . JUST RIGHT FOR A PLANE RIDE, OR, INDEED, A CRUISE."
—*Los Angeles Times*

"A SHARP AND SATISFYING MYSTERY."
—*People*

"UPBEAT, FAST-PACED."
—*New York Times*

"SPOONS IN A BIT OF BAWDY, A SOUPCON OF SLAP-STICK. . . . NO ONE CAN READ JUST ONE PAGE."
—*Washington Post*

"FRESH AND FUNNY, *SNAGGED* KEEPS YOU THOR-OUGHLY ENTERTAINED."
—*West Coast Review of Books*

"BREEZY AND HUMOROUS . . . *SNAGGED* OFFERS A RUN ON FUN AND ENTERTAINMENT."
—*Fort Lauderdale Sun Sentinel*

"A SUSPENSEFUL CLIMAX."
—*Publishers Weekly*

"A FUNNY, LIGHT SUMMER READ."
—*Hartford Courant*

"ENJOYABLE . . . HER SENSE OF HUMOR . . . CARRIES THE DAY."
—*Greensboro News & Record*

PRAISE FOR CAROL HIGGINS CLARK AND HER NEW REGAN REILLY MYSTERY
ICED

"IT'S A DISTINCT PLEASURE TO READ A NEW MYSTERY BY CAROL HIGGINS CLARK. She has created some delightful characters who frolic through her well-crafted stories, creating humor and satisfying reading in the midst of mystery and mahem."
—*Chattanooga Times*

"I LOOK FORWARD TO SEEING REGAN BATTLING WITS AND BRAINS IN THE NEXT REGAN REILLY MYSTERY. Carol Higgins Clark tells a fast-paced, suspenseful story with never a dull moment and a refreshing sense of humor."
—*Mostly Murder*

"FUN AND FROLIC! Clark had penned a frothy . . . funny story of art theft and kidnapping in that winter playground of the rich, Aspen."
—*Princeton Times*

"TOLD WITH SUCH APPEALING SIMPLICITY IT'S IMPOSSIBLE NOT TO LIKE. . . . An unpretentious book that promises little and delivers more."
—*London Free Press*

"CLARK WRITES WITH SKILL AND HUMOR AND HAS A NICE WAY WITH CHARACTERS."
—*Miami Herald*

more . . .